Strange Bedfellows

Foul Play Fair Play Foreplay

John A Lamb

For Rob
Come aboard for a journey with
a father Brother

Barnstead Press

ISBN 978-0-615-40772-2

Also available in digital formats
at
www.barnsteadpress.com

Cover artwork by Randall McKissick
Book design by Melissa Darnell

For Nanette's legibility, Gerda's lucidity, Maggi's love and loyalty, and Chris who made this book come to life.

Chapter 1

"Stroke—stroke—stroke," the coxswain barked for a quickened cadence. "Pick it up lads, or we'll capsize in the wash of those American buggers next week. Stroke, stroke, stroke." The count was raised to a rate with almost imperceptible intervals between the single syllable commands as the five-feet-four bully tongue-lashed six rowers twice his size to exceed human capacity. "Come along now, Swan," he snarled through the megaphone strapped to his face. "Move it if you want to hold your place as stroke oar."

Elliot H.N. Swan responded to the heckler by whipping his blade through the water with such power he caught the crew off guard, veering the boat's course before the rowers compensated for the deviation.

"Let's get to the finish line straightaway, shall we lads? It's faster that way." The coxswain's sarcasm might have been lost on some rowers strained to the limit, but not on Elliot H. N. Swan, who repeatedly wondered why he tolerated, no, submitted to any abuse, for he was not a violent man. Winning a race was much more than the adrenalin rush of a sportsman's kill; it surpassed the achievement of superiority—it was independence.

Another three hundred yards full out, then the merciless count ceased and hearts no longer threatened to burst. Now with the turn of the rudder, the boat drifted shoreward, all blades held in precise perpendiculars, the exhausted oarsmen bowed like supplicants before some fierce, ancient god whose face they dare not glimpse. In the afternoon on the river all was silent; the boat parted the water without a wake, the breathing of the men returned to the quiet of post exertion. The sky was undisturbed except for the watery jewels dripping from the uplifted oars—the ritual fulfilled.

As they floated into the gloom of the boathouse, the crew, in dutiful response to the coxswain, shipped oars, disembarked in unison by the numbers, lifted the boat to a storage rack. There would be another punishing drill tomorrow and the next day and the day after that, as there had been an unbroken series of tomorrows for the last two months—always with that devilish coxswain exacting more. And his parting words continued his badgering even after they'd landed, "Lads, tomorrow *promptly* at one thirty." Elliot wondered if all coxswains were as obnoxious as this one; sitting passively at the rudder would not satisfy most competitors, and the sole release for a coxswain's frustrations was to verbally browbeat the muscular oarsmen. Possibly this tension between coxswain and crew was the origin of a time-honored tradition for celebrating victories by throwing the helmsman into the water.

Preparation for racing demanded a dedication so intense the actual competition seemed an anti-climax, coming and going almost unnoticed. In reality, Elliot had been preparing for racing as far back as he could remember. As soon as he could swim, Father had taught him to scull in a single-seat boat, its razor thinness skimming the river's surface graceful as a dragonfly, leaving no evidence of passage. Now three years on a winning crew had earned him his position as stroke, and in his last season before graduating from the university, he was not about to be replaced at the number one seat. His retirement would be voluntary—to distance himself from depending on others, for the exhilaration of sole responsibility. After graduation, he'd return to his single-seat boat, an extension of his muscles and nerves and will to resume the impossible challenge of conquering himself.

Elliot was never perplexed by the unexpected. Freed of naiveté and introversion's burdensome afflictions, little separated him from reality, at least reality as he perceived it. Tempted neither by palliatives of ethical or religious doctrines, nor captive of predestination's debilitation, he was secure in the notion that life's anomalies could not be contained with anticipation or guile but demanded each moment be met with experience, gratitude, and indomitable optimism. Those trying to assign arrogance or ignorance to Elliot's modus operandi were on a fool's errand—keener perception would detect he'd escaped false credos and petty indulgences. Life happened, and Elliot H. N. Swan was in the middle of it.

While quite young, a curious style surfaced of being blunt without intended malice. One day while accompanying Mum to tea at the parsonage near their home in England, the newly installed cleric's wife gushed a welcome to mother and son before dispatching Elliot to play with her boy, several years his junior, while the adults became acquainted. At the appointed hour when English teas end and Elliot and Mum were leaving, the hostess asked her young guest if he would care to come again and play with her child.

"Not with that snot-nosed, little rotter, thank you very much," Elliot replied matter-of-factly.

Mum, always at a loss for words in such situations, beamed at her hostess and said, "It's been a lovely time. We must do this again at our home." Then, as she hurried Elliot out the door, realizing her parting remarks might be inadequate, added in a menacing tone for all to hear, "We'll just see about that, young man."

Though she secretly concurred with her son's appraisal, Mum felt obliged to carry on the charade of parental anger until they were out of sight. Then, no longer able to control a grim face but still repressing a chuckle, she asked Elliot why he'd said such a dreadful thing.

"Because he really is a snot-nosed, little rotter." Besides, he was obeying Father's rule of always being truthful.

Thus began Mum's long and sometimes confusing explanation of tact and candor to Elliot.

With the awakening of his libido, Elliot reached the age when children are in conflict by the realization their existence depended on the union of a man and woman but resist the notion their parents had sex. Logically progressing to the conclusion they might still be doing it, he was perplexed that he had no brothers or sisters. Finding his

Father always at sea when such life-defining moments arose, he dragged Mum from her genealogical mountain of charts and text to resolve his predicament.

"Oh Elliot, not now, I'm about to establish the Swans are direct descendants of Sir Francis Drake, and well they should be with such similar names. You know how happy that will make your father, the dear man."

Realizing Elliot would give her no peace until she answered his question, Mum straightened in her chair, put aside the wallpaper-sized chart, plucked off her glasses and gazed into the distance at some nonexistent object to emphasize the insignificance she attached to the response to follow. "Come along now, dear, you needn't bother your head with such things," she said as a last effort to deter her son.

But seeing his determination to pursue the subject, she in a moment of inspired invention fabricated a tour de force of fact and fiction. She narrated how her ovaries, inspired by perfect alignment, collaborated in a last heroic effort to produce a truly one-of-a-kind original and, unable to improve on perfection, withdrew to retirement. Finding her son's attention diminished by satisfaction or boredom, she concluded her deceit, saying, "Your father and I have done our part to carry on the lineage; now it will be up to you."

Elliot wandered away, considering when he should petition the pretty girl next door.

Having acquired the restraint to hold his peace with contemptible annoyances, Elliot, a talkative youngster, discovered the mutual felicity of expressing approbation. This new aptitude was first tested one morning while observing his neighbor's voluptuous teenage daughter tending her garden. As she bent to kneel, her open-necked blouse fell away, revealing ample breasts.

Stupefied by a surge of testosterone, Elliot blurted out, "What wonderful melons you have," then instantly prayed she'd construe this as a compliment to her gardening skills.

She glanced up without any change in posture and immobilized him with a smile of gratitude.

Thirteen, a landmark year, witnessed the conflicting rhythms when puberty subsides and parental restraints are replaced with privileges—responsible behavior rewarded with kudos. Sometimes Mum, getting ahead of herself, confused Elliot's partial observance of the rules with exercising good judgment and accelerated cutting the umbilical cord of parenting. Summing up, on balance, Elliot's successes far outweighed his failures, and he grew towards manhood in increasing knowledge and confidence. He now fully understood Father's mantra each time he left for a voyage. "You're the man of the house now. Take care of Mum." These simple words stated Father's loving concern for his family but also put his son on notice that becoming an adult was not optional. Both father and son understood no one, in the conventional manner, could take care of Mum. She evaded all conformity—her style made idiosyncrasy an art form, the bizarre commonplace, and Elliot had learned to navigate around her aberrations as skillfully as Father cleared reefs and shoals.

Apparently, it never occurred to Mum that when the time came for Elliot's departure to a proper public school, more would be required than putting him on the train with a box of cookies in his Gladstone bag, a reminder to write weekly and a parting kiss. In Elliot's instance, suitable institutions were first visited by father and son, and then the whole family returned to those of interest for interviews and tours. It was not uncommon that the academics were interviewed more rigorously than the applicant. One of England's most prestigious public schools was the object of Elliot's scornful rejection when his tour of a lower form dormitory disclosed the boys bathed in tin basins neatly aligned on a long soapstone trough and slept in a large hall, each separated in curtained cubicles. At last, Harrow enrolled Elliot, and his parents packed him off with a box of cookies in his Gladstone bag, a reminder to write weekly, a kiss from Mum and a "Harrumph. Good show, lad," from Father.

Elliot's initial presence at Harrow was perhaps as disconcerting to the masters as the student. Freedom of expression practiced at home was often discouraged or prohibited in his new environment, but by mid-term he found an appropriate forum for his discourse in the debating society. In short order, his eclectic knowledge, unique conceptualization and forceful delivery demolished most he opposed. One time, his interest flagging with the trite thesis advanced by his challenger, Elliot at the rebuttal stage reversed his position to argue against himself, throwing the judges into a state of pandemonium. Finding no precedent for this highly irregular behavior, the masters moved to redirect Elliot, appointing him president of the society and coach of the debating team.

Elliot's unorthodoxy permeated all his Harrow experience as he continually sought to break lockstep instruction in the belief that he should know the benefits of conclusions before laboring through the process of solution. The application of this concept was not novel, but extant in only a few writings such as newspaper articles where the last was the summary paragraph. Discovering his concept was not applicable in the sciences, he advocated abandoning texts and promoted learning by doing—a technique already employed in some quarters. But introducing this protocol to Harrow's curriculum was limited by its resources, such as the hands-on course on mammals with but a few specimens to study. Some disagreeable resolution was gained when Elliot constructed a tea table in his manual training class. The tyrannical instructor's requirement that all work be done with hand tools ended Elliot's enthusiasm for on-the-job training, at least in fine cabinetry.

His independent behavior and contrarian beliefs made him an admired fellow by most classmates but a constant irritant to all but a few masters who were discomforted by a student's probing intellect. One unreconstructed traditionalist, angered by challenge in a literature class, accused his pupil of impudence and defiance of authority.

Elliot listened attentively to a tedious reprimand then, when asked for a reply to the charge, said, "Sir, I was not defying authority, only defining authority."

In one sentence, Elliot had declared his manifesto.

The incident precipitated a request that Father and Mum meet with the school's administration to discuss their son's inconsistent academic record and questionable conduct—erratic, brilliant, abysmal. In summary, his divergence from Harrow's tradition was adversely affecting his education and unsettling those about him. With Father as usual at sea, Mum alone kept an appointment with the authorities and attempted to make all the appropriate responses to each predictable and superficial charge.

Manipulating the conservative school's aversion to potential gossip generated by an expulsion, implying the school had failed, Mum said, "Why don't you give him the boot?"

The master recoiled as though witnessing a violation of the Queen.

"Oh no," he replied, "We'd never do that. What we're thinking of is moving him to a lower form. Of course that has its drawbacks because Elliot would have to give up crew."

Mum, in typical fashion, concluded the meeting with, "Thank you, it's been a lovely time. We'll see to that young man."

She immediately went in search of her son but, unable to locate him, left a note. "Dear Elliot, you simply must do as well with your lessons as you do with crew or you'll get the boot. Love, Mum."

And so Elliot graduated with distinction.

Self-sufficiency was the norm at Oxford with only the most disputatious conduct drawing attention. Entering the less turbulent years of his late teens, a maturing perspective allowed more tolerance for foibles, and his witness of offensive absurdities registered no visible reaction. Having learned people rarely appreciated a response to their questions or had already made up their minds, his views were mostly unknown, but persistent pursuit of mindless inquiries drew a withering response framed in a tolerant smile, signifying he was pleased you'd no longer squander his time. An activist fully engaged in life without the shrill of protesting exhibitionism, he'd freely leave the secure dwelling of majority's conformity for a cause defended by few. At one with nature, he delighted in observing without judgment the endless peopled pageantry, preferring to interpret this cavalcade as the human condition, not the scornful cynics' human comedy. It was no wonder Elliot attracted a diverse coterie of acquaintances, many of whom tried to define him within the confines of their imagination but in the end always failed.

Elliot devoured Oxford's nine century harvest of knowledge. His first startling revelation upon admission to the university concerned the institution's selection of applicants. Candidates were accepted subject to minimum education qualifications and the results of special examinations, which made him wonder why he'd endured so many regimented years at Harrow. The news of the university's liberal admission policy irritated him and provoked memories of his failure to circumvent Harrow's old-fashioned instruction. But life would be different at Oxford, for students were housed with and taught by tutorial fellows closer in age and more collegial, and their twenty-four-hour availability gave Elliot an information source limited only by his initiative. He'd found his Rosetta Stone.

Well oriented by his second year, interested in expanding his enlightenment beyond insular academic loci and seeking practical applications of experience including pleasurable pursuits, pedagogy he'd always endorsed, Elliot devoted his attention to the university's sister colleges. His Mediterranean good looks and humorous views contrasted favorably with British stereotypes, winning him easy admission to the company of select female students where he became identified as the gorgeous puzzle. Crew-muscled six feet, black curly hair and boldly chiseled features supported Mum's genealogical legerdemain of Sir Francis Drake ancestry and, if liberties allowed, the admiral's assignation with a Spanish contessa bearing issue who unexplainably arrived in England. The initial thrust of Elliot's debut was to correlate the range of Oxford women's academic pursuits with their levels of self confidence fostered by the venerable institution. He assumed, unlike recent combinations of many American male and female institutions where one or both of the mixed sexes felt like intruders, Oxford's nineteenth century women's college had resolved such anxieties long ago.

Armed with this insight, Elliot developed a design for his study on the premise young women constantly displayed repetitive cues, which predicted their matured personae. As his observation of the feminine landscape accumulated ever-increasing data, unable to mentally retain an orderly catalogue, he developed a journal indexing all the information under headings of Profiles and Hypothesis, summarized as follows:

—Women who wear flat heels and large-rimmed glasses are sexually repressed.

—A woman who buys her own meal on the first date wants to be a friend.

—A woman who pays for her escort's meal on the first date wants a return engagement.

—If she reaches for the entire check on the second date, she's a control freak.

—Cat ownership indicates a homebody (introvert).

—A cat, vast quantities of houseplants and limited toilet paper predict a divorce.

—Dog ownership indicates she enjoys walking but on an either/or basis will exchange canine for homo sapiens protection.

—Without incident, a woman who bursts into laughter seeks an audience; one who bursts out crying should seek a doctor.

—A female student using a backpack for books expects accolades for her industry; one using a book-strap or carries them loosely held earns good marks.

—A woman who constantly arranges her hair or picks lint off clothing doesn't get most jokes.

—Those who bed on the first date will never be as good again.

—A woman who changes her street attire several times a day may have a messy house.

—One not embarrassed by singing off key often shows unusual compassion for others in all things.

—A woman who shows off her body in public may be embarrassed being nude in private.

—Women will talk with men but rarely other women about their sex lives.

 —A woman with a large appetite while dining out never cooks a good meal at home.

 —Most liberated types expect men to hold doors for them but seldom reciprocate.

 —Women who can only tie a man's tie when he's lying down may become undertakers.

 —One who talks about her course work is a bore; one who talks about his course work is a diplomat.

 —If a woman buys something because it's on sale, she's a woman; if she buys it because she needs it, she's abnormal.

 As the document lengthened, becoming progressively inconclusive with no end in sight, Elliot acknowledged he might be a gifted explorer, but conceded failure as a social scientist and looked for a source he might draw upon without revealing his project or compromising his authorship. This deviation from principle marked the beginning of his fall from grace. Within the purview of his inquiry, he'd profiled a particularly winsome sample name Samantha Burridge. She spoke in tones so soft as to command attention. On closer inspection, he learned she was a post-graduate anthropologist major three years his senior who wore flat heels, large-rimmed glasses, and enjoyed a nubile endowment with doe eyes that failed to keep secret a smoldering eroticism. He approached her without revealing his intent, hoping to glean some techniques for improving his study. As they talked, his questions became less skillfully disguised and, sensing she was being manipulated, Samantha asked how he was going to use the information. He decided to tell her about his project after she promised to keep it secret, and a behavioral collaboration became a sexual marathon. In a single stroke, he'd obliterated the first canon of research—the departure from impersonal objectivity to subjective intimacy. Though the yield of much work proved deceptively misleading, not all was lost as he experienced the time honored proverb that a woman reserves the right to change her mind and one should never judge a book by its cover.

 For a while, they met ostensibly to analyze the Profiles and Hypothesis, but that venture became secondary as the intermissions from work previously reserved for lovemaking took precedence—and Elliot's endurance was prodigious.

Samantha, being the consummate anthropologist, acquainted Elliot with the diversity of global fornication, covering two continents in nineteen days; from Oneida community's repressed interpretation of Far Eastern Karrezzo, Hindu's Kama Sutra, Serbia's Srpjkijeb and Croatia's Hrvatskijeb.

Shortly after their passage through the sexual landscape of France while they lay luxuriating in post-coupling languor, Samantha said, "Now I feel I can tell you."

"Tell me what?" Elliot asked.

"About your survey."

"What about it, other than we're not keeping at it."

"I knew what you were doing long before you told me," she answered.

"You didn't," he said, propping up on an elbow to see if her face disclosed a lie.

"I did."

"How could you?"

"Women's intuition," she answered.

"Rot."

"Why do you think I listened to those transparent questions day after day?"

"Why did you?"

"Because I wanted to find out how long it would take you to catch on to me."

"You dirty little voyeur, you're a sneaky socialist," he said.

"Sociologist," she corrected.

"That, too," he said. "Now if you're such an expert behavioral scientist who knows multi-cultural sexual practices as a sideline, tell me who does it standing up in a canoe."

"No one."

"Yes, someone," he replied. "I can."

"You can't," she said, amused he'd now turned tables and might be teasing her.

"I'll bet you."

"You're on—a bottle of Dom Perignon," she answered.

"Two bottles," he countered. "I'll meet you tomorrow night at eleven and we'll bike down to the boathouse."

Samantha, wearing a thigh length crew shirt, stood with her bike, eagerly waiting for Elliot to lose his wager.

"What's that for?" he asked, pointing at her shirt.

"Something warm and dry to wear after you dump me in the river. I don't have anything on underneath."

In twenty minutes they were at the bank of the Cherwell River, looking down at the ancient, rectangular wooden boathouse resting across the shoreline like a beached barn, the lone, triangular window at roof's peak reflecting the full moon's prediction of a high tide. Elliot slid the massive door along its overhead traveler to reveal a U-shaped, wooden interior deck two feet above the river slapping at its pilings. As Samantha's eyes adjusted to the dark, she saw all the rowboats and canoes but one in racks on the long walls of the U.

"Would you like to raise the stakes to three bottles?" Elliot joked. "Pick a canoe."

"This one," she said, pointing to the only canoe set secure in its cradle on the deck.

"That won't be necessary," he told Samantha as she began to remove her crew shirt. "Climb in."

"Aren't you going to launch her?" she jested, trying to be nautical.

"Only you," he replied, helping her into the canoe stabilized to the deck and winning the wager.

The fruition of Elliot's academic life was at hand. In a few days, he'd receive and probably put away forever diploma, cap and gown, marking him a Master of Philosophy. Not one to normally direct his attention to reminiscing, a few memories materialized, however, fragile as a dream in which Elliot remained detached, clinically observing snippets of vaguely familiar experiences. As quickly as they formed, they faded, clearing his mind for new challenges. Tomorrow his father would make port, and Elliot had a surprise for him when he landed his ship.

More knowledgeable about the sea than most his age, each year when his classes ended for the summer, Elliot gravitated to the deep water port near home for employment. His high concentration and quick assimilation caught the attention of the pier manager who advanced him from stevedore through the various duties of increased responsibility to operating a crane that unloaded the ocean fleets. But Elliot regarded these promotions solely as a path to being transferred to a tug that helped berth the passenger liners. Although Mum and Father were aware of his employment at the docks, they never departed from their separate worlds to imagine he was anything but a roustabout, nor did Elliot free them from his deception. Diligence and persistence were not to go unrewarded for long, however, and one happy day Elliot was certified as a tug boat pilot and helmsman. He'd waited patiently for the right time to surprise his father, and tomorrow was certainly the day.

Yesterday's tomorrow was today, a day which found Elliot at the wheel of a tug boat, watching the massive hull of the Queen go in and out of focus as she crept through the patches of morning fog. It was his father's ship in need of the tugs that nosed and pushed the liner to a safe harbor and the shelter of a berth. Elliot watched two other tugs make fast the hawsers thrown down from the steamer's deck fifty feet above. Now the three little floating powerhouses moved in to nudge and pull the big ship through cross winds and tides to a soft, safe landing. When she was secured at the pier and the tugs gave back the hawsers to be free for their next business, Elliot radioed his father. "Captain, this is Elliot Swan, pilot of the tug Tricorn. Your ship has come in."

The day after Elliot reversed the roles of parent and child to bring his father safely home; Oxford would celebrate their sons and daughters with degrees, some honorary, and uninteresting, fusty speakers mumbling unintelligible petitions. Congratulations would be exchanged by recipients of degrees with such gusto a disinterested third person would never guess the two graduates barely knew each other. Then Elliot would join the family for dinner at the club, return to the inn, pack his gear and in the morning leave for home. He wondered in what direction his degree would take him, only certain he had no appetite for returning to the classroom for a doctorate. Now he had neither the credentials or gray beard to attract a publisher, and research was too passive as prescribed by academia, unlike his independent foray in which he'd encountered the feminine mystique. Perhaps his initial science major could be effectively combined with his philosophy degree in today's holistic world. It would work out as it always had and would. He had no regrets.

The next challenge was Henley, and he was ready for it.

Chapter 2

Rowing: Moving a craft through water with oars is one of the oldest means of transit known and undoubtedly among the earliest sports in which men participated running and perhaps horseracing date from earlier times. Ancient tomb carvings depict rowing before the earliest of most recorded history, and it is a fact this locomotion was used for transport and warfare even after the introduction of sailboats. Rowing events were probably inaugurated by professional watermen on the Thames, providing England's earliest taxis. It is generally accepted that the first formal race was sponsored in 1716 by Thomas Doggett, an actor, for apprentice watermen, with the winner receiving a silver badge and livery, a requirement for employment. Rowing races on the Thames have been held every year since their origin except during the two World Wars. The second oldest continuous contest is the Cambridge/Oxford race started in 1829, ten years before the first Henley Regatta.

American rowing competitions, begun by professional watermen at the end of the eighteenth century, took place in New York Harbor, one of the most memorable being a race of whale boats between New Yorkers and Cape Codders, with the latter claiming victory. America's first intercollegiate contest was the Harvard/Yale race held on Lake Winnipesauke, New Hampshire, in 1852. Since 1895, regattas have drawn competitors from Pacific Coast, Midwest and Eastern universities, and since 1922, when the sport became an Olympic event, the Naval Academy, Yale, California and Washington Universities have won gold medals in the World Games.

The first boats were lapstreak construction; later the outside keels were removed and the bodies made of one skin. Today's largest rowboats, weighing less than three hundred pounds, are approximately sixty feet long with a twenty-four inch beam and a ten inch depth. Constructed of redwood cedar skins joined with waterproof glue to the ribs of spruce frames, they hold eight oarsmen using twelve foot long solid and laminated blades. A light metal outrigger attached to the frame of the boat holds the oarlock out from the boat to provide maximum rowing leverage. The oarsman sits on a sliding seat, moving fore and aft to optimize the stroke.

The actual act of racing in an eight man boat is not a conventional rowing motion but rather a setting of the blade in the water and then pulling past it. There are four phases to each stroke: the catch, pull through, finish and withdrawal before the oarsman repeats the motion—his body sliding forward in his seat to cock his legs before extending his whole body backwards, straightening his legs and pulling with his arms to complete the cycle. An expert eight will slide in and out of the stroke without altering their rhythm to check the run of the boat.

"Not bad, lads, for a Sunday row in the park," the coxswain taunted as the crew lifted the boat from the river. "Remember, we're just starting the qualifiers and we won't make it to the finals with a run like that. You need to pick it up and row together. Your rhythm is way off the mark. Your coordination is so bloody bad you'd think you'd never met before. Swan, when I call for a step up, I want to see your blade bite that water before the words get out of my mouth. If you all don't put out better, you'll be spectators next week."

Elliot slung a towel over his shoulder and started for the showers, cursing under his breath this antagonizing man who clearly believed in negative motivation. At this stage, it was not possible to calculate the number of boats they'd need to best to reach the finals. He'd win this regatta if he had to row the 2,310 yards by himself, then with a victory he could drown the bloody coxswain.

Bathed and dressed, Elliot started toward the river, thumbing through the official Regatta catalogue. The cover proudly proclaimed the races had been held annually since 1839 except during the two World Wars, and that Prince Albert had become a royal patron in 1851, bestowing the official imprimatur of Henley Royal Regatta forever more. No matter how often Elliot crossed the Henley grounds, he felt a sense of discovering this preservation of nature's beauty for the first time. The Regatta's Stewards justly deserved their title, for they were responsible for the removal of all land and water installations at the end of each racing season to return the site to its ecological origins from September to March.

Selecting a good point for appraising the crews still to qualify, he skimmed the catalogue's lore during the five-minute intervals between trials. More than seventy international teams were registered in the classes of Eights, Fours, Doubles and Singles, and Henley's two at a time boat races, unlike the international multiple lane contests, stretched the length of the Regatta over two weeks. In his impatience, he almost missed scouting some of his potential rivals, but he did see the strong races of America's Harvard and Princeton in the qualifiers. For the first time, it occurred to him that he might have been better off entering the Singles, dependent on none but himself. But he'd trained to stroke the Eights, and his brain and body were committed to win the big boats. As he watched the last trial heat of the Eights, he wondered how his crew, drilled for Henley's 2,310 yard course, might perform on Boston's Head of the Charles 5,632 yards of water.

When the qualifying heats had narrowed the field to two competitors from each class for the following day's finals, Elliot waited at the pier to watch Princeton's challengers pull their boat from the river for inspection and storage. Their coxswain moved among the rowers joking, making suggestions or encouraging them with a pat on the back and a good word. Though Elliot had watched the Princeton team from the riverbank, this was his first close-up look at the big, boyish, blond stroke whose face expressed continued amusement.

On their way to the showers, their paths converged.

"Welcome, Yank. I'm Elliot Swan in the Oxford boat," Elliot said, offering his hand. "Same class as yours."

"Glad to meet you, man. I'm Steele, Rich Steele, Princeton stroke," the American replied, smothering Elliot's hand in his.

"I know, I watched you stroke through all of the qualifiers."

"Oh, that was nothing. We were just running on half power," Steele replied with a mischievous grin, leaving Elliot uncertain if the Yank was really arrogant or just pulling his leg. But the possibility Rich was overbearing gave Elliot the added incentive to win the race with Princeton, then drown the bloody coxswain.

The day of the Oxford/Princeton finals dawned with a greenish-yellow sun appearing at a false elevation because of haze-induced parallax. In times past, a waterman's measurement of the sun to determine his bearing would have been imperiled by such a celestial anomaly. Things were also amiss for some of Henley's watermen as other days' inconsequential annoyances, now distorted by the lens of anxiety, became insoluble problems. A broken shoelace or a toilet that wouldn't flush was catastrophic, and the afflicted, unwilling to acknowledge stress, let the tension build up, risking a faulty performance in the race. In general, the Oxford and Princeton crews exhibited even more nervousness and withdrawal than the other teams; theirs was the last race of the day, and the wait seemed interminable.

The day wore into the afternoon without improving; the air thickened with hanging rain, precariously suspended as though a sudden jolt would jar it lose on the Regatta, which was usually the fate of all England's outdoor events. The hour of the last race neared with palpable excitement rising in the spectators, who'd grown in number with each previous heat. Now packing the riverbanks for the final event, the carnival mood crowd raised a great din, which the normally reserved English most probably attributed to the multi-lingual tourists.

Earlier that day when crews traditionally make repeated inspections of their boats to calm nerves, ever confident the previous check was insufficiently thorough, Elliot and a shipwright had made an adjustment to the rigger holding his oarlock, but once completed, subsequent scans proved everything was ready to go.

Half an hour before starting time, boats, slider seats and oars were rechecked, and finding inadequate distraction for pre-race nerves, some resorted to calisthenics.

On the ready signal from the officials, the boats were launched and began circling around each other behind the starting line like two great water bugs performing some ritual that precedes mating or combat.

Another whistle signifying 'get set,' and the contestants moved to the starting line, jockeying to gain an advantage from sudden gusts of wind that turned the river into corduroy. Elliot loved the spike of excitement whenever he was about to be tested—perception's stimulus transformed into instantaneous reflex, muscles and sinews exploding into the starting stroke.

The 'pop' of the starting gun, almost indistinguishable from a child's cap pistol, sent two boats of superbly conditioned human machines straining for the next 2,310 yards as though their lives depended on it. Elliot, squinting against the glare off the river as he rocked back and forth, felt the tension of anticipation release with every stroke. He was pacing the crew in perfect rhythm, and as they passed the second of the ten course markers, the lead over the Princeton boat seemed too easily gained.

At the third marker, Oxford still maintained its lead, but the gap was beginning to close. Another one hundred yards and the Oxford coxswain moved the count up to lengthen the lead, but Princeton met and bettered the challenge.

For the first time, Elliot felt demands on his body, but he had much more to give. Sweat began to wet his scalp, blur his eyes, and trickle down in ticklish rivulets between his cheek and nose. He thrust out his jaw, extending his lower lip beyond the upper, and attempted to blow the sweat off his face, but it only spattered his eyes with the salty stinging liquid, so he abandoned any attempt for relief. Out of the corner of his eye, he saw an unbroken wall of spectators...a jumbled frieze capturing unity of purpose for but seven minutes then dispersing unchronicled. Without turning his head, he flicked his eyes toward the competition's lane to see Princeton pull even.

At the halfway marker, his breathing was still regular; no body cramps. From what he could tell by looking at his crew seated with their backs to him, none were in trouble. Again the coxswain raised the count for Oxford to regain a marginal lead before Princeton again edged ahead.

Elliot's hands began to burn, his rocking motion in and out of the stroke became uneven, his legs, gut, shoulders and arms burned with pain. He could see nothing, hear nothing but the cadence of the devil whipping them toward purgatory.

At the three quarters marker, the Americans committed to making their all out move. Now they were five feet ahead, eight feet, ten. Why didn't their coxswain call for a spurt for the finish line although they had little left to give? Elliot cursed silently. He thought of stepping up the pace and forcing the rowers to follow, but that unexpected move could throw them off their rhythm even more. Now they were three hundred yards from the finish line and losing the race.

"Go get them," the coxswain yelled, "full bore." The rowers seemed crazed as they thrashed the water. "Finish them off, lads. Faster, faster, faster."

At fifty yards from the finish, Oxford had nosed ahead of Princeton, when Elliot's rigger broke, disabling his oar.

Shocked, thousands stood silent in disbelief as the Princeton boat crossed the finish line uncontested, showing Oxford their wake. Dejected, but never impolite, the English applauded the Americans then turned their backs to put the loss behind them and went their separate ways.

Oxford's humiliated crew was reduced to paddling their crippled boat to the pier, but they remained impassive until they reached the cover of the boathouse. Once out of public sight, some vented their anger on the shipwright for the equipment failure, one insisted on self-incrimination as a purgative, while others withdrew to be privately punished by their own feelings.

The sight of the spectators turning their backs and walking away from a lost race continued to intrigue Elliot. He saw no act of disloyalty towards their Oxford team but a prescience that the only reasonable course was to put the disappointment behind them and get on with life—an affirmation of his view. In an act of bringing the day to a close, the Oxford crew pulled the shell from the river, prepared it for shipment to their home club and left for the showers.

Along the way, Steele saw Elliot and stopped to wait for him.

"I wager I'll even trail you to the showers," Elliot said with a wry smile. "Congratulations, Yank."

"You Brits gave us a helluva bad time. Being used to the longer courses back in the States, we had trouble pacing ourselves. The tendency to hold back for a stretch almost put us out of business on the shorter Henley run. Sorry you had such a bad break."

"Me, too, literally and figuratively."

They talked for a while, becoming more comfortable with exploring a friendship. Short but increasingly personalized anecdotes swapped in good humor helped bridge the winner and loser from two different cultures. As they dressed, Steele, in what Elliot regarded as typical American spontaneity, invited him to Princeton's party scheduled for later that evening. The words 'victory party' discreetly left out caught Elliot's attention.

"I'd like that," Elliot replied. "My family came up for the races and expect me for dinner; please join us. Then on to the party."

"You're on," Steele said as the two former arch rivals left for dinner at the club.

Father arrived for dinner in the full regalia of a captain of an H.M.S. Queen; Mum, in an indescribable challenge to prescribed garden party ensemble, swept in full of entertaining absurdities.

Before Elliot could introduce his companion to his family, the Yank in his typical American way stuck out his hand towards Mum. "I'm Steele."

"Mr. Steele," Mum inquired, "do you have a first name?"

"Oh, yes, a first and middle with a lineage marker at the end as well. James Rich Steele the Third, but I'm known as Rich Steele."

"How interesting," Mum replied, "I don't believe I've come across any Steeles in my chart."

"My family came from Ireland."

"How unfortunate," Mum said before realizing how insulting that might sound. "I mean, the poor dears live such dreadful lives. But somehow I think they bring it on themselves. They're all Catholics, you know."

Elliot's finely tuned ear diverted him from a conversation with his father to effect a life saving intervention. "What are you two up to?"

"We're playing a genealogically advanced version of 'who do you know'. It's called, 'who are you,'" Steele replied impishly. "We were discussing names, and while I'm on the subject, I noticed Elliot's listed in the Regatta catalogue with two middle initials. What do H. N. stand for?"

"Oh my dear boy, for Horatio Nelson, of course." Mum beamed as she jumped back in. "The Swans are a long line of seafaring men. I've just verified Sir Francis Drake is a forbearer although it's not yet in the official register. Tell me, Mr. Steele, what line is your family in?" Mum said, breaking all British etiquette with her inquiry into something regarded as socially off limits.

"Indirectly we've been involved in one way or another with the sea since we first came to America."

"You don't say," Mum replied, her interest picking up.

"But I do say," Steele answered, having always wanted to correct such a silly conjecture and knowing the likeable, outlandishly engaging woman with whom he'd established a rapport would be amused. "My great-great-grandfather built the U.S. yacht that won the first American Cup Races."

"Did you hear that, Father? The Steeles built the first winner of the American Cup Races. Are you still building ships, Mr. Steele?"

"No ma'am, most of our work now is waterfront construction, piers, dry-docks, that sort of thing."

"Father, did you know Mr. Steele's firm builds dry-docks? If the Queen ever needs to be laid up, oh dear, if your ship ever needs to be put up, I'm sure Mr. Steele will find a lovely dry-dock for you."

Father had long since reduced his social vocabulary to the non-committal ambiguities of 'mmm,' 'harrumph,' and 'by Jove'. In larger social gatherings, his inscrutable good looks and heroic naval bearing made his stoic silences even more intriguing. It was common knowledge the good captain rarely spoke and never raised his voice to transmit his intentions to the crew—unmistakable facial expressions clearly conveyed his expectations.

It was well past nine when after-dinner coffee talk ran down and Steele realized he knew nothing more about the captain than the thousands of transatlantic passengers who caught glimpses of him, a competent but remote figure on the bridge of the Queen. Nor was Mum any less transparent, erecting private reserve markers reading 'No Trespassing—Keep Out'; she guarded an unusual intellect with diverting genealogical trivia. It amused Steele to imagine the Captain and Mum in a typical Alec Guinness farce where the mystery could only be resolved by Elliot and his parents submitting to DNA analyses. Trying to decide which parent Elliot resembled the most was a pointless exercise because in reality, he was an alloy—just more socially adjusted. Elliot was someone Steele wanted to know better, but that would be unsatisfied as long as the son was with parents.

"This was a real treat for me," Steele said to the Captain and Mum as they rose from the table, signifying the dinner had ended.

"I do hope we'll see you again before you return home," Mum said.

"I'd enjoy that, Mrs. Swan, but we're leaving early tomorrow to tour some of your country before flying back. I know my family would enjoy you as much as I have, and you're most welcome to stay with us any time you go to America. I'll give Elliot our address and phone number. Good night, Mrs. Swan. Good night, Captain."

By the time Elliot and Steele joined the American crew's party, the collision of physical exertion and alcohol was beginning to reduce the celebration to an endurance contest. As Elliot and Steele moved from rower to rower for an introduction and brief chat, Elliot was acutely aware of the contrast in moods between the victors and the vanquished. With the loss, the Oxford crew went through all the motions mechanically, from preparing the equipment for shipment to exchanging farewells and dispersing in defeat, while the Americans wanted to continue fraternizing, although it was unlikely they would ever again row together now they were entering the world of career building. Steele steered Elliot to the least noisy corner of the pub where they could sit back undisturbed and observe the revelers.

"What are you going to do now you're out of school?"

"I'm not sure yet—muck around for awhile, I suppose."

"Will you follow in your father's footsteps?"

"I would think not. Taxiing tourists back and forth to the same place year after year without exploring the visited country beyond the harbor doesn't appeal to me."

"Does your mother go with him on these trips?"

"She did once when I was old enough to travel but was so bored with the passengers, she never went again."

"How long has he been at sea?"

"This is his thirty-fifth year. Qualified for captain's license at twenty. I don't know how he does it. Sometimes I think he's been unfair to Mum. Don't know if her genealogy is the chicken or the egg."

"Have you ever thought of going to America?" Steele asked.

"No, but there's nothing to prevent me now I'm finished with school."

"You know, I purposely haven't talked about today's race. You came so close to taking us. It must be very hard for you," Steele said.

"I mainly wanted to win so I could drown the bloody coxswain. But we'll never know what the outcome would have been if the equipment had held up."

"Maybe we can find out. Come to the Head of the Charles this fall and we'll race again," Steele said.

"I doubt if I could reassemble the crew and get a sponsor."

"So you and I will race in the Singles."

"It's a deal," Elliot agreed.

Chapter 3

Alexandra Appleyard, alternately known through the years, dependent on the venue, as Apples, A. A. and Alex, devoted much of her formative days trying to distance herself from nicknames incompatible with her vision of *une femme des belle lettres*. She viewed her given and proper names as perfectly appropriate for all successes along her carefully constructed career path and discouraged any deviation from being properly addressed. Alexandra Appleyard was two degrees removed from becoming a snob. Family on her mother's side, scions to the founder-publisher of New York's most prestigious newspaper in the late nineteenth century, deftly continued to conceal their connection to the publishing empire. A distant black-sheep cousin once said Alexandra's congenital heritage endowed her with printer's ink in her veins, to which she reacted with mixed pride and revulsion.

A graduate of Smith College, majoring in literature and creative writing, her stories and poetry were welcomed by the school's newspaper but found no publisher identifying an impatient market waiting to empty her work from the shelves into the nation's bookstores. Never one to quit, only reorganize, Alexandra recast her resume to feature summer internships at a fashion magazine and an advertising agency, which provided admission into the newsroom of the family's newspaper without revealing her identity. Determined to sustain this sub-rosa separation, she reluctantly encouraged the newsroom people to call her Alex, knowing most would never bother to look beyond that for another name. Not unexpectedly, she was designated newsroom grunt, fetching coffee, supplies and backdated issues from the paper's morgue. Bitter java, stale cigarette smoke and raunchy jokes comprised the trinity for many fellow employees. In the beginning at the first sign of Alexandra each morning, some self-appointed wit would announce loud enough to override normal chatter, "The Ice Maiden approaches," signaling his co-conspirators to pretend to pull their coat collars tighter about them as they said, "Brrr." Then in unison, they'd yell, "Here comes Alex," and burst out laughing. For a while she ignored this hazing until their none-too-subtle remarks were directed at the various parts of her anatomy which might need warming. The following morning at the regular coffee break, she distributed to the four offenders coffee frozen hard as iron in their mugs, saying, "See if you can warm those up?" The crude remarks dwindled to only an occasional expression of disappointment that her wardrobe was not more revealing, but she had gained confidence from their behavior. Her security had not been breeched.

For four months Alexandra sat in the newsroom without a news assignment of her own, reading the city desk's bulletins and reporters' stories and checking punctuation, spelling and grammar until her eyes crossed. At times she couldn't wait to visit Smith and tell the bright-eyed literature undergrads what it was really like in the outside world. Each morning when she reported to the chief, it was a repetition of his previous day's pep talk. "Alex, the paper couldn't run without dedication like yours. Our reputation is dependent on the news we uncover and the accuracy of its presentation."

"I thought the accuracy of its presentation was based on the validity of the facts and reliability of its sources."

"That too, Alex, but dotting every 'i' and crossing each 't' is no small matter. Be patient, I'm sure something right for you will come along in time."

With each of his evasions, she felt betrayed by her college teachers who'd implied her magna cum laude was license for entry into any publication of her choice.

At a recent major gathering of the clan, an uncle, chairman of the board and more than a substantial shareholder of the publishing conglomerate, asked Alexandra in an offhand manner how things were going. Much as she wanted to vent her frustration, to do so might cause her uncle to intercede, and she would never know if she'd made it on her own.

"Fine," Alexandra answered as casually as the question had been asked, and the subject was dropped.

One day, silently and as mysteriously as an apparition, a woman adorned with a dramatic hat and high priestess-like garments entered the newsroom. Mistress of an Olympian demeanor, her commanding yet graceful figure followed a mixed-breed miniature dog to a desk distant from most newsroom occupants. The dog, clearly an extension of the owner's fashion statement, jumped onto the chair next to the desk and went to sleep as the woman removed a portable air filtering device from her black bag and began an ongoing battle with cigarette smoke. Alexandra considered it remarkable none of the others in the newsroom found this ritual as fascinating as she had. Adjusting her chair to a comfortable height and distance from the desk, the woman rolled a sheet of paper into an outdated upright typewriter and wrote without pause for two hours. At exactly 10:30 a.m., she leashed the dog, removed a disposable plastic envelope from her bottomless carry-all bag and left the newsroom, to return in ten minutes and repeat the exact entry of two hours earlier. At exactly twelve forty-five, the woman covered the typewriter, neatly inserted her typed copy into her bag, leashed the dog and left for the day. Alexandra had been so occupied watching this stranger her day's copy proofing had piled up, requiring her to work furiously to finish by press time. For a while, Alexandra wondered if this surreal travesty was contrived by the four reporters in retaliation for the frozen coffee she gave them.

For a week, the woman arrived and left on the same schedule, each day costumed in a different but equally arresting version of the ensemble worn the day Alexandra first saw her. It was apparent by the lowering of lewd decibels whenever she was present that the newcomer was a woman of considerable substance. Self-sufficient and intensely focused, she made no effort to cultivate acquaintances nor leave any trail to track. Not surprisingly, she disappeared from the newsroom as unexplainably as she entered. For all puzzles there are solutions, and this one was resolved in the executive women's bathroom. When the newsroom's women's toilet failed one day, those in need were granted temporary use of the prestigious key marking success. On entry, Alexandra encountered the enigmatic woman and introduced herself. The woman responded graciously, revealing she was Wysteria Marchant, food editor, who'd been temporarily exiled to the newsroom while her office was being redecorated.

"How long have they had you doing those menial tasks?" Wysteria asked.

"Since I arrived four months ago."

"Tell me about yourself," Wysteria said. "Better yet, come to lunch with me and we'll talk. I'll let your boss know you're with me, so don't worry." That simple statement seemed to indicate she enjoyed an important position on the newspaper's masthead, which explained the newsroom's deferential behavior.

At twelve forty-five, Alexandra and Wysteria Marchant left the building for a five-minute dog-walk before proceeding to a fashionable East Side restaurant where the maitre d' welcomed them with obsequious attention, hoping for a good review in the newspaper's food section. Wysteria seemed satisfied with the limited biography offered by Alexandra, who placed considerable emphasis on her eagerness for a story assignment.

"Let me level with you," Wysteria said, failing to achieve the get tough tone intended. "Those guys in the city news are going to lay off their work on you as long as they can get away with it. Tell the assistant manager you're through getting their coffee and correcting the reporters' copy, which they're being paid to do. You were hired to be a reporter. Now act like one. Go out and find a story if they don't have one to assign to you."

As they parted after lunch and Alexandra repeatedly thanked her hostess, Wysteria said, "I'll bet they won't fire you, but check in with me from time to time."

Alexandra, never one to let impatient enthusiasm compromise good timing, waited until the morning after her talk with Wysteria to approach the newsroom chief. Convinced by several rehearsals that her petition might sound whining, or even worse, apologetic, Alexandra settled on a simple extemporaneous summary of her disappointment that, to date, her responsibility in the newsroom did not meet her qualifications. Prepared to discuss her position in detail, or as a final resort resign if her assignment request wasn't met, she checked her hair, wet her lips and entered the chief's glass-enclosed office.

"Come in, Alex," he said without looking up as he scribbled some notes in the margin of the paper he was reading.

"Chief, I..."

"Sit down, Alex. Understand you had lunch with Wysteria. Very independent woman. Smart as hell, too. Started here the year after I came, but that's another story. Now, what can I do for you?"

"Chief, I'm sick of this coffee..."

"I agree it's pretty bad, why don't you get another brand."

"No, I mean I came here to become a reporter not serve coffee, and for almost five months some of the men have been giving me work on their stories they should be doing. I want an assignment. Anything to show you I can write for a newspaper."

"Alex, this has certainly got to be your day, because I've got a story all the guys are too busy to cover and it's perfect for a starter. It might take a couple of days to wrap it up, and it could probably run four or five column-inches, but then we'll look for something else for you."

"What is it, Chief?" Alex asked, finding it difficult to believe the interview had gone so well.

"It's an environmental thing. The city has passed an ordinance requiring all dog owners to keep their animals leashed out-of-door and pick up their droppings from curbside or face fines."

"That's it?" Alexandra asked, somewhat deflated.

"It's a start. Let's see what you can do with it. Now get on it and let me get back to work."

In fewer than three paces from the Chief's office, Alexandra admitted to herself she'd been had—a crappy assignment both literally and figuratively around which the jerks in the newsroom could build their pitiful jokes for weeks. She wondered if she was subconsciously setting traps for herself along her way—first the identity quagmire, which seemed insoluble, and now her commitment to a worthless piece of metropolitan trivia nobody else wanted. To make it newsworthy was as likely as turning a sow's ear into a silk purse.

After indulging in five minutes of self-pity, Alexandra went to the newspaper morgue to memorize the specifics of the canine sanitation ordinance. It took two readings of the regulation before she could decode the political lingo and learn what the authorities really wanted to state. It seemed sensible to solicit some public reaction to the new ordinance before approaching any city officials, which Alexandra intended to do by talking to dog owners in three different demographic locations. Her first stop was the Upper East Side, an affluent residential area where both genders walked their pets day and night.

"Hello, I'm Alexandra Appleyard," she said, introducing herself to the first prospective candidate to be interviewed. "I live just a few blocks away, and I'm thinking of getting a dog for the nights I walk."

"Good idea," the skinny, gray-haired man in the double-peaked Sherlock Holmes hat responded, "although I can't understand how there can be any crime in this neighborhood with hordes of dogs around. It looks as though the Westminster Kennel Show had moved here."

"Incidentally, what's your reaction to the new ordinance requiring owners to clean up their dog's droppings?"

"It's about time they got after these people who think the sidewalks are canine toilets. It's terrible out here, at times reminds me of my war days trying to pick my way through a minefield. Good luck, young lady. Don't buy a miniature canine abomination," he lectured, hauling off his bloodhound as he tipped his hat.

Half a block further, Alexandra encountered a svelte, blonde, pony-tailed jogger keeping pace with a stylishly groomed poodle.

"Pretty dog," Alexandra said, quickening her stride. "May I ask you a question?"

"Shoot," the blonde answered.

"What do you think of the new regulation requiring all pet owners to pick up their dogs' messes from the street?"

"Don't know anything about it. I just let Ginger do her business in the gutter by the sewer grate and the rain does the rest."

"You'll be fined for that."

"They'll have to catch me first. Besides, there are never any cops around. See ya."

Alexandra interviewed several more people in the same area before continuing her survey in other sections with different ethnic and economic characteristics. Had she thought about it, she wouldn't have been surprised to find a lower dog census in poor neighborhoods, as most couldn't afford the luxury of a pet, and streets were relatively clean because much of the residents' free time was spent in front of their homes. Reviewing her notes on the day's investigation, three issues dominated the verbatims concerning the ordinance…people didn't know about the regulation, they'd probably ignore it, and there was no tangible enforcement to change current practices. Alexandra was satisfied she had enough data to take the next step—an interview the following day with Frank Callahan, Commissioner of New York City's Sanitation Department.

"Good morning. I'm Alexandra Appleyard from the Times."

"Good morning, Ms. Appleton. I heard you wanted to talk about the new ordinance holding owners responsible for cleaning up after their dogs or face a fine."

"Appleyard," Alexandra corrected.

Callahan rudely ignored his mistake with Alexandra's name and transported to his own special world by fury generated from the dog sanitation issue, launching into a diatribe on pet owners. As he spoke, his voice mounting in anger with each recalled sanitation violation, he cracked his knuckles as though punctuating the end of each sentence with an aural period. Having conveniently forgotten his offer to hear the petition of a citizen, he was well into soliciting sympathy for the hardships of his office.

"Last year," he reported, "we received thirty-one demands for financial restitution from people who reported injuries from skidding on canine feces to ruining a new pair of ballet slippers. Do you have any idea how time consuming these nuisance claims are? This year to date we've received twice as many. Now you tell me why anyone needs a dog in this city. I see career women come home and first thing they do is walk the dog. Why do they have a dog when they only see it a few hours a day? Maybe they're so bossy they can't keep a husband and dogs don't talk back." Suddenly Callahan realized he might be on shaky ground with Alexandra and changed the direction of his monologue. "So, I say if we can't get rid of the dogs, make the owners get rid of the mess."

Alexandra was intrigued by the commissioner's monopolizing the entire time without once inquiring why she wanted to meet with him—and his capacity to talk was unlimited. She'd watched TV moderators interview political candidates and office holders who'd skew their answers to a question away from the subject or totally disregard the program moderator, but this face-to-face encounter with a civil servant gave her a whole new perspective on being talked to death. When she resumed listening to Callahan, she was determined to simply interrupt and offer him the results of her survey. He was somewhere in the midst of recapitulating the woes of an increasing dog census, a 'dog epidemic' he called it, when Alexandra broke in.

"Commissioner, I wanted to meet you and review some results of a survey you may find interesting."

"What survey is that?"

"Yesterday, I talked with residents in several different parts of the city, and here's what I learned." She spread the notes on the desk before him and waited for his reaction.

He squinted through his glasses, rocking slightly side to side, and muttered unintelligibly to himself before jumping up to say, "You got it, sister. I told the Mayor, measly one hundred dollar fines won't do it. One thousand dollars is more like it and nuke any second offense animals. Sister, you put your finger right on it, enforcement is the issue. You gotta have cops, cops everywhere, handing out tickets right and left." Callahan was becoming euphoric with the prospect of a dragnet that would ultimately make streets dogless. "One thousand dollar fines and a cop on every corner. I won't get any argument from the Mayor with these interviews to back me up. It's about time he got that publicity-happy Police Commissioner to give Sanitation the support we deserve. Yes, sister, one thousand dollar fines and police on every corner. No more 'need a cop, call the donut shop' business as usual. Ms. Appleton, I'll give you a scoop on the story when it breaks. Now we'll see who gets the press coverage, Mr. Police Commissioner Carmine Delisio."

"Appleyard," Alexandra corrected.

When Alexandra returned to the paper, she was greeted with exaggerated barks from the four irritating reporters, followed by a stream of suggested headlines for her story—

Canine Feces to be Wiped Out
Police Organize Poop Patrol
Sewage Scofflaws Down the Crapper

—and of course, her antagonists even supplied a sub-head for the response to counter the canine counter culture—

Puppy Poets Publish Protest Doggerel

Lest Alexandra's colleagues be accused of ignoring the nurture of a cub-reporter, the lead to the first of a series of articles was provided. "Last night while citizens slept secure in the vigilance of the city's administration, Mayor Morris Abramowitz formed a task force, co-chaired by Police Commissioner Carmine Delisio and Sanitation Commissioner Frank Callahan, for the protection of a majority of our residents who believe a dog isn't necessarily man's best friend."

Alexandra filed her article with the newsroom chief and, without waiting for his response, left for the streets to develop her story.

Callahan was correct. At the fifteen locations she quickly toured, no foot patrol officer was visible; two spiritless meter maids ticketing cars and the shriek of a distant police siren were the only indications of law enforcement's existence. For a while she occupied herself with additional interviews, but the dog walkers confirmed the previous day's survey, leading her to look elsewhere for a story in how people collected and disposed of the waste. Most used makeshift equipment such as sticks and folded paper, while the more sophisticated used household utensils…spatulas, tongs and plastic baggies. At one place Alexandra noticed a clean-shaven, neatly-dressed young man with a box-type suitcase, studying the law-abiding minority. As soon as the retrieving ritual was complete, the young man approached the owner and spoke for a few minutes before opening his case filled with shiny aluminum implements specially manufactured to ease the task just completed. He pointed out the tool's ergonomics and spring loading features. Money and product were exchanged, and the young man resumed his surveillance of prospects.

When Alexandra introduced herself, he apologized for not facing her directly as they spoke, saying he needed one eye for customers and the other for cops. She replied that most of her day was spent looking for a police officer, which she had yet to find. He explained he was creating a whole new cottage industry with his invention of the 'pooper scooper.'

"But there are a finite number of dogs. Won't you ultimately saturate your market?"

"Yes, but there is the refill market which is even bigger. The razor companies learned to make more money with the blades than with the holders. As soon as I get a concentration of customers in a neighborhood, I offer biodegradable dispensing envelopes delivered door-to-door. Then there are deodorizing wipes, also biodegradable, and so on. I build a business, they obey the law and become congratulated, model environmentalists to boot. Everybody wins."

In a half hour, Alexandra entered the headquarters of the New York City Police Department and climbed a grand marble staircase to Commissioner Carmine Delisio's office. After stating her business and showing her identity card to the guard outside the door, she was admitted into a white-walled, mahogany-trimmed room and spoke to a blue-uniformed receptionist.

"I'm Alexandra Appleyard from the Times. I'm covering the enforcement of the new canine ordinance holding owners responsible for cleaning up after their dogs. I have a four o'clock appointment with the Commissioner."

The receptionist whispered something over the phone to a blue-uniformed secretary sitting ten feet away, who rose to speak with Alexandra.

"I'm afraid the Commissioner will have to see you another day. He's in a very important meeting right now."

Alexandra, irritated by this inconsiderate rebuff, decided to stand her ground. "Perhaps he'd be interested in knowing there was a survey made which recorded multiple violations at each of fifteen locations and not one officer to ticket the offenders. He might also like to know I've had a meeting with Commissioner Callahan at Sanitation."

The secretary disappeared into the office behind her and instantly returned to say the Commissioner would see her if she could wait.

Before she had leafed halfway through a racecar magazine, the door to the office opened to dismiss a small, wiry, bespectacled man burdened with multiple books of clothing samples, followed by the Commissioner, dwarfing his tailor. Carmine Delisio, large in every way, moved with uncommon agility toward Alexandra, a photo-op smile splitting his clean-shaven, tanned face.

"Good afternoon, Ms. Appleyard. Sorry for the mix-up. My tailor was supposed to be here at five. Anyway, come in and let's talk. I understand you've seen Frank Callahan, great commissioner if there ever was one. Did he tell you how closely we've been working with his department on this dog thing? May I get you a cold drink? Our officers have been out there day and night, stretched to the breaking point. We're badly understaffed but new appropriation bills keep dying in the Council. Now let me show you the geographic impossibility we're always working to overcome with understaffed force. This map will give you an idea of the deployment problems we face with each new enforcement assignment and no more men."

There it was, Alexandra thought. The agenda to discuss an overworked police force had been set in twenty-nine seconds, and she'd bet the little remaining time of a token interview would be used by Commissioner Delisio to ingratiate himself with the press. Again, Alexandra took the initiative in response to Delisio's seventh example of the department's manpower shortage.

"Commissioner, I've heard many think the one hundred dollar fine for violation is much too low—for that little money, people will go on taking a chance they won't be caught. And the city won't get any significant revenues at that rate. Some have suggested one thousand dollars. It seems to me that one thousand dollar fines could pay for more meter maids, maybe even officers, and if the problem went away because of the size of the fine you wouldn't need additional personnel. Now if I may, let me show you the fifteen neighborhoods where high numbers of offenders are disregarding the law with impunity."

Alexandra felt slightly manipulative for using a word probably unknown to the Commissioner simply to impress him, but it seemed to have the desired effect because he quickly scribbled a note on his pad.

Relenting, she rephrased the thought for his understanding and said, "Some people are acting as though they're exempt from punishment."

Signaling the meeting was coming to an end, the Commissioner said, "You're lucky to be working for such a fine newspaper, and they're lucky to have you. If there's anything more you need for your story, give us a call," and opening the door, continued, "if you want to witness the force in action on a real crime, get Jessup at your place to take you with him. He's an old fixture around here."

Alexandra's story ran the next Saturday on the City News page with follow-up reports on two successive weeks, and she became a reporter.

Chapter 4

Except for the dim light emitted on the aisle from the fixtures in the bases of the seats, the passenger cabin was dark. After boarding, passenger lights were extinguished one by one as travelers put away books, switched off televisions or whispered conversations were traded for the rhythmic breathing of sleep. Released from his seat belt, Elliot rolled away from his neighbor to discourage conversation and stared out the windows at England's lights disappearing in the night. Bound in a new direction, it suddenly impressed him as strange how he'd traveled throughout the British Isles and much of the continent, but never to the United States. Somehow, this trip seemed ordained. At first, responding to Steele's challenge to race Singles in Boston provided all the required impetus to make the trip, but beating the American was now yielding to the expectation of exploring a new direction demanding agility and improvisation. In occasional contemplative moments, he was pricked by the prospect his British reserve would erode him into a stereotypical Colonel Blimp, so he prepared to guard against this with unconventional pursuits.

In the weeks following Henley, Elliot and Steele had begun an effortless long-distance dialogue which led to a friendship of growing importance and ease demonstrated by good-humored quips and serious exchanges, all in brotherly affection. Both knew that they would soon meet, and Steele's invitation for a visit had made final the travel arrangements.

The British Airways jet whined as the engine pitch was adjusted to descend from cruising altitude to enter Kennedy's controlled airspace. Elliot awoke before the flight attendant reached his section to advise in a gentle but insistent voice the estimated time of arrival in New York. The large, blowzy woman in the seat next to his snorted, yawned and sank back into a deep slumber. Apparently this behavior was not unusual because the flight attendant spotted the recalcitrant and returned to repeat the announcement louder and closer to the woman's ear.

"I heard you the first time, dearie," the woman scolded in a voice loud enough to rouse any other sleeping delinquents before rummaging through her pocketbook, spilling much of its contents in the process. Heaving her bulk out of the seat, she stomped off to the lavatory, grumbling all the way.

The flight attendant's low, persuasive voice and puckish expression conveyed her preference for all to enjoy the flight, but unquestioned authority in the five-feet-four-inch curly head easily outweighed any of the passengers'. Trifling with this attractively disguised taskmaster was not advised.

Elliot watched her collect and store pillows and blankets in the lockers, moving with the efficiency of two hundred flights of practice. In minutes she and her associates restored the cabin to order and began to move along the aisle offering coffee and tea. He tried to guess how many times she'd crossed the Atlantic and if she'd continue this work until retired by age. Did she ever explore beyond the airports the countries she flew to, or was she a jet age version of his father, never venturing beyond the boundary of the familiar?

"Miss, how may times do you think you've landed in New York?"

"Let me think, I'd guess one hundred and fifty. No two hundred."

"Would you ever like to go sightseeing in the city or even further?"

Misinterpreting the question as an approach for a date, she replied, "No sir, it's against company policy to fraternize with the passengers," and moved along the aisle with the carafes of coffee and tea.

The savory aroma of the steamy brew did not exaggerate its taste. Who said the English were limited to tea? Each sip of coffee released him from the beguiling luxury of drowsiness, heightening his sense of the immediate. Predictable England was passing into a memory three thousand miles old. Soon, the native tongue he would share with a country he was about to enter would mark him as a foreigner. The words would be the same, but accent and inflection would set him apart. He found it a paradox that in Europe so many different languages spoken in poor grammar or faulty accents attracted little attention, but Americans in their homeland immediately singled out linguistic counterfeiters.

The sudden, increased illumination in the cabin disrupted his ruminations and frustrated his search for America's border lights by flooding his window with distorting reflections. He pulled a jacket high on his head to form a hood-like light barrier and pressed his face against the glass, straining to find pinpricks of white in the darkness. His reward, seen through tired eyes, was a smudge of gray, like a giant chalkboard hurriedly erased. The ashen smear fanned slowly across the sky in an arc—the Kennedy beacon reaching out to welcome wayfarers. His trance was broken by the captain requesting passengers return to their seats and buckle up.

"We are now about to enter our Kennedy traffic pattern which will offer a splendid view of New York City," he reported. "Please follow your flight attendant's instructions."

The information immediately stimulated a flurry of activity, particularly among those first-time visitors to the United States. The blowsy woman, having returned to her place, struggled into a seatbelt and began devouring a box of chocolates, oblivious to all around her. The din of the passengers rose to drown out the loud thump of the landing gear locking into place. On entry into the landing pattern, the captain's promise was fulfilled with a dazzling view of Manhattan's skyline—man's incandescent triumphs thrust high enough to touch. Now the plane staggered ever so slightly as engines roared into full power to maintain flying speed while compensating for the drag of lowered flaps maximizing lift. Elliot noted the optical illusion of landing—the ground always rose to meet the plane, defying the reality of descent. A screech of the tires as the landing gear wheels rotated instantly to one hundred sixty miles an hour from zero.

"Welcome to Kennedy Airport, New York. The time is ten thirty a.m., Wednesday. Thank you for flying British Airways," said the captain as he parked the jet at the gate and shut down engines.

"Hi guy!" Elliot yelled to Rich Steele who was waiting for him to clear customs.

"How was the flight?"

"Piece of cake. Slept right through it without one nightmare about you."

"Well, it's good to see you even if you've left your British manners at home."

"You know that old bromide," Elliot joked, "when in Rome, do as the Romans do."

"We'll see how quickly you adjust. Any jet lag?"

"Not yet, but your prattle may put me to sleep."

"Prattle is definitely not an American word. Over here we say 'bullshit,'" Rich said.

"In the company of ladies?"

"No, we say B.S.; the ladies say bullshit," Rich replied. "How long before you clear customs? Or are they holding you as an undesirable alien?"

"I think it may be guilt by association," Elliot answered.

By now, passengers waiting for their baggage inspection clustered around Elliot as he traded quips with Rich on the other side of the barrier. One onlooker offered to bet his companion on the length of time this repartee could be sustained.

"How much longer are you going to be with customs?" Rich inquired again.

"The man says they can't find you on the F.B.I. wanted list for harboring aliens, so I'm free to go." Elliot loaded his bags on a luggage dolly and stepped out of the customs area into the United States. The two rowers stopped in the middle of the concourse and hugged for the delight of being reunited.

"See," said the bespectacled, sallow faced man, who with his companion had listened to the two rowers joking, "I told you they were queers."

"Where's your shell? We have a race next week, or are you trying to weasel out of it? Maybe you'd like to concede and save yourself embarrassment," Rich teased before realizing he might have gone too far.

For a moment, Elliot felt stung—oversensitive to the poor showing at Henley or maybe culture shocked.

"We'll see. We'll see," Elliot replied, shaking off his irritability to remember Rich was his friend. "My boat arrives tomorrow. By the way, is there a place nearby to row?"

"Cold Spring Harbor. It's only five minutes from the house. I usually get in a half hour after work when the club members have come in from sailing and tied up at their moorings. If you don't think Long Island Sound is big enough, it's only a half hour to the Atlantic Ocean," Rich said, inviting Elliot to return to their banter.

It was exactly eleven p.m. when they loaded the baggage and circled the parking lot to the northbound exit.

"How far are we from your home?' Elliot asked.

"Less than forty-five minutes if the traffic has eased for the night. It was pretty bearable when I came to get you."

"Is your company located near your home?"

"The headquarters is in downtown Manhattan near the Battery but our sand and gravel plant where I work is in Smithtown, less than—"

"I know," said Elliot, "less than forty-five minutes from home."

"Dad commutes by train to the city most days and I go in for a review meeting every other week for a few hours. I'm also out on site when we have a job and material estimates are needed. Our equipment depot is just across the Hudson in Jersey City. That's about it. Oh no, I forgot. About a year ago, we started a brokerage business to handle our insurance coverage. Originally, it was intended for our purposes alone, but knowing the marine construction field as we do, others in the industry came to us because we can provide the service they require and save them money as well."

"Is this going to be your life work?" Elliot asked.

"I don't know. I've worked for the company since I was sixteen doing every dirty job. I used to get pissed off being moved form the bottom of one section to the bottom of another, but now I'm glad because I learned where trends started and I can predict most of the industry's developing problems. For example, there are finite reserves of sand and gravel, which are major components of our material requirements, and zoning restrictions on many quarries and deposits compound the problem of future supplies. And that's before you even consider foreign competition, which is undercutting pricing with lowball bids. You ask me if this is going to be my career. I don't know, but I'm sure we've got to diversify if we want to grow or perhaps simply save our business. When people in the company find this hard to accept, I remind them we used to build boats, now we build bridges."

Rich spoke with increasing passion as he navigated the tangled spaghetti of Long Island's highway system, deftly entering and exiting connecting roads so intertwined the novice would find it hard to believe the next turn wouldn't return him to where he'd come from. For a distance, Elliot tried to memorize the route for his return to Kennedy to pick up his boat. Finally unable to untangle the labyrinth he said, "I have to retrace this route by myself tomorrow to pick up my boat—you may never see me again."

"You don't seem to be adjusting very well to America," Rich replied, "but I'll chalk it up to fatigue this time. Not to worry, I'll go with you."

Rich turned off the interstate to a secondary route crossing the Long Island Railroad onto a country road to Cold Spring Harbor, past the yacht club, and up a private drive of crushed oyster shells to a large brick Georgian house set on the top of a rise.

"We're home," he said. "I'm sure my parents are in bed, but you can meet them at breakfast, or if you want to sleep in tomorrow, at dinner."

"This is where you live?" Elliot asked, more overwhelmed with the imposing home the closer they came to it. "This is where you live?" Elliot repeated, losing some of his British reticence.

"For the moment. Now I'm finished with college and working full time, I'll find my own place, probably nearer the plant in Smithtown." Rich rounded the circle in front of the house to a garage inconspicuously placed behind a bank of rhododendrons and parked the station wagon in the only vacant stall. "Looks like a used car lot, doesn't it? This wagon is mine, but I guess you already know that from the stuff lying all over. The Mercedes is Mom's, the BMW sports car is my sister Laurie's, and the ten-year-old, black, plain vanilla Ford is the old man's. He always drives a junker, says it keeps him humble."

They crossed the oyster shell driveway, a luminous white ribbon defining the Steele's affluence. Even the crunch under their feet sounded like money. "Where do you get all these shells?" Elliot asked, sounding foolish trying not to say something foolish.

"A lot of our jobs require dredging and they come up in the mud, so we just dry the silt and screen them out. Come on in." Rich opened the front door into a circular hall three stories high with a spiral staircase leading to the floors above. "Want something to eat or drink?"

"I'm for bed. I must be hallucinating," Elliot said, gesturing at the beautiful space where they stood. Then concerned he might have been rude by implying it was ostentatious, added, "It's pure symmetry."

The four-poster was high, firm and welcome, bringing immediate sleep. Elliot awoke in a noiseless house, the sun announcing its arrival with pink and purple swaths across a lemon sky. Through the slightly parted, fine linen curtains he could see a few hardwood trees showing different progressions in their fall coloring. Within days, he and Rich would drive to Cambridge, and for a few minutes at the Head of the Charles Regatta, three months of friendship would be excised as they went head-to-head in single boats. Perhaps it was a mistake to have accepted Rich's invitation to his home before the race. Elliot wondered if he'd be welcome after he beat Rich and then decided that was silly because their meeting and subsequent friendship had evolved from his Henley defeat. He checked his watch and realized he'd not reset it. Still on London time, he moved it to New York Eastern Standard time, seven a.m. His internal clock was not yet adjusted to new surroundings, and he decided the sooner he was active, the sooner he'd be in sync. Hoping to have breakfast with Rich and his parents before they went their separate ways, Elliot bathed and dressed, delaying unpacking until later.

At the bottom of the corkscrew staircase he heard conversation coming from the rear of the house and traced the voices to a plant-filled solarium. About to enter the room, he almost collided with a fifty-year-old edition of Rich: big, trim, athletic, blond going gray, friendly, vigorous.

"You're Elliot. I'm Jim Steele. Glad you're here. Rich told me a little about you, but we'll catch up with each other later. Gotta go or I'll miss my train. Welcome. If you don't see what you need, tell Danvers here," Mr. Steele said, indicating the butler busy at the hunt table, "he'll take good care of you. See you tonight." And he was gone, leaving Elliot certain this introduction had to be the shortest and most hospitable he'd experienced.

"Good morning, Sir," the butler said, bringing Elliot back from his thoughts about the similarity of the father's and son's styles. "What is it you'd like?"

"Good morning, Danvers. I'd like to start by nibbling around the edges of everything before I make a choice."

"Very well. I can recommend the kippers. They were Mr. Richie's idea to make you feel at home. Mr. Steele's preference is for Eggs Benedict. Mr. Richie is eating more carbohydrates than usual as he gets fit for the race."

"How long ago did you leave England, Danvers?"

"Twenty years this October, but I go back every five for visits."

Elliot watched the butler move quietly and skillfully from the hunt table to his place with the appropriate china and silver. If the butler hadn't been talking, he could almost go unnoticed.

"There certainly is no shortage of choices," Elliot said, noting the silver hoods on the steam trays. "If I had to guess, I'd say you were from Cheshire."

"You have a keen ear, Sir."

"Could you just call me Elliot?"

"As you would, Mr. Elliot."

"Danvers, you have a very distinctive name. Danvers, Danvers," Elliot said, trying on the sound to appreciate the authority implied. "Is there a surname?"

"That is my surname, Mr. Elliot."

"And a given?"

"That's my complete name. Scottish ancestors apparently practiced frugality to a fault, and my parents saw no reason to do differently," the butler said, pleased with his jest.

"How do you fill in forms?" Elliot asked, seeing difficulties satisfying the bureaucracy.

"It's a bit of a problem, Sir. Immigration clerks got into an awful row when I wrote only Danvers on the application—weren't going to clear me and all that rubbish."

"How did you manage that?" Elliot persisted, eager to learn the resolution of the impasse.

"The first clerk brought in another and after blustering about, called in their supervisor. After searching the regulations and finding no solution to the case, they all reluctantly agreed to notify the regional section chief. He arrived, obviously irritated by having his after-lunch nap disturbed, grabbed the application, looked me over and said, 'Pass him. He's as dangerous as a Sunday school teacher, and mark 'One Name Danvers' in the first, middle and last boxes on the form.' Relieved to be rid of the problem, I was rushed through the remainder of the processing with only the reoccurring annoyance that many call me 'One Name' as though it were a title."

"Perhaps you'd like me to loan you a name. I have a rather large supply."

"No, Sir. Everything is pretty much straightened out, and I pretend I'm a one name celebrity like that Picasso fellow. That seems to do the trick."

"Now, let's see about breakfast," Elliot said, savoring the aroma of the delicacies beneath the silver hoods on the steam trays.

"May I help you, Mr. Elliot?"

"Thank you. Now I'm ready to concentrate, but I'd enjoy talking with you while I eat if you have the time. Is Rich coming down soon?"

"Oh no, Sir. He left an hour ago," the butler said, checking his pocket watch to verify the time. "He asked me to tell you he'll pick you up about two and you can see about your boat."

"Have you ever attended the Henley Regatta, Danvers?"

"Once when I was a little boy. I didn't much like it—all that pushing about and everyone stepping on me because I was so small."

"That's where I met Rich," Elliot said. "His Princeton team beat ours and that's why I've come to race him again, but this time it will only be the two of us." For a few minutes, Elliot concentrated on the fresh strawberries before taking a large helping of waffles and sausages. Until he started to eat he'd been unaware of his hunger, then his appetite, once primed, tried to compensate for the time lag.

By mid-afternoon the two contenders, having retrieved Elliot's boat from Kennedy, plunged back into the nightmarish cat's cradle laughingly called a highway system. Seeing in daylight the circuitous route Rich had navigated the previous night impressed Elliot even more, and he determined to concentrate on mental mapping until he was no longer dependent on others for transportation. He forgot the turn off the secondary highway to cross the Long Island Railroad tracks, but he picked up on the country road to Cold Spring Harbor and was correct on the rest of the course.

At Elliot's earlier suggestion, they went directly to the yacht club, changed into racing clothes and in minutes were on the water. A few full sweeps to clear the Beetles and Day-Sailors at mooring loosened up his plane-cramped stiffness.

"I'll pace you," Rich called to Elliot as they reached open water, setting the two on a mile stretch across the harbor.

The sun, lowering towards night, had lost its midday heat and the breeze off the water was a prelude to autumn. The two rowers stayed even at a moderate warm-up measure.

"You seem to be faltering," Elliot joked. "Would you like to go back, or maybe a tow?"

"I've been paddling with only my hands. Wait till I put my oars in the water. I'll row your English ass off that slider seat."

"I've been dragging my anchor to slow down for you. Would you try to go a little faster on the way back?" And so the two exchanged banter, knowing as race day approached, rising tensions would need a harmless outlet.

Elliot's first dinner with the Steeles, less than twenty-four hours from his London departure, was a sleep-deprived, murky tableau. To date, his own mother and father had been his principal reference to family dynamics and over time, their quirky behavior had become predictable, ranging in a pattern of slight variations within one basic theme. The Steeles, as he soon would observe, were an uncommon union of diverse individuals constantly reinventing the formula for family without compromising their unconditional mutual love and respect. Spontaneity was part of their metabolism; good will towards others and trust in even the least gifted they encountered, more frequently than not, gave most the incentive to play at the top of their game. Rich had told Elliot that one time as a young boy he'd complained to his father how his best friend Sam had asked to borrow a baseball mitt then lost it. Rich, hurt and angry, told his father he was never going to trust anybody anymore, to which his parent replied, "You're going to have a very lonely life with no friends. Just because one does something mean to you, there's no reason to distrust others. Sure, things don't always work the way you think they should, but there are many more that work right. But the most important thing is to let no one change your behavior because of the way they act." And that was Elliot's profile of the senior Mr. Steele.

Exactly at the stroke of six, Mrs. Steele, exquisitely groomed, came down the spectacular staircase to signify the cocktail hour was at hand. Elliot's first sight of her was unforgettable—a beautifully graceful, dark-haired woman moving mysteriously in and out of the shadows in her circular descent. Her close presence, even more stunning, revealed steady blue eyes, patrician nose, high cheek bones and a firm but kind mouth—all in perfection to exceed her portrait in the library. Her welcome, genuine and warm, unmistakably conveyed an invitation into the family. Her splendid naturalness overcame Elliot's momentary concern that his informal attire might be unacceptable despite Rich's assurances to the contrary. For a few moments, she spoke in subdued, warm tones to Rich and Elliot as a mother respectful of two sons, holding their attention with sheer charm. The discordant crunch of oyster shells beneath car tires announced the arrival of her husband.

"With a driveway like ours, one doesn't need a burglar alarm system." She laughed, rising to greet her husband who entered, shedding his brief case and several New York newspapers along the way.

"Hello, dear, how was your day?" he asked after a kiss. "Did these fellows take care of you? Everyone have a drink?" He poured himself a Chivas Regal and sank into the couch next to his wife.

"Elliot was telling us a little about his family when you came in," Mrs. Steele said.

"How long are you over for?" Mr. Steele asked.

"I have a six-month visa, sir. I think I'll travel a bit after getting even with your son, then I'll go back."

"What will you go back to? Rich tells us your father is a captain of the Queen. Will you follow in his footsteps?"

"I think not, sir. Doing the same thing over and over doesn't appeal to me. When I left Oxford I went back to my previous summer job of working in Southampton's port, berthing large ocean-going ships. I have my pilot's license for tugs and I like the sea, but not for long stretches."

"I suppose Rich has told you about our business. You might want to drop by before you leave and see what he's being overpaid for."

"We've talked about that—the work I mean," Elliot said, catching himself on the verge of insulting his host. "I mean to say—"

"Hello everybody. Hello Mom, Dad, Rich." The young woman sang her way around the room, at first not seeing Elliot hidden by the back of his wing chair. "Oooh," she cooed, "you must be an import. I'm Laurie. Is this the love child you never told us about, Mother?"

"This is the daughter we keep on a remittance out of the country so she won't embarrass the family." Rich said to interrupt his non-stop sister, "Where have you come from and where are you going next?"

"I've been in Maine at the Outward Bound Reservation where I met the most divine man in the whole world. At least until now. What did you say your name was?" she asked, turning her attention to Elliot.

"I didn't, but it's Elliot."

"Like T.S. Elliot?"

"No, like Elliot Swan."

"And what do you do, Elliot Swan?"

"I row."

Rich and his parents, content to witness the verbal tennis match, waited for a missed shot while Elliot remained amused by Laurie's child-like persistence.

"What do you do when you don't row, Mr. Elliot Swan?"

"I practice rowing."

There was a momentary pause in Laurie's inquisition, allowing the maid who'd been patiently waiting at the door to break in. "Mrs. Steele, Danvers just telephoned to say his train broke down near the Jamaica station and he can't get home in time to serve dinner. All the other trains are backed up and there's not a cab to be found."

"Don't worry, Mary. We'll manage," Mrs. Steele said quietly to put the young woman at ease, assuring that neither she nor the cook would be held accountable. The maid hurried away, glad to be rid of bad news.

The family conversation resumed with Mr. Steele asking his daughter about her Outward Bound course.

"It was a real confidence builder," Laurie explained. "Gave me a whole different perspective—new direction to my life."

"Which is?" Rich asked.

"I'm going to dedicate myself to the environment. I'm going to quit Barnard and join Green Peace."

"That's a lovely idea," Mrs. Steele said, "but don't you think you'll be of more value to the environmental effort with the credentials of a degree?"

"Your mother makes a lot of sense, Laurie," Jim Steele said. "If you quit school before you graduate, it may make people wonder how serious you are about things."

"What would you do, Mr. Elliot Swan?" Laurie asked, in part to avoid responding to her parents' common sense, in part seeking an ally.

"I would listen carefully to what your parents say, then I'd try to decide what I'd tell my daughter before making up my mind, knowing the decision and responsibility for doing whatever I wanted would be mine alone."

"Oh, you're deep, Mr. Elliot Swan," she said.

"No, just English."

There was a pause in the conversation as Mr. Steele poured everyone another drink while Laurie puttered over some exotic concoction, presumably the current beverage of choice at Barnard College.

Once again from the doorway to the library, the maid timidly waited for recognition. "Excuse me, Mrs. Steele. We're having duck for dinner and neither cook nor I know how to carve it."

"I'll take care of that, Mary," Mr. Steele volunteered, "I shot the damn thing and I guess I can cut it up."

"In that case, sir, dinner is ready."

"Bring your drinks," Mr. Steele suggested, draping his arm over Laurie's shoulder as they walked towards the dining room. "It's good to have you home, Laurie."

"You know, Daddy, when I become an environmentalist, I'll probably have to sue you for digging those big holes in the earth," she said, visibly worried. "Or at least picket the company," she added, seeking a less harsh alternative.

"I know, honey. You have to do what you have to do."

Chapter 5

Five days remained until Elliot and Rich, their boats secured atop the station wagon, would drive two hundred odd miles to join the score of rowing teams cheered by three hundred thousand spectators at the Head of the Charles in Cambridge, Massachusetts. Rich, having resumed daily practice and Elliot, completely adjusted to the time zone change, now felt ready for the race. Each afternoon since Elliot's arrival found the two skimming across the harbor taking turns setting the pace and matching it. Although neither spoke of it, there was no doubt the competitors understood the leader never rowed his fastest and the follower always lagged slightly behind, thereby concealing the best effort of both. Secretly, each knew the charade was ridiculous, but they perpetuated the transparent duplicity, fortifying themselves with expressions of grim determination and choking back uproarious laughter.

In that same week Elliot, responding to Mr. Steele's persuasive invitation, toured the company's facilities. Starting at the heavy equipment depot in New Jersey, Elliot's concentration was captured by Mr. Steele's enthusiastic, detailed description of the marine construction business. Leaving New Jersey, they crossed the Hudson River by ferry, bringing to mind the history Elliot had read of early U.S. rowing on the mighty river. From the landing at the downtown terminal to company headquarters on Whitehall Street was a few minutes' walk where the old-fashioned, iron-grilled elevators ascended seventeen floors to J. Rich Steele, III and Company offices and a magnificent view of New York Harbor. For a moment, Elliot stood entranced by the miniature, otherworld-like scene below, guessing at which dock his father berthed the Queen.

Steele, as though reading his young guest's mind, pointed upriver to a large wharf with a shiny metal roof. "That's where the Queen ties up."

Only Elliot's introduction to key employees interrupted Mr. Steele's informative monologue supported with facts and figures on every department. The management's systems in place were designed to optimize initiative while providing instantaneous tracking of all work in progress. Mr. James Steele, not a man who left things to chance, constantly considered alternative actions to recover from inevitable mishaps. It was during their visit to the company's marine terminal on Long Island that Elliot showed his keenest interest. As Steele, with faultless accuracy, inventoried the barges, lighters and scows by capacity and use, Elliot's eye drifted towards the tugs tied up at the other side of the yard, his excitement almost palpable.

Again, Steele's perceptiveness read Elliot accurately, and pointing to one of the network of gangplanks providing access to the crafts, he said, "Let's take a look over there," as he headed towards the tugs.

"Seems to me I heard you know how to master these bulldogs," Steele continued, indicating the powerful, stubby boats.

"Yes sir, I was fully licensed last year and spent most of this past summer berthing large ships at Southampton."

"Ever sail an ocean going tug?"

"No sir, all harbor crafts, but I'd like to try."

"How about right now? I see Jack Willard, the skipper of our fleet is on deck. I don't think he'd mind us borrowing one for awhile."

Willard looked up from some maintenance reports as the two approached. "Morning, Mr. Steele."

"Closer to afternoon, Jack. I haven't done a lick of work because of this fellow. Elliot, this is Jack Willard, captain of our fleet and head of the yard. Jack, meet Elliot Swan from England. He's skippered harbor tugs but wants to give your ocean boat a try."

"Fine with me, Mr. Steele. If you don't mind, I'll go along just to be sure he doesn't take over my job."

After studying the instruments and checking minor operational procedures with Willard, Elliot called for the deckhand to stand by to cast off. A slight press on the starter and the deep throaty engines came alive, sending vibrations through the leashed craft. Hawser-freed, Elliot put his drive in reverse and slowly backed into the yard's cove, cautiously respectful of the boat's latent power and quick response. Feeling his way into controlling the boat, he swung the bow towards the channel of the East River and headed downstream towards the harbor. For awhile, he maneuvered through shipping traffic, passing under the Williamsburg Bridge to catch a glimpse of the Statue of Liberty before coming about to turn upstream alongside the decommissioned Brooklyn Navy Yard. When a stretch of river cleared before them, Steele encouraged Elliot to run at full power. For a moment, the force of the high speed propellers scooped out a hollow in the water to keep the tug from swamping as it buried its stern. Then as the boat's speed picked up, it righted and plowed forward, leaving a deep furrow in the slick, dark river before being skillfully maneuvered to the dock to be tied up.

"What do you think?" Steele asked Elliot as they went ashore.

"Thank you, sir. She's a beauty. I think ocean-going tugs are the only thing for me from now on," Elliot replied over his shoulder as he walked ahead of Steele and Willard.

"We better be on our way. Thanks, Jack, for the use of your yacht."

"Anytime, Mr. Steele," Jack replied and then lowered his voice to add, "He's a good pilot. Wish we had more like him."

Elliot and Rich left on a clear, crisp, Tuesday fall morning to enjoy a leisurely drive along the New England coast with plenty of time to become settled before the start of the races. There had never been any exchange but teasing about the outcome of the contest, perhaps because neither wanted to risk a word, misunderstood or carelessly spoken, to jeopardize a friendship still in the process of being built. For twenty minutes they drove west from Cold Spring Harbor to cross Throgs Neck Bridge connecting Long Island with The Bronx. From the middle of the span crossing the water, one could look down and never see the thumb-shaped land neck from which the westernmost tower rose to support the bridge.

The sense of the impossible moved Elliot to mention the illusion.

"That tower rests on a pier the company built when the bridge was constructed a few years back. From here, it looks as though the tower goes into the water, but it actually rests on Throgs Neck—a tract of land that juts out into the channel," Rich said. "Dad has an English eighteenth-century map on which this piece of land is named 'Frogs Neck.' And the Saw Mill River, which runs about twenty miles west of here, is marked navigable for ships of the line for thirty miles up from the coast. The truth is you probably couldn't get a canoe past five miles."

"I wager the cartographer caught hell if his charts were used for military operations," Elliot added.

"Let's take Route One," Rich said. "It's slower than Ninety-Five, but it pretty much follows the Boston Post Road Ben Franklin laid out for the first federal highway."

"Fine with me. You're the tour guide."

For several miles, Elliot lay back in the seat, absorbing the sights and sounds of a land settled by his countrymen three centuries earlier. With each mile distant from New York City, manufacturing plants gave way to office buildings and an occasional time-worn residence predating and stubbornly resisting the intrusion of commerce.

"We're now passing through New Rochelle, the site of Thomas Paine's farm where he retired and died. In case you didn't know it, he was a Brit who saw the light and came to this country to serve us during the Revolutionary War—wrote *Common Sense and the Age of Reason* and generally pestered people into waking up and sticking up for themselves."

Related to nothing in particular, Elliot asked, "Do you have a girl?"

"I always have a girl but nobody in particular," Rich answered. "Why do you ask?"

"I don't know. Just wondered if you had someone special who'd go to Cambridge to see you row."

"Oh, there'll be plenty of girls to see us row—just don't know their names yet. You'll do fine with that accent and British manners."

"Does your family ever watch you race?"

"They used to, but every time they were there I lost, so they stopped coming," Rich joked. "Oh, look to the left. See that old red house in the trees at the edge of the ravine?"

"What about it?"

"Israel Putnam, an American general in the Revolution, escaped your bunch as they were coming in the front door by going out the back and riding his horse down that embankment. The old guy must have had nine lives. Before that, he was almost burned at the stake by Indians and one of the few who survived a shipwreck in Havana Harbor."

"You're certainly giving me a non-stop lesson in American History. Now I know why you wanted us to come this way."

"Well, I thought sooner or later you'd see the wisdom of staying over here and working, so I decided to hurry you up a bit."

For the next half hour, they wound along the coast to New Haven, where Rich made a slight detour to the Yale campus, explaining, "This is where you go to college after you're rejected by Princeton."

"What trivial tidbit do you have for me at this landmark?" Elliot mocked.

"There was a fellow named Nathan Hale who went to Yale and graduated at age fourteen, but you can't hold that against him because he did some pretty good spying."

"Don't tell me, I know, against the British in the Revolutionary War and was captured and hanged."

"He was only twenty-one when he died, but he sure left an impression on every schoolboy with his dying statement that he, 'regretted he only had but one life to lose for his country.'"

"I've read he would not have been convicted if incriminating papers hadn't been found on him. That should teach you to never keep your love letters," Elliot said.

For a while, the perfection of the day occupied their senses before Elliot asked, "What did you think of Princeton, I mean, now you've graduated and no longer need to defend it."

"They have an excellent divinity school which you can guess never would have accepted me even if I'd changed my profligate ways."

"Of course, you didn't apply."

"Never," Rich answered, "I rather visualized I'd blaze a new trail where Einstein left off. He did special work there for several years before my time. But to answer your question, I think the first three years were the best in my education; the school doesn't demand enough in the fourth. It's like they know you're going to graduate, so 'let's not do anything to prevent him from getting out of here so we can clean up his room for the new guy.' What about Oxford?"

"I quite liked it. Nobody seemed to find me eccentric and the studies were worthwhile. One or two of the dons were a bit touched but quite harmless and very amusing. I suppose in their day they were challenging teachers."

"If I remember, you told me you switched your major from science to graduate with a degree in Philosophy. What do you plan to do with that?"

"Right now, I'm searching for how to best console you when I win on Sunday," Elliot said.

"If you're looking for me at the end of the race, you can find me in the showers where I'll be long before you cross the finish line," Rich jabbed back.

For the next twenty-five miles after crossing New Haven's Quinnipiac River, Elliot amused himself trying to pronounce the Indian points of interest on the highway signs and counting the number of towns along the coast with English names.

"Time for your hourly history lesson," Rich said. "We're about to enter New London on the banks of the Thames River, founded in 1656. Benedict Arnold, arguably the best American general in the Revolution, beat you Brits at Fort Ticonderoga, Danbury and Saratoga—then went over to your side and burned New London down to prove he was really pissed off with the way Washington had slighted him."

"How much more folklore have you left for the trip?" Elliot asked.

"A couple historical and one contemporary," Rich said as he turned off onto Route One-A. "We'll stop and have lunch near a town named Weekapaug, home of the Blackfish to you people who don't speak Indian. When Ben Franklin traveled from Boston to Philadelphia, he'd always stop at Weekapaug and some cutie with strong arms would row over from Block Island for a little extracurricular activity. He was then well into his sixties."

"What a man," Elliot responded.

"What a woman," Rich replied.

"Then further along, we pass Green Hill Beach which I think would be of interest to you—nudists far as the eye can see, but probably too cold for them now," Rich explained.

"At least this landmark doesn't discredit our team."

"But the best I've saved for the last. After we cross the Black River from Providence into Pawtucket, lots of dirty limericks made up with that name, you can see Samuel Slater's mill built in 1790. He memorized the English Machinery plans for spinning cotton thread and came here to start America's textile industry. Today we raise hell when the Chinese steal our intellectual property, but back then we thought it was okay for us to do it."

"Where did you get all this information? Did you major in history?"

"No, historical road markers. And there are lots more when we get to Boston."

"No thanks. I'll do my own exploring of this country after the race."

And that was the way they drove to Cambridge Town.

Early Wednesday morning before the river became cluttered with rowers, the rivals were working the Charles, feeling for currents and dead spots that might make a difference. It was the first time Elliot and Rich went separate courses, each seeking to exorcise the devil's handiwork of idleness with lonely exertion. When they weren't rowing, they watched TV, took short walks, sometimes together, more often not, reserving impersonal conversation for meals. As expected, they advanced through the qualifying heats of the single boats to Sunday's finals.

The day began with a chilling rain, driving many spectators from the river's edge to view the events on TV in nearby bars over a hot cup of coffee or more muscular potions. By noon, the weather system had blown out to the Atlantic, leaving the riverbanks bright but cool and returning thousands to the races.

To Elliot and Rich, it seemed they suddenly were called without warning to face off in a contest neither was sure they wanted—as though each was almost afraid of winning. They shook hands, launched their boats and moved to the starting line.

The judge's gun fired too soon; their boats felt unfamiliar, uncomfortable. Opening sweeps of the long oars were sloppy, and they were near the five-hundred yard marker before either settled into the smooth, continuous, rolling motion of a skilled oarsman.

For most of the course, they stayed even. Occasionally one stepped up the pace to draw the other into spurting ahead prematurely using valuable energy.

By the three-quarters marker, Rich was half a length ahead of Elliot, convinced his rival, trained on a much shorter course, was tiring.

With four-hundred yards to go, Elliot began to close the gap.

With two hundred yards to go, the boats were even.

A hundred yards left in the race, and Rich was slipping behind when he yelled out in pain. He had dislocated his right shoulder. The boat skidded helplessly to the river's bank as Elliot crossed the finish line.

With one giant sweep of his oars, Elliot returned to Rich to take care of his injured friend.

"Of all the rotten tricks, dislocating your shoulder when you knew you were done is the dregs," Elliot said as he and Rich left the emergency room. "You knew I'd win. Why didn't you just concede?"

"Listen, Limey, I would have busted your balls in my last hundred-yard sprint if my wing hadn't gone out. You're lucky, it saved you from two straight losses. Then you'd have gone home hanging your head in shame."

"I might just break your good arm. We're even in two races and you know it. I'll drive you back to New York and then I'm off to see if there's an honest loser among you Yanks."

"There's an old Chinese proverb that declares 'if one disgraces another by overcoming him in public, the two are bound until forgiveness is granted,'" Rich recited.

"Bullshit!" Elliot shot back. "You just made that up."

"See, you're getting the hang of it. I'll make an American out of you yet. Yeah, I just made it up, but not bad for the spur of the moment."

"Sounds about as genuine as your excuse for dropping out of the race."

Elliot exploited Rich's limited mobility, smugly pronouncing his friend was in no condition for the long ride home at this hour, adding in the most obsequious tone he could master, "Where to now, sir?"

"Let's look for some women. They always go for a wounded warrior."

"More so than a winner?" Elliot questioned, emphasizing his victor's status. "Besides, only the motherly type would be interested in you now."

"Oh, yes," Rich answered, "you can try that phony English charm, but you'll probably do better if I tell them you're not playing with a full deck. Then they might feel sorry for you and give you a break. In your case, sympathy will do better than suave."

Freed from the tension of preparing to race, Rich and Elliot returned to their relaxed camaraderie, both inwardly disturbed they'd doubted the durability of their friendship and risked alienation with such carelessness. In the harmony of true friendship, each silently pledged to never again shut down their communication.

Elliot, confident an Englishman could drive in the right-hand lane as well as any American, made the transition with more optimism than success. Rich expressed fearfully to his friend this might be the last car ride of his life, though it would be a well-spent demise to expose Elliot to the civilities of Cambridge and Boston. In rapid succession, they passed Harvard Yard, MIT, Boston's Public Gardens and Common, Symphony Hall, Northeastern University, Boston University and Fenway Park before returning to their room for the night. By ten the next morning, they were closer to reaching home than an agreement.

"Elliot, we're never going to settle this single shell thing."

"You're trying to make me feel sorry for you. It won't work."

"Think about it. Whoever loses the next race will want a rematch and on and on. How about joining forces and racing in the two men shells?"

"Explain to me how that's going to work with you over here and me in England."

"That's the point. Come with our company while you're getting your citizenship."

"Hold on, man. Who said I wanted to be an American?"

"Then do it until your visa runs out. Dad told me about your visit to our Long Island marine site, said Willard was impressed with you. Why not find out if there's anything open there? You could get a pad near work and we could party on weekends," Rich emphasized the social life.

"I suppose I could give it a try. There are almost six months left to go on my visa. No, no," Elliot said, having a change of heart. "I came over to beat you and have a look around, not to work."

"Think about it. If we teamed up, we could win at Henley and the Head of the Charles."

"You know, Rich, you're a real shill. You should join a carnival."

"Then you'll think about it?" Rich asked, attempting to coax an affirmative answer.

Elliot stayed silent long enough for Rich to notice and, realizing he was thinking seriously about it, did not intrude.

"Okay," Elliot said, "as long as I don't have to report to you. Some self-appointed sage once said 'a partnership is the worst ship in which to sail.'"

"Did you just make that up?"

"Yes," Elliot admitted.

"Then it's a deal," Rich said, extending his hand. "Shake."

"Shake," Elliot replied, grabbing hold.

"Watch it! I don't want your clumsiness to permanently injure my arm."

"Don't worry, I'll be stroke in all the doubles we race."

Chapter 6

"Captain, Mr. Steele told me to report bright and early this morning to see if you could use another hand," Elliot said as Willard made his routine 6 a.m. entrance into the ramshackle, two-story, corrugated metal building that served as office, warehouse, machine shop and record storage without any discernable architectural demarcation for each function. A quick glance around the building's interior revealed little order in the terminal's stores, supplies and equipment; items from every section were scattered throughout the building. From Elliot's observation of Willard, it was a good bet the captain could retrieve items with minor difficulty, but there was no evidence others had mastered this casual housekeeping. It was a situation with such obvious pitfalls, Elliot branded its existence a probable sacred cow and postponed any mention of the subject for the time being.

"I guess you've already met Ned," Willard said, gesturing towards the night watchman. "He checks in at 6 p.m. and leaves when I arrive in the morning. Incidentally, what time did you get here?"

"Five-thirty, Captain."

Willard made a mental note of Elliot's respect for punctuality.

"As you might imagine, Mr. Steele and I talked about you and I told him there might be a few things where you can help. I understand you're only staying over here for six months, so I don't want to involve you in some project that runs longer than that. I already know how good you are with a tug, so maybe a walk around the terminal is the place to start. Then you can tell me what you see—where you think you can help." With that, Willard started single file, sure-footed and swift-paced along the narrow planks with Elliot trailing, registering impressions as he navigated the higgledy-piggledy footing.

In half an hour, the two were back in the multi-purpose building, Willard trying to swat the summer's leftover flies as he listened to Elliot. The captain, having made his final kill, sat back to give his full attention to the matter at hand when the whine of a grinder in the machine shop drowned out any incentive for an exchange of ideas.

"You see anything that strikes you?" Willard asked.

"Yes, sir, for starters I'd get a door for this office."

"Take care of it," Willard replied. Then rising from his perilous perch on an exhausted swivel chair, Willard suggested, "Let's go across the street to the Greasy Spoon and get a cup of coffee while we talk." To Elliot's surprise, the coffee shop was in fact named 'The Greasy Spoon,' but maintained an immaculate standard throughout. For privacy, Willard chose a booth at the end opposite the door and, over searing black coffee, began their meeting.

"There are two projects I believe deserve your consideration. I'll start with the easier because its success may give you confidence to go on, and it should gain the yard hands' willingness to help me on the bigger projects. First, I'd reorganize and provide simple weatherproofing for some of the stock stored outside. The top layers of several items are getting sunburned and bent out of shape. Consolidation in designated places and tarp coverings could reduce the labor of locating items and limit spoiled inventory. I think that will take six man days and a fork lift."

"That sounds about right," Willard said. "I'll assign a couple of men to you—you run the project."

"I'd rather you didn't," Elliot interrupted. "I'd prefer to tell them about it and see if anyone wants to help me. That way it's their success."

"Okay, you do it your way, but keep me up to date."

"The second is more complex and will take planning, but it could make a profitable impact on this division. I estimate you'll need twenty-five man days, but that can be spread over the months before winter sets in. It involves a redesign of the fleet's harbor moorings, access gangways and the vessel bumpers. My guess is that some of the bumpers were meant to be moved from their original position for a short time only and were never returned. Anyway, some placements are not giving adequate prevention from damage to the hulls. It would seem sensible to reset your vessel moorings and the gangways to them based on frequency of use and the types of jobs they serve. Probably your records of the equipment configuration for past bids will help. And of course, the gangways to access the craft will naturally depend on the mooring design if we want to optimize the effort. It would seem the change can be least disruptive if we return a vessel to its new site every time she comes in from a job. I'll give you a more detailed plan before I ask for approval."

"A pretty detailed analysis for your first mooring," Willard commented.

"Not really," Elliot replied. "Some of these I thought of when I visited you last week."

Honest too, Willard thought to himself. *He didn't try to lead me into thinking he'd come up with all that in the last hour; must be sure of himself.*

"I'll think about the second phase," the captain said. "Put your plan together and we'll talk." Willard had never hired anybody so well organized, and he was unsure how he felt about it.

By noon Elliot was back at the Greasy Spoon, watching the terminal yard crew straggle in for lunch. In general, they were an undistinguishable collection one would have difficulty describing, unless it was for an errand such as Elliot's. They were good people of moderate intelligence and limited education who'd accepted the niche society had assigned to them. Probably defensive, easily threatened by the unfamiliar, it was likely they were xenophobic and would be wary of him. Only a few minutes of observing their body language suggested no obvious pecking order. The overweight, continually smiling sycophant waiting to hear what others thought before committing; the glamour boy, losing his battle with middle age, preening even as he engaged in body building, obsessed with cleanliness amidst the dirt of his workplace; the elder, long employed and long-of-tooth who dispensed wisdom in garbled aphorisms; the wheeler-dealer, constantly alluding to his unbroken record of achievements told in such a fashion as to defy any verifications, and several more colorless players content to provide a human backdrop for the tableau.

A few minutes later, in what appeared to be unrehearsed ceremonial order, Izak the yard boss, accompanied by Rube and Lou, tug boat pilots, arrived to take a booth distant enough to discourage thoughtless intrusions, but not so far as to flaunt rank. Having already received no objections from the three supervisors for recruiting help for his first project, Elliot approached the crew as they finished lunch.

"I'm Elliot Swan from Southampton, England," he said as thought they didn't already know. "I'm over here for a few months to learn the tricks of the trade from you Americans. While I'm getting the hang of it, I'll try to earn my keep by being helpful and do some housekeeping you've probably been too busy to bother with." Elliot chose his language carefully and emphasized the appropriate words to relax their guard. "The captain thinks it would be a good idea to get a door for his office so the machine shop won't have to worry about how much noise they make. I thought I'd give it a try, but I'm not much of a carpenter."

His admitted deficiency in carpentry skills drew no reaction. Helplessness did not awaken any Good Samaritan stirrings.

"I rather thought it might be nice to attach a little plaque to the door naming those who built it. It would probably be okay with the captain." The pick-up in interest registered among several of the men who glanced about to solicit support for the project. "Maybe someone in the machine shop might take a stab at engraving a metal plate with the names. If not, I'm sure I can get one outside."

Two of the least conspicuous in the group, indecisive about making a commitment, finally said in voices barely audible, "I'll help with the carpentry," "Me too," and were joined by a machinist who offered to make the plaque.

By the end of the third day, the door with the inscribed plaque was hung with all the solemnity of a ship christening as Elliot jokingly proclaimed it was land worthy.

When each of the three who'd built the door checked on the inscribed plate, one said to Elliot, "How come your name isn't on it?"

He thought for a moment and, unable to come up with the right way to explain that everyone should know it was their project, answered, "Because we English are a timid lot."

Thursday, a week following the door installation, the wheeler-dealer seeking to be included in those sure to be recognized for the proposed terminal face-lift joined the carpenters, the machinist and the body builder to reorganize and weatherproof stock and supplies stored outside. The project was completed ahead of schedule, and after inspecting the job, the captain delivered a witty speech observing everything was so neatly organized, he couldn't find anything, but it was important to be as tidy at work as in their personal lives. He continued to extol the virtues of good housekeeping, closing by apologizing that there could be no marble inscribed tablet identifying those who participated because stone did not easily attach to tarpaulin.

Nearing the end of his first month at the terminal, Willard scheduled Elliot to skipper a sand and gravel haul from the Northport plant to a construction site in Port Chester. It would take a full two days with an overnight aboard the sea tug. Elliot was assigned the wheel with a back-up from Willard, who would also navigate. Rube, all around sailor, would handle the engine room, the pick-up and drop-off of the towed barges and just about anything else needed on the trip.

"You run the whole haul," Willard told Elliot, "from picking up the barges to delivering the load. These tubs react a lot different loaded and unloaded, and you need to get the feel of them. You may be doing more of this on your own pretty soon. I'll try to stay out of your way, but if you need help, don't be bashful."

Elliot had not embarked from the yard since his trial run with Mr. Steele and Willard on the East River a month earlier. By now, his acceptance by the terminal crew and Willard nudged him toward the next challenge and made him inwardly impatient to work on the water. Besides, his proposal to reset the fleet had lain on Willard's desk without comment for a week, and indecision was not Elliot's favorite condition. Yet, he knew he must appreciate the captain's hesitation in rushing into a major reorganization when the chief's instincts had served him so well for many years. It was wise to be patient and let Willard work it out at his own pace. Then Elliot indulged in rationalizing, remembering he'd be going home in a few months.

The trip to Northport was uneventful. Good weather and moderate traffic in the East River and Long Island Sound simplified towing the two stubby barges, trailing like a child's string pull-toy as they were meant to. At mid-afternoon, Rich, all smiles to see his friendly antagonist, met them at the Northport plant dock, the giant conveyor belts were extended over the barges and the loading began. Later, the loaders still clanking in the background, the two friends sat with Rube and Willard to eat steak and French fries washed down with beer.

"Did you take my advice to get a pad in Jackson Heights where all the stewardesses live?" Rich asked Elliot.

"You're a sexist," Elliot replied. "Haven't you heard, 'flight attendants' is the politically correct term. But to answer your question, they all tell me any friend of yours is not a friend of theirs."

"It's been three weeks since we rowed," Rich said, pretending to change the subject.

"Since I rowed and you foundered," Elliot interrupted.

"Whatever. Do you want to come out on Saturday and scull for a couple of hours?"

"On condition I get to set the stroke."

"Yeah, yeah. We could take in the last clambake of the season, and I can give you some pointers on attracting women."

"And I'll tell the ladies you dislocated your shoulder arm wrestling with the weaker sex."

The repartee went on while they cleaned up after supper, with Willard and Rube so amused they forgot to tune in to their favorite TV program. When the kidding began to run down, Willard outlined the next day's schedule and, noting they'd have an early start, went off to his bunk. Rube, anticipating the two friends would renew their foolishness, hung on for another half-hour, but when that didn't happen, he turned in for the night.

Rich had hoped he'd have some time alone with Elliot to candidly discuss work, but the lack of privacy prevented that. Before he went home to Smithtown, Rich made a final check on the progress of loading the barges, reporting to Elliot that everything was in perfect shape for any early morning departure, adding he'd personally balanced the loads with his shovel. "Now all you do is point the tug at Port Chester and you'll glide over smooth as glass. Try not to mess it up. Good night. I'll see you Saturday at Huntington Station at 10:30 a.m."

By the end of Elliot's second month, the harbor moorings had been reset well before winter weather. Although many prime contractors slowed or stopped new building starts, a considerable amount of supplies remained to be transported to the New Jersey, New York and Connecticut sites accessible by water. One of his favorite hauls was up the Hudson River to Newburgh, which reminded him of his vacation trip along the Rhine. Near Newburgh, coffer-dams were being constructed to provide watertight enclosures into which concrete would be poured to form foundations for a bridge across the river.

His first of several hauls to the upriver site was without backup from Willard or Rube, and cruising out of the terminal with two deckhands depending on him was exhilarating. Passing under the Brooklyn Bridge, he watched the rising sun gild a cloud of pigeons as they performed acrobatics, changing from one course to another. Rounding lower Manhattan to pass the Statue of Liberty, he tipped his cap although nobody had told him such a common courtesy to this lady was expected. Two hours later, the barges, loaded with equipment from the Jersey depot, headed up the Hudson passing deserted, rotting piers, monuments to the demise of ocean-going transportation. At morning coffee break, they passed the George Washington Bridge and ran beside the Palisades, a forty-mile-long fault, walling the western side of the Hudson with sheer, russet stone sheets rising hundreds of feet above the water. Several human specks swung along the precipice, defying gravity, suspended on spider-like filaments. Elliot put rock climbing on his mental list of things to do. The passage upstream was so well charted and the day so serene one could easily forget a cardinal rule of seamanship—sailing is a series of surprises that don't give you a second chance. When they reached Newburgh, fall's shortened daylight was disappearing from the tops of the steep riverbanks, leaving the docks in darkness. With typical Steele efficiency, crews were standing by to unload the heavy equipment to set it up for immediate use the next day. One by one, brilliant floodlights turned the riverside bright as men moved in industrial choreography.

On the return to the terminal, a major weather system swept in from the east and, trapped by the west banked Palisades, directed its fury on the river below. Drenching rains, driven by near hurricane winds, built up walls of water to split on the bow of the tug and wash over the pilothouse, reducing visibility to zero. With no harbor refuge near, they'd have to ride out the storm. Periodically, Elliot checked the two crewmen under the guise of knowing the status of the tug and barges, but his real purpose was to determine their morale. One, an old sea dog, took the experience as routine, the other, a landlubber, was unsure if he'd leave the machine shop again soon. Elliot never doubted the powerful tug would weather the nor'easter, but the empty barges, bobbing like corks, needed constant surveillance to prevent them from ricocheting off waves and slackening and tightening the towlines until they snapped. He concluded the only way to get all three craft through the blow was to give the tug full power and keep the towlines taut. As they passed the section of the Palisades rimmed by the Storm King Highway, Elliot quipped it was well named for such a foul weather place.

Until late fall, there was enough work to keep the terminal running at full force. In early winter, Elliot filled in for Willard, Rube and Lou who took year end vacations when most customers were partially shut down. Weekends, weather permitting, he and Rich joined the sailing "Frostbiters" and sculled in singles or occasionally doubles with both keeping records of whose turn it was to occupy the stroke seat. Elliot became increasingly satisfied with life in the States, and the idea of taking his philosophy doctorate at Columbia appealed to him. As for his future at the Steele firm, he was realistic enough to accept he would never be chosen over Rich to run it and more importantly, he wanted no appearance of sub-rosa rivalry between them to endanger their friendship. So as winter and his six-month visa expiration approached, he planned to return to England for a summer with Mum and Father before returning to the States for another Head of the Charles and the fall semester at Columbia.

Chapter 7

The phone rang once, twice, six times before Commissioner Callahan could sort through the bucket of rusty nails lodged in his martini-soaked brain and reach across the bed to grope for it on the nightstand. As he lay on the pillow next to his, the smell of perfume, unlike any on his wife's vanity table, rose to offend his already queasy stomach. Seven, eight, nine times the demon's bell penetrated his trembling body. The God damn phone never rang Sunday morning at 6:25 or any other time before noon. The office had specific orders to solve all problems themselves until noon.

On the tenth alarm, Callahan unglued his tongue from the roof of his mouth, and with a voice that cracked, whispered, "Helloo" to the caller.

"Callahan, where the hell have you been?"

"Who is this?"

"Who the hell do you think would be calling you at 6:30 Sunday morning, Mother Theresa? Do I sound like Mother Theresa? It's the Mayor."

"Oh, yes, Mr. Mayor, I ate something last night that disagreed with me. Now I recognize your voice, Mr. Mayor."

"You better recognize my voice because you're going to hear a lot of it."

"What can I do for you, Mr. Mayor?" Callahan asked timidly.

"What can you do for me? It's more like what can I do for you to save your skinny ass from that Appleyard broad at the Times putting us in the headlines."

"I don't understand."

"Of course you don't understand, but you sure as hell will if the Governor gets wind of that stinking mountain of garbage in Queens and it comes from a story in the newspaper."

"Sir, we're already taking care—"

"Then the next thing you know, the Feds will be in here snooping around and the environmentalists, too, if they're not already planning a protest."

"Well, sir, if you'll hear me out, we're going to burn it."

"Well, sir, you're not going to burn it. It's against the law."

"We've been burning it right along in the old equipment waiting for the new EPA-approved incinerators to go on stream."

"You're going to land your ass in jail yet. Don't you read the papers? It's obvious you didn't bother to read the judge's cease and desist order, but I thought you at least would see the newspaper article. You'll find it. It's right next to the comic strips."

"Maybe we could—"

"No. You can't burn it in the old furnaces, and you can't dump it in the ocean, as you did five years ago, so figure something out and fast," the Mayor shouted and hung up.

Callahan fell back on the pillow exhausted. As he lay there trying to reduce the anger he could still hear in the Mayor's call and gain some perspective on the problem, the strong, unfamiliar scent returned to distract his concentration. Everything was shapeless and unmanageable. He needed peace and quiet and most of all an aspirin. The jarring jangle of the phone caught him again off guard.

"And another thing, Callahan," the Mayor's tone was low and ominous, "get this done pronto or there won't be any 'commissioner' in front of your name, or did I say this before?"

When the line went dead, Callahan wiped his arm across his sweaty forehead and rolled on his side away from the rising sun pouring in his window at eye level. Seeking to shade his eyes, he turned to look at the shadow side of his bedroom to see a woman's thong and bra hanging on the antenna of the TV set and a moment later, over the drone of the water hitting the shower door, heard a female singing off-key. He rose to dispel what he hoped was a bad dream, but the realization of his infidelity weakened his body, forcing him to sit down. *I'm really a good person,* he repeated to himself, but it did nothing to purge the guilt. The voice in the shower came alive again with a second tune unimproved over the first. He panicked at the thought his wife would surely hear her from a second bedroom she frequented before he remembered she was out of town with some women friends. Just as he was beginning to get control of his thoughts, the bathroom door opened, framing a tall blonde, generously endowed, reveling in her nakedness and laughing at the effect it had on Callahan.

"Hey, Comish, you don't look so good. You probably need some breakfast and a little 'pick-me-up'."

"You have to leave, my wife's on her way home."

"At 6:45 a.m.? Nobody arrives anyplace at 6:45 in the morning. Besides, last night you told me you weren't married."

"I lied. Well, I have to go to church anyway."

"I bet you haven't gone to church since you were married."

How could the woman know that? She was beginning to annoy him, and the sooner he got rid of her the better. Now that he thought about it, church might not be such a bad idea. It never hurt to get a little salvation insurance.

"Here," he said, handing her a wad of bills, "You have to go."

She took the money and counted it before saying, "Is this for a quickie?"

"No, you have to leave."

"Okay, Comish, you're the boss." In one continuous motion, she slipped on her clothing, picked up her coat and bag and, with Callahan trailing, headed for the door to the apartment.

"We'll have breakfast next time," he said weakly, not knowing why he spoke. For a moment his stomach knotted, afraid someone would see her getting on the elevator, until he remembered with four apartments on each floor, no one could be sure which she'd come from.

As he fumbled with the crook-lock, she said, "Comish, do you always give your dates presents both at night and in the morning?" Before he could answer, she asked, "and do you always pass out on your dates before you get undressed?"

Then she disappeared into the elevator.

Callahan lay against the closed door, losing his battle to hold back nausea, then stumbled to the bathroom to throw up. Several times he vomited, disgorging part of the previous night's indiscretion before he found the palliative benefits of pressing his head against the toilet bowl's cool porcelain. Slowly, the recuperative powers of fear revived his senses—the first of which was self-preservation. Even the slow return of Callahan's reasoning did not muddle his primitive instinct to conceal his assignation from his wife. Only partially recovered from his hangover, he searched the apartment for the most minute clue that would expose him. Lipstick impressions on tissues were retrieved from the waste basket and flushed down the toilet. The pillow and side of the bed slept on by the woman caller were sprayed with mosquito repellent although it was only a week past New Year's; towels were laundered and floors vacuumed for loose hair. The deception would be flawless, Callahan thought, as he waited for his wife's arrival and moved to the problem of the city's garbage.

It was mid-afternoon when Mrs. Callahan barged through the front door wheeling a suitcase large enough to accommodate three weekends' worth of clothes. With uncommon consideration, her husband rose to greet her.

"How was the trip?" he inquired.

"Don't kiss me, I have an awful cold. My eyes are bleary from watering and I can't smell a thing."

By Sunday evening, Callahan's ministrations to his wife's misery sufficiently assuaged his guilt to address the foreboding garbage accumulation. His mind, now returned to the full capacity of its limitations, strained to judge the mayor's threat to fire him. With next year's election nine months away, Abramowitz would be expecting Callahan to influence his constituents to back the mayor. The Commissioner was also aware of the rumors Delisio would quit the police department to run as a replacement for Abramowitz. Callahan, at times departing from reason, considered hinting to Delisio he might throw his support behind the police chief if the favor was returned by arresting environmentalists for unlawful assembly when they showed up to protest the garbage accumulation, shifting the public's attention away from his incompetence to the Sanitation Department's concern with possible personal injury and property damage.

Another alternative, to which Callahan assigned special merit, was to give that Appleton woman at the Times an exclusive on his plan to call the governor at the New York State Capitol and request an emergency permit to dump the garbage in an Albany landfill. The more he thought of it, the more it seemed like a perfect solution. The newspaper article would congratulate Callahan for his vigilance and imagination in heading off an emergency, and the governor could hardly refuse to rescue New York City, which had given him an overwhelming plurality in the last election, and his standing with the mayor would be restored.

As Callahan was preparing for bed, the phone rang but once before the commissioner picked it up.

"Callahan," he said in his most business-like tone, having just congratulated himself; he was now back on top of things.

"One ring, that's better," the unmistakable growl of the mayor acknowledged.

"We're close to solving the problem, Mr. Mayor."

"How?" Abramowitz asked and, without giving Callahan a chance to answer, went on. "I had my usual Sunday breakfast with the city fathers," he said, referring to a regular after-mass gathering of the Catholic political establishment, "and I can tell you our friends from Queens are not happy about having their borough stunk up."

"We're going to get on it tomorrow morning, pronto," Callahan said, borrowing a favorite word from the mayor's vocabulary to assure his boss he understood the urgency of the matter.

An early Monday morning call to Delisio's office disclosed he was marlin fishing in Florida for a week. Callahan quickly regrouped with the Appleton Solution, as he liked to call it. He was confident his three meetings with Alexandra had built mutual trust and cooperation, emboldening him to reveal everything.

At nine-thirty, Alexandra was in Callahan's presence, reminding him her name was Appleyard and listening to his flight of fancy. "Commissioner, I can't plant a story intended to influence a condition. I'm a reporter. I'll get you the coverage the newspaper feels it deserves, but I'll have to pass on your idea. I'm not an investigative reporter, or I'd be unable to keep silent on our meeting until some action was taken, but I can't touch this. Sorry. Goodbye."

Callahan sat back in his overstuffed chair, his best chance for redemption walking out the door. He cracked a few more knuckles and switched on the TV to take his mind off a mountain of worries big as the garbage pile in Queens. Trying the time-tested sedative of inane daily TV talk shows, he turned to his favorite channel, propped his feet on the desk and concluded this form of solace was less demanding than the pilgrimage to church he'd considered. As he let his mind drift, the show's M.C., plastic as an inflatable doll, grinned his way across the set to welcome his next guest, a representative from some Federal agency controlling the disposal of toxic waste. The little, balding, bespectacled man immediately began to deliver a scientific treatise guaranteed to drop the audience ratings to zero before the M.C. rescued the program with a series of direct questions requiring 'no/yes' answers. Contrary to the M.C.'s previous experience, this public servant was in no way disconcerted by his host's abrupt intervention but settled quickly into a comfortable, informative discussion in which the guest listed the states prohibiting importation of hazardous materials. Callahan noted they were mostly northeastern, Midwestern and west coast locations.

The M.C., anxious to speed up and end the interview on a positive note, asked, "What about the southern states?"

The guest replied that there were still a few that had toxic storage, but they too were disappearing. Now the states from

Delaware south were concentrating their environmental resources on garbage disposal in landfills or incineration.

The commissioner yelled 'Yippee' so loud his secretary checked to see if he'd had a seizure.

"Gretchen, get me the mayor," Callahan ordered. In a moment he was connected to Abramowitz. "Mr. Mayor, the problem is solved."

"Which problem, Callahan? All I have is problems. That's what I was elected to do—solve problems. Anyone who can run this city can run the country," he added, expanding his political horizon.

"The garbage problem. All we do is load the stuff on trucks and haul it down south. They'll take anything and burn it or make landfills."

"Callahan, have you lost your mind? You can't put that smelly crap in perfectly good trucks and haul it all over the countryside."

"We'll put it on a train, then."

"Same thing. It would stink up the train as bad as the truck, anyplace it went. Call me back when you get a better idea."

"No, wait, Mr. Mayor. We could use these old freighters on the East River and ship it down the coast."

"You can't. They're decommissioned, but I'll bet we could get some barge towing company to take it."

"Well, I guess I'm elected then," Elliot said in his phone call, explaining to Rich why he wouldn't see him the coming weekend.

"Yeah, I heard," Rich replied.

"But I'd planned to return to England shortly, and my visa expires in a couple of months."

"Oh, you'll be back in a few weeks, and Dad really needs you on this one. He promised to help the mayor out, and then Willard gets sick and Rube can't take over for him without Lou and Izak."

"Did you hear what I'm hauling?" Elliot inquired.

"Tootie-Fruitie," Rich answered. "You'll always be upwind from it."

"You hope."

"Elliot, think of it as a winter vacation in the south. You might want to take your shell along and help tow."

"You know, Rich, you are a wretched human being."

Chapter 8

Before the dark had given way to morning, the first to arrive at the terminal was Commissioner of Sanitation Frank Callahan, anxious and distracted by the most minute irregularity. The hour and his demeanor hinted he had not slept well and was guarding himself against some fateful event that would undo him forever. He shivered against the cold, cracked his knuckles and paced the pier with such visible agitation the night watchman was concerned and required identification.

"Of course, I'm Commissioner Callahan," he said, annoyed anyone would question his authority. "I'm here to supervise the elimination of noxious waste."

"There's no noxious waste here," the suspicious watchman replied.

"No, not here, in Queens."

"Well, whataya doing over here then?"

"One of Steele's tugs is going to take care of it."

"How do they do that?" the watchman questioned, sure the Commissioner was a real loony.

"Never mind about that. Where is everybody?" The Commissioner was convinced his premonition of disaster was becoming a reality. Nothing was working the way he'd planned it. Nothing could rid him of the putrefying monument to the martyrdom of a public servant. He continued his pacing as though his activity would hasten the arrival of some angelic deliverance. As the steely-gray winter dawn signaled another day, Elliot and Rich arrived, followed by two dissimilar men toting duffel bags, who boarded the tug and disappeared below deck.

Callahan, unable to conceal his disappointment that his vision of a heroic captain was not among the foursome, approached Elliot to ask, "When will the captain who's running this show arrive?"

"He's here. I'm it," Elliot replied.

"I was expecting someone older," Callahan said tactlessly.

"I can assure you with time I'll age," Elliot answered. "What would you like to know? Have I ever hauled a loaded barge? Yes. Have I ever been a garbage man? No," he added, making it clear he thought the job was demeaning. "I've studied the list of ports you gave us serving the cities that accept garbage for incineration, and you can be sure we'll unload at the first opportunity."

"You'll be doing me a favor and saving New York taxpayers' money if you can get rid of it at your first stop."

"We'll try. Now, Mr. Callahan, perhaps you'd like to go in the office over there and have a cup of coffee while we prepare to get underway. When we leave the terminal, we'll go upstream and pick up the barge, so we should be passing here on our way out in about two hours. I must get on with our final check of stores and equipment to be sure everything is ship-shape." Elliot was almost ashamed to be so trite, but the expression had the desired effect of calming and confining the disruptive Commissioner.

Rich, who'd quietly watched the exchange between Elliot and Callahan, now turned his attention to the two seamen and their new skipper absorbed in a detailed stem to stern check of the tug's readiness for an ocean haul. Even to Rich, little experienced with the open Atlantic, it was obvious the two hires were longtime seafaring men. The first to be noticed was a giant of a man named Bones because of his acromegalic affliction, causing an abnormally large head and deformed hands and feet. His congenital defect apparently caused no limitation on his physical activity, however, because he moved like a ballerina; heavy and fragile objects alike were handled with careful ease. His partner, Mac, a cherubic, middle-aged, walking marine encyclopedia, knew the specifications of every vessel built since World War II. His work specialty was marine propulsion, and at one time or another he had rebuilt or repaired engines on tall ships, ferries, yachts, Coast Guard cutters and tugs. Both men, previously employed for several years by the Steele Firm, simultaneously contracted wanderlust and left the terminal only to return after nine months of seeking the elusive greener pastures. They had made a couple of local hauls with Elliot, and their skilled seamanship made him willing to take a chance their loyalty would last long enough for the garbage haul.

While the last item on the checklist was being examined, Callahan again boarded the tug and, giving Elliot two sheets of typed paper, said, "I almost forgot. This list updates the information you have, rating the incinerators now allowed to operate, those identified for upgrading and those shut down by the EPA. The Feds are moving faster to control burning than I thought. Makes our job tougher every day."

"Thank you, Mr. Callahan. That will be all," Elliot replied, his tone signifying he was now about to enforce a captain's prerogative and dismiss the Commissioner. "You must return to the office or we will not be responsible for your safety. If you want us to haul this garbage away, you must not disturb us."

"Oh, I certainly want to see this crap leave here forever," Callahan mumbled, returning to the pier.

"I guess this is it," Rich said, breaking his silence. "But before you leave, I have some bon voyage presents for you." He gave Elliot three festively wrapped packages, which were carefully unwrapped as though they were bombs or Limoges china. The first contained a set of clothespins for the crew to put on their noses, the second a bottle of eau de cologne, and the third a mock-up of the front page of a New York newspaper with the headline, 'Statue of Liberty Drops Torch to Hold Nose as Swan's Scow Sails South.'

Trying to squelch his friend's buffoonery, Elliot said, "In the early days of your country, British ships captured American vessels and impressed their sailors into service. If we'd lived then and I had the misfortune to be stuck with you, I'd pay your government to take you back. Now kindly get off my ship and I'll make New York a better place to live. Cast off," Elliot yelled to his crew.

Rich hugged his friend then jumped ashore.

In two hours the barge had been secured and the grotesque flotilla, provoking derisive toots, whistles and blasts from passing vessels, made its way through the narrows toward the Atlantic. Elliot, ever mindful of the capricious sea, called for another complete check of the tug and the barge before they left the outer harbor. Although he was satisfied all was in order, he wanted to impress Bones and Mac he ran a tight ship. Then he cursed silently to himself for using another hackneyed expression. The thermometer confirmed the sun, though well in its ascendancy, had done little to warm the morning, making Elliot wonder if the trip would be cold throughout. Rounding Sandy Hook to run nearly directly south along the Jersey coast, Elliot saw an endless succession of villages, originally fishermen's ports, giving way to summer cottages yielding to resorts and year-round homes for commuters to businesses in metropolitan areas. Mac said the shoreline road continued south to a mile wide spit of land dotted with small settlements, stretching halfway to Atlantic City and on a clear night looking like a necklace of diamonds. Seagulls skidded in sheets across the ice blue sky to tilt down past the tug to the car-sized bales of garbage, their screeches audible even floating away in a five knot wind.

With the passing of each vessel, the man on watch entered into the log the time, name, registration numbers, class, approximate speed and course. Crews and passengers alike on other ships close enough to see the haul expressed disbelief when they identified the load on the barge. Occasionally a sailboat, its auxiliary engine chugging at full power, strained to speed its owner from a late start to warmer climates. Privileged couples emerged from the cabin, waving their cocktail glasses in a toast before, with one whiff of the polluted air, they vanished below deck.

Four hours out of the terminal, Bones took the wheel, Mac stood watch and Elliot slept, establishing the rhythm of duty and time off that would last throughout the voyage. When he was awakened by Mac, who succeeded Bones at the wheel, the big man slid down the gangway rails on his hands to his bunk for four hours of rest.

Now mid-afternoon, buildings on shore turned on lights against winter's encroaching night. The world was silent except for the constant, deep-throated revolutions of the propeller shaft and the swells slapping along the hull. Elliot made his last daylight check of the boat, paying particular attention to the hawser tethering the barge, and was gratified the automatic running lights showed there was a tow. Elliot cooked supper, setting aside a portion for Bones when he woke up, then took Mac's and his meals to the pilothouse. As they ate, they reviewed their progress and concluded they were making good time, estimating they should round Cape May around midnight for the run up the Delaware River to Wilmington. Docking and unloading could take most of the day, and a layover till the following morning would still get them back in New York in three and one-half or four days.

The moon had not risen by the end of the first day, and the tug and its tagalong, the only visible lights in the black, seemed the last sign of life in an undulating void. When Elliot finished his shift at the wheel for four hours of sleep, he was confident Bones and Mac had demonstrated the skill and judgment to handle any exigency which might be encountered in this cold but stable weather. The local offshore traffic along their route had dwindled to nothing several hours before, and their position inside the open sea lanes made them a solitary convoy. Rounding Cape May took slightly longer than calculated, but it was reasonable to expect they'd make better time when they reached the Delaware River and the incoming tide. One more look at their course on the charts, a quick check to confirm the flashing beacon on the barge was operating, and Elliot went to his bunk.

Waiting for sleep, Elliot scanned the previous seven months filled with uncommon challenges and surprising rewards. It was curious how a contest once so important for him to win now seemed inconsequential and the adversary to whom he'd lost had become his most valued friend. He'd never known anyone like Rich and wondered if it was because they were so alike or so different. He drifted back to his origins—Father and Mum, who from the perspective of time and distance's separation, he now recognized as a dysfunctional couple, which probably made him dysfunctional as well. He called home at the irregular intervals the young allocate for their families, never able to get a precise date when Father would be in New York to allow a visit. Mum, always cheerfully occupied with her genealogy, gave no indication if he was missed, and it left Elliot uncertain if that was because they didn't care or were clumsy in expressing their love or saying goodbye. Perhaps by going their separate ways, they'd said goodbye to each other years before and were simply living in the same house. It bothered him that he might exhibit, or worse yet, be genetically endowed with indifference. He'd not quite reached the point of asking himself who Elliot Swan really was when he fell asleep. It was a restless sleep, coming awake several times to hear the tug's engine and drifting off reassured. Once, the overcast having lifted, an oval of stars shone so bright through the porthole he could identify navigational constellations. He lay back, measuring his heartbeat against the pulsing engine, hoping the coordinated rhythms would lull him back to restorative sleep, but a myriad of restless thoughts made him wide awake. He swung his feet over the side of the bunk into his boots, grabbed a jacket and cap and joined Bones, relieving the big man a half hour early from watch. Bones stood in silhouette on the prow, united to the roll and pitch of the vessel, like a figurehead carved into some primitive craft to scare all enemies. He welcomed the coffee Elliot brought him and returned to the silence he preserved unless asked a question. In a few minutes, Bones turned the watch over to Elliot and entered the pilothouse to relieve Mac for his four-hour rest.

Bracing himself against the cold wind, Elliot toured the tug, stopping at every checkpoint to make the required notations before returning to the bow to spot any obstruction on their course. On the southern bank of the Delaware River, he sighted the distant lights of Dover, the state's capital, and figured they'd land at Wilmington slightly later than their arrival estimate. Bones and Mac would be needed to help make the barge fast to the dock, but they could be idle until the state's loading equipment emptied the barge. The prospect of a three and one-half day round trip seemed realistic.

Elliot watched the sunrise announce an unseasonably warm February day. He noted America's weather ran to extremes even within seasonal variations while England's remained moderate, and he was amused by the thought the inhabitants of both countries exhibited the same characteristics as their native climates. When winter's delayed dawn freed the naked eye's limited visibility and dependence on navigation instruments, Elliot climbed to the pilothouse to complete his watch with an increased range of sight. Bones, ever mum, acknowledged his presence and resumed his total concentration on his task. There was still little traffic on the river, and the movement on land was almost nonexistent. A bend in the river brought them in view of a suspension bridge, fifteen miles ahead, its cables glistening like a silver harp, connecting New Jersey to Delaware. Elliot took the wheel from Bones, knowing there would be more craft in the river as they approached Wilmington and wanting no incident to prevent release from their stinking cargo.

From the sketchy information Callahan's department had provided, the transfer of trash would take place at the state pier located at Marcus Hook, slightly upstream from City Center Wilmington. As he swung the tug shoreward, a launch under full power sped out to intercept Elliot.

"This is the Harbormaster calling the tug in tow," said the tinny tones of an electronically amplified voice. "Swing out of the traffic lanes, cut your engines, drop anchor and secure your haul beside your vessel."

When Elliot complied, the launch came mid-ship to the tug and the owner of the bull-horn voice stepped out on deck to deliver instructions in person. "What's your cargo?" he asked, although the stench and flocks of seagulls covering the mess had already answered his question.

"Garbage for incinerators or land fill," Elliot replied.

"Where are you from?" the official continued, his eyes watering and his breathing becoming labored.

"New York City. I'm looking for the state pier at Marcus Hook to unload."

"There's no facility there to handle this. Let me go in and get in touch with City Hall," the official said, returning to his launch to escape choking as much as to resolve the problem. In a moment the launch backed off and moved to a new position upwind of the barge before the official came back on deck. "Are you sure they didn't tell you to go up river to Chester?"

"No, it was clear I was to discharge in Wilmington, Delaware."

"Well, you'll have to get New York City to contact the Delaware Sanitation Department and straighten this out. In the meantime, your whole operation is dead in the water," the official said, trying to make a little double entendre over the incident while reinforcing his order not to move the barge. "I've already had a call from the City's Chamber of Commerce. They're concerned about damage to our pristine waterfront."

The conversation was barely completed before Elliot was using his ship-to-shore communication system to talk with Callahan. After being cut off and put on hold several times, one of Callahan's minions related the Commissioner would be unavailable for several days.

"I'd suggest you tell him he make himself available unless he wants Elliot Swan to return his load of garbage."

"We'll call you back, Mr. Swan," the voice at the Sanitation Department said and hung up. Elliot kept his line open for an hour before seeking another solution in Wilmington's municipal government, where his call was routed department by department from Public Health to Public Works to Transportation to Sanitation and finally Environment, wasting another hour before learning this was a State matter. He'd always believed that one solves a problem fastest by starting at the top and was almost at the height of frustration where a whim might easily be rationalized as the only course of action left open, leading him to call the President of the United States. But as he savored the fantasy, he remembered this was a man who ridiculed environmentalists, calling them 'tree-huggers', and dismissed the notion. Compromising his top/down philosophy, Elliot began the baffling search for the appropriate authority at the State Capital in Dover, interrupting himself only long enough to make another call to Callahan and receive the standard answer that Commissioner Callahan would be unavailable for an indeterminate period. It was now after four p.m. Friday and there was no possible solution for resolving this stalemate until eight a.m. Monday when the State Capital went back to work. The Harbormaster, making the last round on his day shift, advised them not to move the tug or barge before receiving official approval from the State, which effectively put them in quarantine for the next sixty-three hours.

When Elliot realized they were beached for two days, he and the seamen made a security check over both crafts to assure their stability in any weather. "Well, fellows, the Harbormaster said we can't move away from our anchorage, but nothing about us staying put. Why don't you two go ashore in the 'putt putt' and see the sights? I'll stand watch and take my turn tomorrow night. Go on now. Just be sure to jimmy the engine so no one lifts the boat while you're doing the town."

Elliot watched his two companions lower the 'putt putt,' a glorified, motorized dinghy, into the river on the leeward side of the tug. When Bones, following Mac, added his great bulk to the tiny craft, it looked as though it would swamp, but the gunwales cleared the water by a safe margin and the engine kicked in with a couple of tugs, sending them on shore leave. Never one to become pessimistic with an unexpected deviation from course, Elliot viewed the layover in Wilmington as an opportunity to begin his long-postponed sightseeing of America.

By Sunday evening, Elliot had visited most of Wilmington's tourist attractions among which was one he knew would be of special interest to Mum. Winterthur, a dwelling of castle proportions given by the DuPonts, was filled with the finest examples of period piece furniture in the world. He imagined Mum, who rated antique furniture only second to antique people, could happily spend her next life with the beautiful relics. He also ventured north of the city to Longwood Gardens to see the spectacular winter greenhouse presentations. More than one frequent visitor urged him to return to experience the spring and summer botanical extravaganzas. On his way back to Wilmington, a sign marked 'Brandywine Battlefield, 10 miles,' caught his attention, and his explorer initiative rewarded him with the account of the August 1777 battle between British and American forces, which he memorized in detail for a future one-upmanship contest with Rich. Aware he would soon be captive to his own cooking during the return trip, he dined at the Hotel DuPont and, despite the reaction to his rough seaman's attire, enjoyed a sumptuous meal at the very table, according to the waiter, once occupied by Prince Ranier and Grace Kelly shortly after their engagement. By ten, he boarded the tug, stowed the 'putt-putt' and, hearing from Mac there had been no incoming calls, turned in for the last two hours of his off-duty schedule. At midnight, Bones told Elliot he couldn't sleep and would stand watch for another shift and wake the skipper at four. On the hour, Elliot rose for his watch, checking the tug and barge in the standard procedure. When he entered the galley, Mac offered him a cup of freshly made coffee which Elliot judged, contrary to conventional wisdom that seamen's java is lethal, as delicately brewed. For a few minutes they chatted about their impressions of Wilmington before the ever-present stink from the barge's proximity reminded both of their mission.

"Is it my imagination or have you also noticed how much the gulls have eaten?" Elliot asked.

"I was thinking the same thing," Mac replied. "All we have to do, skipper, is sail around long enough and they'll get rid of the whole damn thing."

"At this rate, neither of us will live long enough. Why don't you turn in and get some more sleep, Mac. Who knows what will happen next."

At seven a.m. Monday, the ship-to-shore phone interrupted Elliot's second reading of the probability ratings for refuse acceptance Callahan had assigned to eastern seaboard ports.

"Hello, Elliot! You're an overnight celebrity," Rich yelled from the other end of the line.

"It certainly took you long enough to admit it."

"No, you're on the front page of today's *Times*."

"What are you talking about? Are you drunk at seven o'clock in the morning?"

"No. Well, it's not you exactly but the garbage that made the news."

"As usual, you're not making any sense, Rich."

"An employee at the Sanitation Department tipped off some environmentalist that they gave you the wrong Wilmington to take the stuff to. You should be going to Wilmington, North Carolina. Now some guy named Axelrod, Alex Axelrod or something like that got a hold of the story. Now you—no, now the garbage is practically world famous."

Chapter 9

"**M**onday, February 19, 12:00 hours, four days out of New York City, marooned in the Delaware river at Wilmington, Delaware," the log entry began. Elliot tapped his pen on the table and gazed up at the weather instruments. Maritime reports forecast the collision of a warm southern system with a polar continental front at an undetermined hour later that day, and if his convoy was to be released, he wanted to clear the Delaware before a blinding snowstorm set in. In a way, he wished Rich had never called; then he might have gone blindly back to New York and dumped the garbage problem on Callahan who'd created it in the first place. On reflection, he knew that never would have happened because Jim Steele had made a commitment to the mayor to help him through a politically sensitive situation, and Elliot couldn't dodge his obligation.

Still there was a sense of unmistakable doom in Rich's words, "Your garbage is prohibited by the State of New York to enter its waterways."

Bones and Mac took the news that the voyage would be extended further south better than expected and at the moment were engaged in their inconclusive poker contest. Again Elliot called the capital in Dover to learn about the tug's release and was told it was no longer a decision of the State of Delaware but now was within the jurisdiction of the U.S. Coast Guard, sorry, no name to contact available.

At 1 p.m. a young, rosy-cheeked Coast Guard officer hopped aboard from a day-glow white launch and told Elliot he was released, apologized for the inconvenience and directed him to a downriver depot for refueling. Elliot thanked him and was in the pilothouse before the day-glow white launch had cast off. Bones and Mac helped reposition the barge behind the tug, and the three sailed away to the accompaniment of onlookers jeering "good riddance to bad rubbish."

Nature, as though compensating for the fiasco of the previous four days, favored them with an outgoing tide, which accelerated their cruise to the mouth of the Delaware Bay, missing the full force of the storm. With more than four hundred miles ahead before rounding the Delmarva Peninsula and sailing up the Chesapeake Bay to Baltimore, they resumed the wheel-off-watch schedule which Elliot named "WOW" in a failed attempt to make their sea duties less monotonous. But their passage, now out of land's sight, grew monotonous. Elliot chided himself for not bringing anything to read. Undisturbed for long periods at a time, it would have been ideal for plowing through some of the philosophy texts required for his doctorate. Mac and Bones seemed content with their lot of stoical observation when they were unable to return to their poker. As with all vessels there were maintenance assignments, but Elliot always allowed enough free time for creative entertainments to be devised. The most notable of these was "Guess the Mess," in which opponents bet on how much garbage the birds would eat each day. Every evening when there was a minimum of light reflected from the water, a telescope reading of the pile was taken from the same place on the stern of the tug. The pole carrying the barge's running light was the measuring stick and Bones, who was not a betting man, was the arbiter of disputes between Elliot and Mac, whose estimates were submitted after dark the night before the measurements were made. As might be imagined, each day's scavenged material was miniscule in proportion to the massive mound on the barge, creating endless challenges between Elliot and Mac on the accuracy of the telescopic readings. Inevitably, there was no apparent winner, but Elliot capitulated to his opponent, voluntarily promising to buy Baltimore-style dinners for Mac's visual acuity and Bone's steadfast impartiality.

Three days after Alex's story broke exposing the bureaucratic bungling of the Sanitation Department's routing of the garbage scow, she walked into the newsroom to find a composter on her desk with a card that read, "Shut Down the Mafia—Recycle." She immediately sat down and wrote a note of appreciation addressed, "To Whom It May Concern! I want to thank one and all for the generous gesture toward me and the utilitarian addition to the newsroom. This device has been long overdue and will provide an appropriate depository for the trash that is sometimes falsely generated under the pretense of news. Alex." After pinning it in a place of prominence, she briefed the newsroom chief on the status of her investigation and left to try and penetrate the stonewalling deceptions so masterfully conceived by politicians as a substitute for doing their jobs.

Two unsuccessful attempts for interviews with officials in the descending chain of command at Sanitation were blocked at the switchboard the instant she stated her business. She assumed reporters from other papers interested in getting a story had also experienced the same information vacuum and were contriving ingenious tactics to scoop the *Times*. Betting her hunch was right, Alex entered the Sanitation Department's reception room and in her best, helpless little girl voice asked to see Commissioner Callahan. As expected, she was informed he was out of town for an indefinite period, to which Alex expressed great bewilderment and disappointment before leaving her card with the receptionist and departing. When she reached the lobby, Alex bought a competitor's paper at the newsstand and scanned the pages as she stood by the bank of elevators watching the building's occupants leave for lunch.

For fifteen minutes Alex monitored the people leaving the elevators, looking for the Sanitation Department receptionist. Deciding she either ate in or had slipped by unnoticed, Alex was about to abandon her surveillance when the elevator doors opened and the voguish receptionist emerged reading a fashion magazine. Lagging some distance behind the woman, Alex followed her out onto the street to a nondescript coffee shop. Allowing the receptionist time to be seated and order, Alex entered, located and walked past her quarry on the pretext of going to the ladies' room. Approaching the receptionist, Alex pretended to accidentally drop her purse, berating her own clumsiness as she picked up its contents. The receptionist, distracted by Alex's distress, knelt to help her without any thought of their meeting again outside the Department's offices.

"I'm such an idiot when I'm upset over failing to get interviews," Alex confessed. "A good reporter must be able to contact principal sources. Thank you for helping me."

"You're welcome. Come here often?"

"Actually, it's my first time."

"Incidentally, my name is Camille. Want to share a booth?"

"Love to. I'm Alex. Do you have lunch here a lot?"

"Only when I don't have a date," Camille said in a manner implying she might be as popular with the men at lunch as at dinner. "You work for the *Times*, right?"

"Yes, I saw Commissioner Callahan when the new dog ordinance went through but can't reach him now."

"Nobody can. You're the fifth reporter today who's asked for an appointment."

"Sounds like he's in demand."

"Only since the garbage crisis. Most days you could shoot a cannon in the department and never hit anybody; except before election, then everyone is here looking for a favor in exchange for a vote. You been a reporter long?" Camille asked, tiring of office talk.

"Not really," Alex replied, seeing an opening to move to a subject of more interest to her companion. "I see from the way you dress you really keep up with fashion."

"I try but there's not much incentive to be particular about clothes where I work. That would surely be different if I had a job with some fashion business."

"Once I worked for a fashion magazine," Alex said casually.

"You did?" Camille's eyes sparkled, anticipating the inside story on the glamour world. "I've always wanted to do that. What's it like?"

"It's hard work because you're dealing with a lot of temperamental people who pretty much get their way on things or they leave to work for another magazine."

Camille, entranced with the expose, let her soup grow cold. "But not everyone's like that, are they?"

"No, there are always some good guys in every business; the trick is to find them. Now take the Sanitation Department, I'm sure there are some other conscientious people besides you who realize it's a government agency whose only purpose is to serve the citizens of New York the best way possible." Alex's voice lost its helpless, little-girl tone as she took command of the situation. "For example, some employee knew about the mix-up of Wilmington, Delaware and Wilmington, North Carolina and how that could cost taxpayers money and thought it was his duty to get that out in the open before there were any more mistakes. Somehow he told the ReGreen Environmentalists and they contacted us so we could run the story." Alex stopped talking to eat, shifting the conversational responsibility to Camille.

"But how could anyone get information to the newspaper without being connected with passing it along? Wouldn't they be named in the article?"

"As long as they asked to be held anonymous, only the reporter would know their identity."

"I guess you can imagine in my job I know who's coming and going. Sometimes people let slip things they wish they hadn't said and a lot of them forget to close their doors before they start a conversation."

"What I want to find out is how long after the garbage left New York did they discover the mistake, and why wasn't the captain of the tug notified? The ReGreen Environmentalist people couldn't tell me, so I guess the Sanitation Department whistleblower didn't know either," Alex said, attempting to get a reaction from Camille that might indicate her involvement.

"I think to answer your questions you first need to know who worked on the search for possible disposal of the garbage."

"Is that a secret?" Alex asked, sensing Camille's fascination with an intrigue in which she might be key.

"It might be. I'm not saying this is so, but I might be the only one who knows about Commissioner Callahan's new girl—"

"Stop right there, Camille. Do you want to be an anonymous source giving me allegations? Besides, plenty of married men have girlfriends. That's nothing new."

"What's an allegation?"

"It means something has been stated but not proven."

"Would my name have to be mentioned?"

"Not if you don't want it."

"What would you do if you knew something wasn't right?"

"I don't know, and I can't tell you what to do. I believe from what you've told me, you're not happy with your job at the Department and you probably ought to make a change."

"Will you help me get a job in the fashion business?"

"I can't guarantee the job, but I will give you introductions."

"Okay, I'll do it. Callahan's new girlfriend is his executive assistant. Nobody knows this but me. She made up the trip schedule for the tug which included seaports that had operating incinerators or landfills or were distribution centers for inland cities that had these facilities. Each was supposed to be rated by type of waste processed and the current EPA classification of acceptable, undergoing upgrading or shut down. Some of the centers checked had been shut down and many weren't contacted before she released the list for the department's contract with the Steele firm that is transporting the stuff because Callahan wanted the garbage to disappear in a hurry."

"When did the commissioner know about the Wilmington mix up?" Alex asked.

"As soon as he arrived in the office after seeing the garbage leave, but he let it go anyway hoping they'd take it at Wilmington, Delaware, as long as it was there. When they didn't he hinted to a few in the department the captain of the tug could have made a mistake or it might have been a clerical error made by the people who write the contracts. He also said Wilmington, Delaware could have changed their agreement to accept the junk but he didn't know it till two days after the tug landed there. It seems to me he's doing everything possible to confuse the situation. And he even persuaded the Port Authority of New York to classify the garbage as toxic waste, prohibiting the barge from reentering any of New York State's waterways."

"Where's his girlfriend in the mess, now it's coming out in the open?"

"She's sitting tight. She knows Callahan can't fire her because she'd spill the beans to his wife."

"Can you get me a copy of the schedule, Camille?"

"I'll try but if I can't, remember it has about every seaport on the Atlantic coast."

"Thanks, Camille, I'll certainly try to help you find a new job but until then stay at the department and don't talk to anyone. You'll only see me at the department requesting interviews with the commissioner or other officials. Call me at the newspaper once a week or more if it's an emergency. Use a different pay phone every time and say you're Mitzi. I'll work on your interviews, and the fashion companies interested in you will call direct. Goodbye for now and thanks."

When Alex left the coffee shop she realized she might have been too melodramatic at their parting for an incident of this nature. Still, she could have made Camille vulnerable by persuading her to speak so openly and accepted the responsibility for protecting her. Now the next phase of her investigation was to identify the member of ReGreen Environmental who'd been contacted by the whistleblower in the Sanitation Department and arrange a meeting with him to try to corroborate Camille's story.

Elliot awoke to stand his four to eight p.m. watch as the tug left the expanse of the Chesapeake Bay to wind twenty miles up the Wicomoco estuary to Salisbury, Maryland. Warned by the setting sun to find safe haven till the morning, the few remaining laggards on the river seemed oblivious to the risks of night navigation. Objects were more difficult to distinguish in day's fading light as shadows vanished, leaving no contrast to activate the eye's depth perception, and the similar sepia of water and sky dissolved the horizon. As he waited for dark to restore visual differentiation, he reflected on the Wilmington botch and assumed the Sanitation Department had painstakingly reviewed the port schedule to prevent a recurrence, and having found no other errors on the list, they had seen no reason to contact the tug. It was dark when they reached Salisbury, a port of surprisingly extensive harbor facilities for a town its size. Barely moving, they searched the shoreline for some indication of appropriate docking and finding none, turned downstream for a distance that brought them away from the most active part of the waterfront. Unlike Wilmington, no official sped from the shore to intercept Elliot, which he interpreted as a good omen, signifying the port regularly handled imported waste. They dropped anchor and were mindful they lay at a mooring with an offshore breeze, minimizing the town's exposure to the barge's stench. In port and secured for the night, they temporarily discontinued their sea duty schedule. As a substitute, each advanced an entertaining rationale for the routine of his choice until by unanimous decision they agreed Elliot should be off from the present time of eight p.m. till three a.m., Bones off midnight to seven a.m. and Mac three a.m. to ten a.m. With this parliamentarian compromise accomplished, Elliot turned in while Bones and Mac renewed their fight to the death poker.

The next day at six, Elliot, now up for three hours and about to make breakfast for Bones and himself, watched in wonder as morning tinted the sky. In recent years, he rarely enjoyed the luxury of looking at the sky for no special purpose, the most important reason of all. Mostly he searched for weather signs and not the child's business of finding animal and people-shaped clouds. But the beauty of the dawn was soon to be disturbed by another of nature's less elegant constituents as hundreds of gulls found the barge and argued in raucous shrieks over who could eat the most garbage in ten minutes. Among the scores of gulls that blanketed the refuse one, before feeding, flapped up fifteen to twenty feet over the swarm to reconnoiter then plunged down to wrest a scrap from a luckless member of the flock as though it were the last of the garbage before repeating the cycle. *How similar to humans,* Elliot observed.

Attracted by this aerial circus, people on their way to work in the harbor stopped to remark on the staggering size of the garbage mound on the barge and the avian acrobatics.

As Elliot and Bones began eating breakfast they heard, over the din of the scavengers, a motorboat come alongside the tug and a genteel hail directed toward the captain. "Permission to board, sir?"

Elliot went out on deck to greet his visitor, discovering a sole, elderly man making his boat fast to the tug. "Welcome, come aboard."

Receiving permission, the septuagenarian turned off his boat's motor and, as cheerful about his infirmities as he was nimble, hopped aboard to extend his hand in genuine courtesy.

"That's quite a mountain you're moving, Captain. More than the entire Delaware peninsula can pile up in a year, I'd guess. My name's Randall Towson, like the town but different from the Washington's beltway mentality."

"Come in and have a cup of coffee," Elliot said to the dapper man in pressed khakis, tie, blazer and boots. "What can I do for you?"

"I was wondering if you were off course and strayed in here to see our pretty town."

"No sir, I'm here to unload the garbage for incineration or landfill. New York City's Sanitation Department was supposed to have Salisbury's agreement to accept this haul."

"Well, Sir, they're about seven months too late. We stopped taking imported trash the middle of last year. In fact, we ship all of Salisbury's refuse to Cambridge for consolidation with other communities' material, then off it goes to somewhere." Towson sounded a little like a foxy grandpa pulling the wool over the eyes of another municipality. "So, much as we'd like to help you, there's nothing we can do. You might like to catch the outgoing tide, it's due to turn in half an hour, help you along to Cambridge that way. I'll say goodbye now, Captain. Thank you for visiting our city. Oh, by the way, what did you say your name was?"

"Elliot Swan. Elliot Swan from England working for the J. Rich Steele firm in New York City. Thank you for your help. I must say you're much more courteous than the Wilmington, Delaware people."

"That's because we're south of the Mason-Dixon Line," the old man said with a wink as he lowered himself into the motorboat and headed up the river.

At the tug's speed of eight to ten miles per hour measured against the estimated distance to Cambridge, it seemed reasonable to expect they could put in by four p.m.—earlier should insure a place in tomorrow morning's line for unloading, later could delay them to the following day. Randall Towson had been right about the outgoing tide speeding them south down the Wicomoco River, but when they turned north in the Chesapeake Bay, the emptying of this huge water mass was coming head on and it was five p.m. by the time they entered the Cambridge Harbor and Elliot went ashore to make arrangements.

In half an hour, he'd located the harbor master and was directed to the manager of Cambridge Waste Products. The man was well informed on EPA regulations, organized in business procedures and polite. Within the last month Dorchester County, in which Cambridge was located, had modified disposal regulations to require that no trash would be accepted unless accompanied by certification that it was presorted. Aware this excluded the haul from New York, the Cambridge Waste Products manager thoughtfully suggested Talbot County as an alternative, as it had not yet instituted sorting requirements in the Easton landfill. Elliot, feeling like the ancient mariner cursed forever to sail with the albatross around his neck, immediately set out for Easton north up the Tred Avon River.

Once again they made a port entry at night, but Elliot took comfort in knowing they'd probably be first in line for unloading in the morning. Elliot went ashore at dawn anxious to get rid of the haul before another weekend when all the reception centers seemed shut down. After an hour's unsuccessful search for the official responsible for landfill management, he went to the police station for assistance and learned the manager was out of town, but his secretary, located in the county clerk's office, might be of help. From the woman's take-charge deportment, it was evident she ran the department and her supervisor was a political appointment. She confirmed they still accepted unsorted material for landfill, but volume was a consideration. After a few minutes of discussion she grabbed her purse, ushered Elliot out to her truck in the parking lot and raced to the riverbank opposite the barge.

"My God," she said in a soft Maryland accent, "did you have to bring all New York City down here?"

"It's rather large," Elliot agreed and, anticipating her resistance, added, "it compacts down a good bit as it dries."

"I'd really like to help you, pal, but this batch would fill up our site faster than we're allowed. It's way over the quota for a single drop. Come and see us again when you have about a tenth of that load." With a southern 'Bye y'all' she jumped into her truck and was gone.

"Mr. Steele, this is Elliot. We've been out almost two weeks and five ports on the incinerator schedule refuse to take our load. I'm convinced the Sanitation Department's list is worthless."

"That's what some reporter at the *Times* is suggesting. The paper keeps digging into the way Commissioner Callahan manages the department, questioning his competence and integrity. He's been temporarily suspended. This is becoming an embarrassment for the mayor, and that's why he wants the garbage legally disposed of as quickly as possible."

"What do you want me to do, Mr. Steele? The Sanitation Department never returns my calls about the list."

"Where are you now, Elliot?"

"Just left Annapolis on the way to Baltimore."

"I'm surprised Annapolis wouldn't take the stuff," Steele remarked. "They certainly must know how to handle harmful materials with the Navy right there spilling pollutants all over. At any rate, lay over in Baltimore, and I'll get back to you in the morning. Goodbye, Elliot."

"Goodbye, sir."

Elliot piloted the tug-towed garbage all along Baltimore's waterfront, weaving through the active shipping looking for the trash collection pier, located at a most improbable place near the inner harbor. Though he passed the decommissioned 1797 frigate Constellation, now a museum tracing the ship's battles with the African Barbary pirates, he could never find Ft. McHenry, whose siege inspired "The Star-Spangled Banner." He chuckled as he remembered how he had teased an American classmate at Oxford by telling him the music for his national anthem was originally an English drinking song. Once more the garbage was rejected, and after all three ate a hearty Baltimore seafood dinner, Elliot bought a copy of *Moby Dick* and boarded the tug, convinced he'd be at sea long enough to grow a beard.

As Elliot had expected, Jim Steele called back within twenty-four hours.

"Elliot, my people have contacted all the incinerator operators on the East Coast. Some are going through bureaucratic slow-motion routines, and who knows when I'll hear from them. Others are vague but might be shamed into taking the load when you show up. The rest won't commit 'till they see the stuff. The mayor knows all this and still wants to go ahead on our cost-plus contract. So there are your marching orders. Keep me posted."

"Thank you, sir."

"Chief, this garbage story is really heating up," Alex said. "For all intents and purposes, Callahan is out and everyone else must have been sworn to secrecy. No one in the department will tell where the garbage has been or is going, if they even know."

"What about your source, did she get you the boat's schedule?" the chief on the city news desk asked.

"She did, but that was before things tightened up. It's too risky for her now to draw the slightest attention to herself. I've tried to get the environmentalist guy to introduce me to the leak inside the department, but he's afraid we'll screw it up. There's no way at this point to confirm any source's story."

"How many other papers are following this story?" the chief asked.

"Two of the tabloids and one Brooklyn paper."

"Have any approached you and offered to pool information?"

"No."

"Then you can figure they think they have better connections than you. Has this ReGreen Environment Group got an in with any papers in particular?"

"We seem to have been their favorite paper since they first contacted me with the whistleblower's leak."

"And they still won't hook you up with the Sanitation guy?"

Alex shook her head, indicating no success. "Chief, I called on the mayor right after the boat was rejected in Wilmington to get his reaction to that screw up, and he acted as though nothing had happened. When Callahan was thrown out and his deputy took over, I asked his secretary to set up a meeting with the new guy. It's been four days now and no word. I'm going back to the mayor's office and ask for a meeting with him and if I get the runaround, I'll set up some surrogate to sue under the Freedom of Information Act."

"You can't do that, they'll make a journalistic leper out of you and you'll never get in the front door any place you go."

"What would you do?" Alex asked.

"I'd nose around some other department that's regularly in contact with Sanitation and doesn't like them."

"Such as the police?"

"Such as the police," the chief affirmed.

"You're right. They might know something. Despite Delisio's public statements that he respects Callahan, I don't think they like each other. On top of that, Delisio's announcement that he'll challenge Abramowitz next fall for the mayor's job makes it more likely he's been in Sanitation undercover looking for some scandal to bring Callahan down and make the mayor look like he's not on top of things."

"That's a possibility," the chief replied. "Incidentally, your garbage story is getting a lot of attention in the out-of-town editions, and the national news chief would like you to switch to his department. What do you think?"

"No thanks. I've just learned how to tame your pen of oversexed turkeys. I don't want to break in a new animal farm."

Alex was not surprised at how easy it was to obtain an appointment with Police Commissioner Carmine Delisio. After all, he was running for mayor of New York City. It was also not unexpected that he expressed vigor, optimism, confidence and a constantly smiling face to at least one constituent. He repeatedly stated, in various ways, how he would never neglect his public duty as police chief while seeking higher public service. With that, Alex, looking for an indirect route to question him about the possibility Sanitation's scheduling disaster might be symptomatic of something more serious, asked if the police department thought that incident should be investigated.

The chief leaned forward as though to take Alex into his confidence and said, "Ms. Appleyard, our department exists for the prevention of crime, protection of citizens and bringing anyone who breaks the law to justice. Now would you like to talk about the mayoral contest?"

Potential sources left for advancing her investigation were few, and the prospect of shutting down her story seemed an imminent reality. Quitting was unacceptable to Alex, and even though the odds of finding a new lead were tenuous, she found no alternative but to keep searching. As she frowned over burnt toast and cold coffee at a flow chart mapping her investigation to date, one input was suddenly conspicuously absent. She had never interviewed the carrier transporting the garbage. Knowing it would be useless to request this information from the Sanitation Department, Alex went directly to the U.S. Customs House and discovered the carrier was J. Rich Steele, III, and Company with corporate offices on Whitehall Street. Having learned it was always more effective to request the first interview in person, Alex entered the Steeles' reception room, presented her employer and personal I.D. with its unflattering picture and asked to see Mr. J. Rich Steele the Third.

The receptionist, a stylish woman in her forties with twinkling eyes and a friendly smile designed to provide a gentle buffer when necessary, said, "Miss Appleyard, perhaps you'd care to write us a note requesting an appointment."

"Why would I want to do that when I'm already here?"

The receptionist, recognizing the newspaper woman was not to be intimidated, whispered a few words into the telephone and advised Alex that Mr. Steele's secretary would be right out.

As good as her word, the secretary appeared almost immediately and motioned Alex to a couch apart from the rest of the room to ask the nature of her business. After hearing Alex out, she excused herself to see if Steele was free to talk to the reporter. Presumably, the tug's misadventure was gaining so much public visibility, Steele thought it prudent for the press to hear his company's story, and the secretary returned to lead Alex into his office.

"Come in, Ms. Appleyard. Won't you sit down? Now tell me what you think we can do for you?"

Alex repeated in more detail what she'd explained to his secretary and ended by saying, "—and as your firm is providing transport of this material, I thought you might be conversant with the schedule the tug is now operating under and how the original routing list was compiled with so many errors."

"I'm afraid my answer must be no to both questions. The captain is routing the garbage haul at his own discretion, and so we don't make the mistake of thinking what might be a good choice for a port today ends up being wrong tomorrow. The second part of your question you partially answered yourself. You're right, the Steele firm is under contract only to transport the material not supervise the Sanitation Department. I'm aware your paper has eyes and ears in many of the towns the tug may visit, so I would assume when the haul is accepted by a disposal port, you'll know of it before we do."

There was something so genuinely nice about Jim Steele that Alex couldn't resent he'd given her no information about the scheduling blunder. It was apparent Jim Steele was nobody's fool, and she wondered if he'd subtly led her to what might be the only investigative option left.

Chapter 10

"Okay, pilot, that's got to be the garbage brigade way over to your left. Don't go any closer; I don't want it to be obvious that we're tracking them."

"Use my binoculars and see if you can identify their registration number," the pilot said as he held a parallel course to the object of their search.

"Yep, that's it," Alex said. "We got them."

"Now what?" the pilot asked.

"How low to the water can you get?"

"It's pretty calm, so I'd say five or six feet."

"And how far away can your chopper be seen when you're that low?"

"Four to five miles on a flat sea like this."

"I checked it out and that class of tug pulling a load that big can make about nine knots an hour. That means if you get me dead ahead on their course, they could pick me up in half an hour. Let's do it."

"Lady, you're crazy. What if they change course?"

"I'll send up flares."

"Lady, that water's still cold. It's not even March yet."

"That's why I'm wearing a wet suit."

"And you're going to have me let you down, inflate that raft and get your gear stowed, all to be picked up by a floating garbage dump? I can't do it."

"You promised. What's the big deal? You're going to be nearby. If it doesn't work, you can come back and get me. Just be sure you float me right on their course and don't go too far away. Let's go."

Alex didn't want to admit it to herself, but the plan had seemed much simpler when she was in the warm cabin of the helicopter and not dangling at the bottom of the retractable ladder trying to inflate the damn raft. After several frustrating attempts, the compressed gases were released with a loud swoosh and the rubber platform of her survival lay below, pulling at its tether. One by one, the co-pilot handed down oars, flares and a couple of waterproof bags to Alex before the ladder was pulled up and the hatch closed.

As the helicopter skidded away just over the top of the water to evade detection, Alex suddenly felt vulnerable, isolated, immobilized by anxiety. *This was a dumb thing to do,* she repeated to herself. *What if the tug misses me? What if the flares don't work? What if the helicopter can't get back? Nobody will know I'm out here but the fish. Oh my God, what if a whale tips me over? How long have I been out here? It seems hours. Should I try to row towards the tug? What direction is it? How the hell do these damn oars work?*

She kept telling herself people rowed in the ocean. *Why, it wasn't too many years ago some man rowed across the Atlantic. My garbage story isn't worth all this. Who cares what I find out? Everybody just wants garbage out of their sight. They don't care about this garbage barge, so why should I? Where the hell is that tug? I'm getting mad at myself for doing such a stupid thing. I'm not going to wait much longer. If the tug or the chopper don't show pretty soon, I'm going to start rowing towards shore. Let's see, which way is it? The pilot said it was only fifteen miles away. I'm sure to see some other boat if I miss the tug. I'll wait at least a little longer. I'm warm enough and the water's not rough. This raft is really well designed, emergency rations, water filter—I'm surprised the Gideon Society didn't leave a copy of the Bible. Do I hear something or are my ears playing tricks on me?*

The brief appearance of the helicopter did not seem unusual to Elliot as one showed up about every other day, presumably to trace the course of the tug. The other reasonable explanation could be it was searching for schools of migrating fish, or now he thought about it, illegal aliens or drug gangs trying to evade the Coast Guard. Interestingly this, unlike previous helicopters, showed no interest in a close-up fly-by, leading him to eliminate a tracker mission to speculate on the other possibilities. The flat sea made the haul smooth and steady at about eight knots an hour. As he scanned the three hundred sixty degrees of ocean, his eyes fixed on the avian cloud blanketing the garbage, and for a moment he was Captain Ahab, pursued by the great white whale.

It was three in the afternoon, and the lengthening days made positions on the wheel or watch considerably easier than at the beginning of the trip. The entire Chesapeake Bay excursion had been a total failure, and at one point he was tempted to sail up the Potomac to Washington to make an ecological statement. But after some consideration, he recognized his pile of garbage would hardly seem unique in that venue. Upon leaving Easton some time earlier, it became evident that this might be a protracted trip, so the sailing day was reduced to twelve hours except in open ocean, dropping anchor about six p.m. to make frequent stops to keep well fueled and supplies near full when they hugged the coast.

Their inquiries at Virginia's Hampton, Newport News, Portsmouth, Norfolk, and up the James River Richmond had all been turned away with varying versions of 'not in my back yard.' Now they were again in the Atlantic heading towards North Carolina with little encouragement and no prospects.

"Skipper, there's something in the water dead ahead," Mac called down from the pilothouse. "The idiot is trying to stand up in a rubber raft to wave at us, going to get dunked for sure."

"Give a blast so they know we see 'em," Elliot said.

When he focused his binoculars, he saw it was a woman in a wet suit waving an oar at the approaching tug. Mac cut back on power when they were two hundred yards away and, the tug and barge maintaining a constant interval of separation, drifted toward the raft.

As they neared the woman, Elliot coiled a line and called for her to catch it sitting down. Closer and closer they approached the woman, pale-faced and tense.

"Here goes," Elliot called, landing the line in the bottom of the raft. The woman grabbed hold as though she'd never let go. "Fasten the line through one of the ring holes. Tie it tight so I can pull you alongside to the stern of the tug." Elliot secured the raft. "Now throw up the gear onto the deck. We don't want to lose it when we haul the raft aboard."

"Please can you hurry, I really have to go."

"Okay. Here we are," Elliot said, lifting her onto the deck. "The head is down the hatch."

Once Alex was assured of rescue, her survival instincts became subordinate to the suggestive powers of being surrounded by the noise of splashing water. In those few moments of privacy in the head, mounting doubts of acceptance as an intrusive newspaper reporter persuaded her to prepare a recital of lies until the crew found one credible, then having gained their confidence, she would later reveal her true identity. Satisfied with this strategy, she ran her fingers through her hair and went on deck.

Her rescuer, whose name she later learned was Elliot, stood waiting. Seeking to gain the initiative by thanking him profusely, she next introduced herself.

"Would you care to tell me what you were doing out here?"

"I'm a secret U.S. operative waiting to be picked up by a submarine."

"We wouldn't want you to miss your appointment, would we? Perhaps you should get back in your raft."

"No, if they're not here by now they won't be coming."

"Would you like to try again?" Elliot asked, curious to test the limits of her imagination.

"I was scuba diving?" Alex combined a ridiculous possibility and an unimaginable probability.

"You might think I have nothing to do but play this game all day, but there's a limit to my patience. By sea law, I'm obligated to report picking up a castaway."

"Oh, Captain, please don't do that. I'm trying to escape an abusive boyfriend and he's always found me before when I've tried to hide. Don't give me away," Alex pleaded, able to weep a few tears.

"No one could ever find someone with the name you gave me. Alexandra Appleyard, that's a comic book invention."

"Okay, I'm a newspaper reporter," Alex said, not because confession was good for the soul, but believing the connection she'd established with the captain was worth the risk of revealing her identity.

"I liked the abusive boyfriend routine better, brings out the paternal instinct in me. Now let's see what you have in those bags? I don't want you pulling a gun on me."

Alex watched Elliot methodically inspect the contents of her waterproof bags, laying out toothpaste, sneakers, socks, windbreaker, bras, panties, notebook, pen, cap, sun block, sunglasses and wallet. She was glad her I.D. had not been buried at the bottom of the bag but tucked inside her bra under the wet suit. If his uncertainty about her identify became annoying or he had an aversion to reporters, it could end the investigation.

"I'll take a chance on you till we reach our next port. In the meantime, put your stuff out of the way, wash the dishes and clean the head."

"What?"

"Perhaps you didn't understand, this is not a pleasure cruise."

"Well, you don't have to be so rude," Alex replied as she replaced her personal articles in the bags and started below deck.

"Yours is the forward bunk, portside."

"Which is the portside?"

"Left as you face the bow, if you can figure out where the bow is—and don't leave your clutter about."

During the time he was with Alex, Elliot was conscious of Bones' intensive scrutiny of the woman who'd invaded the male domain. No undertones of lust came deep from his eyes, nor any hint of violence in his unwavering glance, only rejection.

Elliot called Bones to join him and Mac in the pilothouse. "Fellows, we need to talk about our new passenger and the trip. I don't know who she is or what she was doing out in the ocean. She claims she's trying to get away from a boyfriend who beats her up, and in the next breath says she works for a newspaper. We can't dump her back on the raft, so we'll have to put up with her till we reach port. Now I know the trip was longer than any of us expected, but the weather's better than in New York and we aren't caught in winter work layoffs, so for a while let's take it a day at a time."

Having no better suggestions, they agreed to Elliot's.

Alex, aware there was limited time to ingratiate herself, worked to surpass the duties she'd been assigned. The dishes now washed and stacked, she swept the galley and sleeping quarters before attacking the head with unaccustomed wonder as she learned the perplexities of sea showers and toilets. Discreetly tidying the cabin with enough order to simplify the lives of four people, but without encroaching on the male prerogative, had the happy result of unearthing fishing tackle, which with the ignorance of an adventuresome neophyte angler, she provided a sea bass for supper. The meal, a departure from canned monotony, was eaten without interruption to completion, registering an approval the crew was reluctant to admit.

Now on a run of open ocean far from a night's mooring, the crew returned to the wheel-off-watch roster rotation, which assigned Elliot to the wheelhouse from eight p.m. to midnight. When Alex had cleaned up after supper, she climbed to look in on Elliot.

"Mind if I come in?"

"Two pairs of eyes are better than one."

"I'll assume that means I'm permitted."

Elliot mumbled confirmation and continued to scan the instruments then the ocean. Standing so the dim light emitted from the instrument graphics had minimal effect on her vision, the infinite, unobstructed, star-sprinkled sky seemed to float the tug through limitless space detached from the world below. She drifted deep into her reverie until the persistent chugging of the engine set her back on the sea.

"Where do you come from in England?" she asked, knowing no other way to start a conversation.

"Outside of Southampton."

"Been there a long time ago, England, I mean. What brought you to the States?"

"Rowing. I rowed at Oxford and came here to race in the Head of the Charles Regatta. You seem very interested in me. What about you?"

"Pretty dull life till lately. Grew up outside New York, went to school in Massachusetts. Met this guy I was crazy in love with before he started beating me. We tried couple counseling but he quit. Made him furious when I kept it up and when I left him, he found me and hurt me badly, so I took a bus to Richmond and another to a fishing village on the coast. Waited for the tide to take me out and rowed the raft to where you saw me. I knew somebody would pick me up, but there'd be a break in my trail and he wouldn't know where I was."

"I know," Elliot replied, "and as skipper I'm required to record your rescue in the ship's log."

"Oh, you can't do that, you'll ruin my cover. Can we talk about something else? That makes me nervous."

"Of course. Maybe you'd like to tell me why you have no bruises on your arms and face. Those are targets bullies usually strike. And as for rowing out to sea, the way you handled that paddle wouldn't get you a mile. Best of all, somebody trying to get lost would never dream up Alex Axelrod for a name."

"It's Appleyard, not Axelrod."

"Oh my God," Elliot roared with laughter, "you're the one Rich told me about."

"What are you talking about?" Alex asked, not knowing anyone named Rich, nor understanding what the confusion of names could possibly mean.

"My friend Rich, Rich Steele, called me when we were two days out and told me a reporter at the *Times*, Alex Axelrod or someone like that had a story about the Sanitation Department's screw up with the tug's routing. You're the reporter."

"I told you I was a reporter the first time you grilled me and you didn't believe it."

"What do you think you're going to accomplish aboard this tug? Your story is in New York."

"I didn't think so or I wouldn't have gone to this elaborate scheme to get on a boat with an arrogant captain and sullen crew pulling a putrid pile to nowhere. Do you realize a shark could have eaten me?"

"I don't think so, their digestive systems reject large concentrations of acids."

"Let's call a truce and consider what we should do," Alex suggested.

"I'm willing to listen to any suggestion, but you're getting off at the next port."

"You know, you have a very closed mind. You asked me what I hoped to accomplish by being on this ridiculous trip, and you won't let me tell you."

"I know one thing you've already done. You've made my crew very fidgety. Sailors are very suspicious of a woman aboard their ship."

"Most men are suspicious of women anywhere. Truce?"

"Truce," Elliot agreed.

"When I first broke the story, an environmentalist gave me Sanitation's phony port schedule. I asked for the contact with the department employee who leaked it, but ReGreen wouldn't tell me. Next I went directly to Callahan to get his version of the mix-up, but he'd barricaded himself. Then I got lucky and found a person who gave me chapter and verse on the incompetence that set you on this wild goose chase. I tried once more to get Sanitation to verify or deny the allegations before I published, but they were locked up tighter than ever. I went to the mayor—nothing, to the Police Commissioner, who can't stand Callahan and might have a plant in Sanitation who'd picked up something—nothing. Finally I saw your boss, Jim Steele. He has a complete hands-off position with anything to do with Sanitation's operating procedures and is acting only as a transport agent."

"So what's that have to do with me?" Elliot asked.

"First, have you been told to stay away from me?"

"No." Elliot stood silent at the wheel, his only expression the constant movement of his eyes as he looked for hazardous obstacles. "Look out there. What do you see?"

"Nothing," she replied.

"And that's what I see my involvement in your project should be. Nothing. Now it's the end of my wheel duty and I'm going to turn in. I have to warn you, I've been known to snore in my sleep."

"And I kick," Alex said.

Alex, giving up sleep slowly, awoke the following morning comforted by the steady throb of the engine as an old man might validate his existence by the pulsing of his heart. She stretched her stiffness against the confinement of the bunk, trying to count the revolutions of the propeller, and wondered what assurance seafarers looked to in days of sails—perhaps the wind song of the rigging, a lullaby for all ages. A glance around the dimly lit cabin revealed the other bunks were unoccupied and her recollection of the assignment roster scheduled Bones to be off duty from four to eight a.m. and presumably still asleep now at seven. Enjoying the unexpected privilege of temporary privacy, she hastily washed, dressed, made her bunk and went on deck. There, pressed against the leeward side of the pilothouse, was a huge mound of mattress, blankets and body— unmistakably Bones.

At the stern, as inexorable as the rudder, Elliot sat motionless facing the barge, watching the gulls feast on the ill-fated cargo.

Unable to conjure up a credible hypothesis for his preoccupation with this current menial errand, she confined her concerns to a more observable assessment of his character. A virile man, his handsomeness did not conform with any conventional standards. His effortless movements disguised a vigorous nature controlling a strong physique. His English accent was untraceable to any particular shire, and a reticence to idly discuss his origins gave him a disarming mystique.

"Good morning," she called, joining him close to where the barge's tow line was tied to the tug.

"Good morning," he replied without a pause in his binocular-aided, foot-by-foot inspection of the hawser.

"Is there a problem?" she inquired.

"No, and I don't want one. If that barge breaks loose, it will not be an enjoyable job recovering it."

"It doesn't smell as bad as imagined."

"That's because we have the wind in our favor. Wait till we hit port and tie up alongside it. But you don't have to worry about that because you'll be with us only long enough to go ashore."

"And that will be the end of finding the bad guys, not just New York City's government incompetence but officials all over the East Coast who haven't the slightest interest in solving this waste disposal problem. Did you find one collection port that tried to help you go directly to a working incinerator or landfill rather than just getting rid of you? Think about this stuff you're towing. What are you doing out here in the first place? I'll tell you. If the city had paid attention to the EPA's early release of proposed standards, they would have had a state-of-the-art incinerator on stream when the old plants were closed down. There would have been no emergency solution like this one. In fact, it isn't even a solution yet, and who knows if it ever will be?"

"You really get steamed up, don't you?" Elliot squeezed in between a couple of her pauses to breathe. Articulating frustrations she'd internalized for weeks extended the scope of her investigation from a metropolitan deficiency to a national crisis.

"Don't you see, Skipper? You're in the middle of it and you're being used."

"I think we need some breakfast and then we'll talk some more." They walked towards the galley to see Bones emerging from his improvised cocoon.

"By the way," Alex asked, "why did he sleep out here?"

"Bad karma when there's a woman aboard."

Again Alex took the initiative for fixing a meal—a breakfast of pancakes, strawberry jam and ham delivered to Elliot in the wheelhouse after the other two in the crew had been served. She returned immediately to the galley, sitting quietly as Bones and Mac finished their seconds of coffee, always waiting for them to speak first, and she was careful to spend little time alone with Elliot out of the sight of others to avoid the appearance of seeking an advantage over them.

In the days that followed, Alex sensed that Bones and Mac had lowered their guards because of her cheerful willingness to cook their meals and do chores, never being pushy or complaining. In short, she was tolerated because she caused no problems and was useful. Gambling to turn this into trust with the next small step, she offered to wash the bunk sheets and any of their personal laundry. Alex noted, with amusement, the hesitation they displayed while giving up their underwear. Elliot's contribution to the wash appeared to be everything he owned. Mac added a shirt, pants, shorts and socks while Bones put in a huge poplin windbreaker and shirt. She may have been pushing her luck when she hung the wash to dry on a line above deck, adding her bra and panties, but Mac and Bones survived and Elliot and she had clean clothes.

Elliot, beginning to think she was a woman to be reckoned with, silently commended her ingenuity which she'd applied so subtly since coming aboard. He recalled her passionate formulation of Sanitation's irresponsible dispatch of the tug to unprepared, indifferent or hostile depository sites as a model of far reaching environmental neglect. She'd behaved diligently if foolishly in pursuing her investigation to his boat, always relying on the power of the press to correct governmental neglect. He was still unsure what she wanted of him other than a sympathetic ear, but his commitment to the firm, the crew and the vessels came before others, and he could not go off on some lark even she hadn't defined. If she maintained a neutral observation of the tug's voyage and found good copy in that, he was willing to accept her presence until they reached the next port, but he would not deviate from his earlier decision. He was reminded his route to Wilmington, North Caroline, a promised unloading site, passed by Elizabeth City, Edenton and New Bern where the woman could be put ashore if need be. In any event, the haul would reach its final destination in Wilmington, and there'd be no reason for her to stay aboard any longer.

"You shouldn't feel obligated to bring me afternoon tea," Elliot said. "That won't stay your execution."

"I really brewed it for myself. You were an afterthought. Besides, I really like to be in the pilothouse and see what little work you're paid to do."

"You couldn't pilot this tug in a straight course for three minutes."

"You want to bet?"

"Yeah, here, take over." As he stepped away from the wheel without her knowing it, he flipped off the mechanism that automatically steered the tug on the desired course. The sea caught the boat broadside and pushed it five degrees to the west of its previous direction. "Bring it about," he directed, indicating which way to turn the wheel.

"That's too much, now take it back till you're in line with the compass route." She eased the wheel clockwise and counterclockwise, maintaining a fairly straight course.

"I have to confess I flipped off automatic onto manual steering just before I gave you the wheel."

"What was that supposed to prove?"

"You did very well for the first time," he said and paused. "In a few days, we'll be in Wilmington. That's the end of the line for the garbage. Then we start back. Tell me one thing. Have you hijacked the identity of someone working for the *Times* named Alexandra Appleyard to get on this tug and if so, why?"

"I'm the genuine article."

"Prove it."

"Okay," Alex said, fishing her newspaper photo I.D. card out of her bra.

"I'll be damned, you really are that reporter. I'll be damned."

"You said that. Now don't you think you should start leveling with me about why you were chosen for this job?" she asked.

"I've already explained the Steele company contracted to transport this waste to a legitimate disposal site and I happened to be the only available skipper for the chore."

Wind whipped white caps, gone as quickly as they appeared, caught and instantly fractured light to dazzle an observer of the spectacle, forcing one to squint in defiance—how different from a rolling sea's mesmerizing undulations that tempted one to break vigilance. Alex's eyes reached for the horizon, not in anticipation of a real sighting, but to clarify her thoughts on her responsibility to others. She'd been raised in a family of wealth, privileged with adventuresome experiences, good schools, special attention to the arts, vacations in exotic venues and even a despised debut. Her family was generous in their philanthropy, but it was always exercised in the form of a grant or some other financial form of largess. If they'd ever engaged in an up-close, hands-on connection, she didn't know of it. Now she felt caught in an undefined cause which compelled her to keep at it when even the markers of progress were indefinable.

Elliot, disturbed by the woman's persistent questioning of his involvement in the matter, was becoming annoyed. The truth, a simple explanation, was apparently unacceptable to a mind fascinated with intrigue. In a few more days she'd be gone, he'd be returning to New York and the whole damn business would be over. His continuously updated weather reports indicated the approach of March had done nothing to mitigate the icy New York blasts, causing him to regard his current temperate surroundings as part compensation for an odious voyage. He assumed it would be even warmer in Wilmington, and when the delivery was completed, stores laid in and fuel tanks filled, perhaps a day or two layover for some sightseeing would be a welcome break. This was not the U.S. tour he'd envisioned, but he'd learned long ago to accept and, if possible, exploit change. Not one to indulge in much daydreaming, he nevertheless let his mind drift back to England to consider what might have happened had he won the Henley Regatta.

Chapter 11

"Like father, like son." It was an expression which, to the best of Elliot's recollection, had disappeared from the lexicon in the last part of the twentieth century. In fact, even the older generation, among whom he rated Mum and Father a prominent personification, had abandoned the sentimentality. A somewhat similar maxim, offering the optimistic possibility of redemption from genetic repetition, suggested 'following in his father's footsteps.' While this did not imply a guaranteed escape from carbon copy lockstep, it offered hope for establishing an individual's identity.

Elliot presumed these aphorisms were descendents of prehistoric times when simple ideas were repetitively communicated within tribal territorial boundaries and some skills became habitually passed from generation to generation. Although the sayings had become obsolete and the father/son succession tradition dissipated, some vestiges defied obliteration even by the advance of depersonalizing information technology.

Because his parents had never pressed him to follow his father to a life at sea, they'd avoided open rebellion, showing great restraint or indifference while allowing circumnavigation different from theirs as he prepared for a career. Although at times they did question the affinity of philosophy and tugboats. Now here he was in a microcosm of his father's world, not placating dozens of disgruntled passengers, but justifying himself to a zealot—not that she wasn't nice to look at. He had yet to see this woman fully aroused, but the passion she displayed in talking about environmental abuse guaranteed she had a stormy side. Curious about juxtapositions and mindful he was not far from hurricane alley, he considered the reason for identifying these violent storms by giving them women's names and indicating their destructive force by categories one, two, three, four and five, the uppermost being catastrophic. He was curious about the category the woman aboard would be assigned if her temper were unleashed. What was the substance of this woman? Did she intermittently suspend her quest for restorative calm or subsist on crusade-stimulated adrenalin alone? It was indisputable that she had pluck, setting herself adrift, risky and foolish as it was, to board his tug. She was intelligent, curious…and occupying too damn much of his attention.

He forced his mind sideways to a more manageable distraction to speculate on the woman he might end up with in the years ahead. No, 'end up with' implied passivity in that adventure, conduct contrary to his nature. It was probable his studies at Columbia would lead him to U.S. residency but unlikely his wife would be an academic, as most arranged their marriages before teaching or pursuing advanced degrees, and undergraduate students were transient. To date, his only serious attempt to characterize women as potential mates was his sophomoric research, flawed from the moment it was designed, but it wasn't until later that the impossibility of tracking the study's participants for twenty years to determine the validity of his hypothesis proved the immaturity of his efforts. Moreover, he'd embarked on a sexual excursion with a member of the study, thereby violating the cardinal rule for objective research. In retrospect, he couldn't believe he'd ever been serious about the project; however, the basic subject of choosing a mate deserved serious consideration…which he could address as soon as the woman was off the boat.

"I'll bet that water is warm enough for swimming."

"What?" He jumped at the sound of Alex's voice.

"I said the water may be warm enough for swimming."

"You know, you talk a lot," Elliot said, cranky for being disturbed in his musing.

"You haven't said anything for half an hour."

"Perhaps I didn't want to say anything for half an hour. You talk when I'm piloting the tug. You talk when I'm reading *Moby Dick.*"

"I can tell you how it turns out," Alex said, meaning to annoy him.

"I know how it turns out. I want to know how Captain Ahab gets to the end of the story," Elliot snapped.

Alex, undeterred for even a moment, replied in a honey sweet voice, "Have I ever told you of your similarity to Captain Ahab and the white whale? Only your white whale is that load of garbage you tow around covered with white seagulls."

"I've already thought of that, but Ahab had a wooden leg."

"You're getting wooden headed."

Elliot stayed silent, composing himself before saying, "Woman, perhaps you're hungry and need lunch."

"Don't address me as woman," Alex said, finally getting nettled. "I'm Alexandra."

"I wonder," he replied, squinting at the horizon. "Sometimes, I wonder."

Alex left the pilothouse for the galley in a fighting mood, the calm of the simple, mechanical process of making lunch restoring reasoning but not certainty about the basis for her irritation. Was it his pejorative use of the term 'woman'? Did he suspect her of a deception camouflaged by a suspiciously transparent news story? Why did he always avoid a detailed discussion of his assignment? Could it be both she and Elliot had an inkling the other was involved in some questionable activity when it was all in their imaginations? Was he struggling with the conflict of his conscience nagging him to support her investigation and his promise to get the garbage evidence away from New York City as far as possible? Instantly, Alex ridiculed herself for constructing a bogus cops and robbers scenario. Was her presence drawing serious rancor from Bones, which she had not detected? Perhaps she should record all these thoughts and experiences for some future newspaper article or memoir. In any event, she decided it was better to switch off the stove and her musing than burn the soup.

On his way to relieve Elliot at the wheel, Bones acknowledged lunch with a low grunt of thanks, more gratitude than she'd heard expressed before. Mac, having eaten with Bones, was now on watch duty and left the galley as Elliot entered, going directly to the business of eating. When he finished lunch, by way of opening a conversation, he asked if any supplies were running low. She answered with a detailed inventory, and both satisfied, sat silent for a while.

"Did I ever compliment you on your cooking?" She shook her head to indicate no before he continued. "You have a knack for making pretty boring grub appetizing."

"Thanks," she replied, guessing his earlier outburst had also been symptomatic of hunger, and left alone, he'd clarified or at least neutralized some issues.

Yesterday she'd been told to get her things together and prepare to leave when they landed at Elizabeth City, an industrial port located on the northern coast of the Albemarle Sound. Like many early settlements, it was at the uppermost reach of one of the estuaries that divides the land into fingers, often separating towns by thirty road miles but only five by water. As they entered the narrows leading to the main harbor, a launch materialized to come alongside and inquire about their business.

"What's going on?" Elliot called down from the pilothouse to the more official looking of the two men below.

"All shipping is restricted from leaving or entering the harbor till the oil spill is cleaned up."

"How did it happen?" Elliot asked.

"Some group trying to make a fast dollar by not bringing their tanker up to code pushed the old bucket too far and the equipment broke during the transfer to the land terminal."

"How long before the harbor will be reopened?"

"At least a week, but it doesn't look to me like your load will suffer from perishability any more than it has."

"Is the port still accepting out-of-state incinerator and landfill trash?"

"Hasn't for months. We're barely able to get rid of our local collections with the reduced quota the EPA has enforced until we work out an agreement with them on new disposal standards. But you're perfectly welcome to anchor downstream a piece and layover for a day or so to enjoy Elizabeth City's attractions."

"Thanks," Elliot replied, thinking what a one man chamber of commerce he was.

Elliot decided to sail for Edenton. It was now almost certain Sanitation's list was nothing more than an identification of Atlantic seaports and no check had ever been made to determine which, if any, were operating disposal facilities. Having grown tired of betting with Mac on the gull's garbage consumption, he devised a new game of chance where one bet on the reception expected at the next port of call. It was a two-part wager, the first simply acceptance or rejection; the second was the manner used by the port officials, which ranged from Scorn, Unsympathetic or Neutral to Regretful or Sympathetically Helpful. Having invented it, Elliot was regarded with suspicion and had no players.

Edenton, a short day's sail from Elizabeth City, displayed a clean, tranquil waterfront unscarred by industrial incursion. No town delegation needed to leave the dock to disabuse Elliot from anchoring in the harbor flecked by furled white sheets of sail boats. Retreating a few miles to moor the vessels in Bachelor Bay as a courtesy to the visual and olfactory sensibilities of Edenton's residents, the four went ashore in the putt-putt, confident the residents' good manners, if not the garbage smell, would deter trespassing on the convoy.

Within a hundred feet after coming ashore at the town landing, the main street offered a small number of tasteful shops and one or two restaurants, indicating this quiet, out of the way community was more comfortable with wealthy retirees than tourists. A stroll through the eighteenth century historic district, displaying the less familiar but classic architecture chosen by owners to represent their individuality, was of particular interest to Alex. Her discerning eye quickly discovered one unusual house with a published pedigree, a short history of the dwelling on an unobtrusive board attached to the façade, which proclaimed it was the first bungalow built. At another point along the way, she learned Edenton had been the original capital of North and South Carolina when they were a combined colony.

Elliot responded to her enthusiastic enlightenment with, "And I thought I'd left all that behind me when I boarded this tug and Rich could no longer give me any more history lessons."

A triumph of Southern-style cooking helped mollify the day's earlier disappointment at Elizabeth City, and a purchase of fresh food to take back to the tug completed their satisfying visit to this small, courteous oasis.

By nine o'clock, they weighed anchor to catch the outgoing tide for their one hundred and sixty mile, semi-circular northwest trip to Washington, North Carolina, just forty miles away by land. Bones, complaining to Mac that his old illness had kicked up, shouldered his bedding to make a human lean-to against the wheelhouse. Mac took his turn at watch, and Alex wriggled under the blankets in the wooden-sided bunk—her coffin as she'd come to call it. Elliot, in unfamiliar waters, cautiously navigated across Albemarle Sound with constant attention to his depth gauge, staying at the wheel for most of Bones' shift. When he was relieved and climbed into his bunk, he'd been up for twenty-four hours. Sleep came instantly, and he didn't move till noon when hunger won the contest of senses. Resisting the rocking of boat which teased him to return to sleep, he saw Alex sitting at the galley table writing in her notebook. He was aware little escaped her mind before she could record it.

His yawn drew her attention away from writing long enough to offer a cheery, "Good afternoon."

"What time is it?" he asked, relying on short sentences to coax him to consciousness.

"It's noon by my time. I don't know how many bells that is in your world."

"I'm starved."

"I saved lunch for you. I'll get it while you return to the living. I've heard cold water works wonders in cases like yours."

"And keelhauling is recommended for insubordination to the captain."

Alex sat while he ate, noting his good manners, unlike those she'd experienced with many of her business associates. When he finished, he tried unsuccessfully to squelch a burp and sat back for a few minutes of idleness.

"You eat too quickly. It's not good for your stomach."

"You're not going to start mothering me now, are you? I liked you better in your protest mood."

Alex let that go by, waited a moment and in a most subservient tone asked, "Where to now, Captain, my captain."

"On to Washington," he shouted, raising his cup of tea, a mixed gesture of leading a charge and making a toast.

When Elliot left to resume his scheduled duty, Alex resumed writing in her journal, an early acquired discipline by which she'd become the beneficiary of the delicate nuances of impressions for future employment. Picking up her pen and journal as many take up the challenge of crossword puzzles, she searched for the precise word to fit in the exact place to perfect the message, not adverse to biting her lip, chewing her pen or resorting to an occasional four letter obscenity when a mental block threatened her manuscript. She remembered the words of a reporter, now long retired, who described each day's activity. "I sit at my typewriter, roll in a sheet of white, unblemished paper. Then I look at my typewriter and my typewriter looks back at me." What an eloquent description of writer's block, she thought. She'd recorded dates, locales, thoughts, views of others—a grab bag from which one day she might make a book but would serve the immediate future when she filed her *Times* story in Washington, North Carolina. Having reduced the last few days to legible notes, she put away the book and joined Elliot at the wheel.

"It's a clear day and an open ocean tells me it's time for my next lesson on steering this tub."

"Tug is the word you're searching for. Here, take the wheel, I'm going below for a nap," he said, pretending to desert her.

"Don't you dare, or I'll turn around and go back to New York."

He allowed she wasn't a bad looking woman, even with no make-up and her hair pulled back tight in a ponytail. Her warm, brown, heavy-lashed eyes gave her a look of perpetual wonderment, like that of a child. Well-sculpted ears lay close to her head, drawing one's attention to her cheekbones that led down to a straight nose and fuller lips than prescribed by today's fashion dictums. It was impossible to guess what the rest of her was like under that oversized sweatshirt and baggy canvas pants. She wore no emblem of attachment on her finger, but that was not uncommon, and rings came off or were never put on in the first place. There was no accent, pretension or reference to her past, other than the sketchy biography she'd offered when she was picked up. Elliot found it curious that, if she worked for a newspaper as claimed, no attempt had been made to contact her employer.

As frequently happens when one is concentrating on mastering a new task, as was Alex at the wheel, another may inspect that person with some intensity before the object of study instinctively senses the gaze and looks up to catch the spy.

"What are you looking at?" Alex asked.

"You. I still don't understand why a woman who's never done any physical work in her life would want to board a tug—particularly this tug just wandering around."

"First, physical activities have always been a part of my life. I play tennis, hike, ski, swim. I used to ride before I moved to the city."

"I mean physical, physical where you get your hands dirty."

"Have you ever mucked out a horse stall?"

"No."

"Tell me, Mr. Physical, what do you do that's so strenuous? Don't tell me steering this boat is strenuous. Any calisthenics? Oh yes, you told me you rowed. Haven't seen you row recently. I guess physical activity doesn't have anything to do with your question."

"Watch it, you're veering off course. Now turn off the engine."

"Are you kidding?"

"You heard me," Elliot said and called down to Mac that there was no problem and he'd start the engine again in a moment.

"My God, we're drifting sideways," Alex said, "and the barge is swinging us around."

"Now turn the engine back on with the lowest power."

"Where?"

"Here, this starter button. Now at lowest power. Gradually turn your wheel back to our course, moving the power up slowly so the tug takes up the slack in the tow line without snapping it."

"Are you crazy? I can't do all that."

"You may have to if the men and I decide we've had it with you and take off in the putt-putt."

"Where to now, Captain, my captain?" she mocked.

"Washington."

Washington, like every old town on the Pamlico Sound, lay up an estuary as though hiding from plunderers and spoilers. Blackbeard, a legendary pirate, reputedly hid in Bath, a tiny hamlet downstream from their destination, exchanging his asylum for the surrounding countryside's exemption from being pillaged. Without the threat of pillaging if no sanctuary was provided for their garbage, the convoy was forced to withdraw to the harbor master's memorable recitation, "Washington, the first town to be named in honor of George Washington, boasts a thriving economy based on lumber, textiles and agriculture but not garbage, thank you very much. Try New Bern to our south, a hog wholesaling market. It's surrounded by pig farms, and you know how pigs take to garbage."

Once again, they turned seaward, with little confidence Washington's "town fathers," though well intended, were actually accurate that New Bern would accept the barge load. A month and sixteen cities separated Elliot from New York, and realistically there was no end in sight, though there was some consolation in the fair weather and the picturesque one hundred fifty mile coastline arc to New Bern. It was debatable whether New Bern lay at the head of an ubiquitous estuary or the confluence of the Trent and Neuse Rivers, a putrid fifty miles of multiple tributaries flanked by the aforementioned pig farms.

Upon entering their destination's harbor, the tug's crew was met by a tall man in a planter's straw hat, standing in the prow of a motorboat approaching at full speed.

"May ah inquire about the nature of your business, suh?" he shouted.

"We've come to unload garbage for the pigs," Elliot told him.

With a nod of the planter's hat, instantly understood by the black man at the outboard motor, the boat backed away, circled the convey and returned. "Suh, ah never saw such dirty garbage. This will never do. We feel our livestock only the highest quality kitchen waste. Ah'm afraid we'll have to decline your offer. Ah bid you good day." And he was gone.

Accustomed to repeated rejections, the crew began sightseeing ashore at each port to save the trip from a total waste of time. Although New Bern might now be captive to the contemporary crassness of pigs, the city's romantic yesterdays were still in evidence. In 1710, Swiss landed in the area and nostalgically named it New Berne, later yielding the "e" to America's fetish with simplicity. Descendants of the founders, determining conditions to be favorable, attempted to make fine fabrics from silkworm cocoons. For a while the venture showed promise, but the silkworms' ravenous appetites for mulberry fruit outstripped the promoters' ability to supply enough of the dark red berries, and the venture literally ate itself to death, leaving only a small grove of trees as a memorial. Somehow, two twelfth century Italian monks knew better than their brother-state neighbors when they smuggled silkworms out of China and broke the Asian monopoly. Had they been alive in New Bern in the eighteenth century, perhaps there might have been no need of sows' ears to make the proverbial silk purses.

Seeking lore of a more positive nature, they turned to a building too imposing to ignore and learned that in the period of 1767-1770

Governor Royal, Lord William Tryon, built a colossal residence for himself, modestly named Tryon Palace. Even in its unfinished state, it rivaled the Governor's Palace at Williamsburg, Virginia. But no good deed deserves to go unpunished, as the saying persists, and Lord Tryon was removed by the Crown to the wilds of upper New York State for some unrecorded reason.

When they returned to the tug and headed toward Wilmington, Elliot's port of last resort, he secretly admitted his discouragement, but remembering he'd agreed with Jim Steele to keep going till they'd legitimately rid themselves of the damn stuff, he sailed full-speed ahead.

For a while, Elliot and Alex listened to a yelling, fundamentalist preacher on the radio explain why the world hadn't come to an end at a time and date previously predicted before going on to assure his listeners his new forecast was the real thing and there was still time for sinners to repent. Alex thought he had things pretty well covered except for leaving out the sins of polluting ourselves to death.

"You're not going to start that all over again, are you?"

"You bet I am, as long as it takes to wake up people to do something about it."

They looked at each other and began to laugh.

Mac called down to them in the galley that he was replacing Bones at the wheel who was experiencing discomfort from his acromegaly.

"I'll take Mac's watch, Skipper. You need to get some sleep while you can," Alex said, slipping into her jacket and going on deck before he could object.

The night was cloudless, full moon bright and mild. She toured the deck, stopping at every station to check as she'd seen the men check countless times. At the stern, she watched the barge's running lights flash to heighten awareness and the hawser, well secured to the tug, leashed the barge in good order. As they approached the channel through the Outer Banks to the ocean, she joined Mac at the wheel to look for debris floating in their path to the sea. The moon at its perigee lit the landscape with dramatic contracts of brilliance and shadows like a surreal stage setting. In an instant they entered the channel carved through a spit of sand less than a mile wide. Just as quickly, they escaped the Pamlico Sound to the Atlantic to sail a southwest diagonal to Morehead City.

Nearing their exit from the Atlantic to Bogue Sound, commercial and pleasure craft began to crowd the four mile wide Beaufort Channel that gave access to Morehead City. Bones slept through two watches trying to recover from his attack but knew rest alone was not a curative. He and Mac, his only confidant, knew that without surgery and drug therapy, his kidneys and heart would be irreversibly damaged, but he was afraid of hospitals and wouldn't seek treatment. When he arose, he was pale and suffering from some lingering pain but said he was ready to resume duty. Elliot stayed at the wheel, piloting them through the busy traffic, and Alex heard no objections to her standing watch.

Late that afternoon just outside the congested Morehead City port, they dropped anchor and waited for the harbor master, but no launch snaked through the water traffic to meet them. Elliot scanned the waterfront with binoculars, finding an array of ferry terminals, docks, industrial buildings and a state pier but no indications of official activity. Encouraged he might reach a resolution sooner if he took the initiative, he lowered the putt-putt and went ashore only to return in half an hour to announce their waste processing facilities accepted no out-of-state materials, and to top it off, there wasn't a single bloody decent restaurant in the town. It will never be known if it was sympathy for his frustration or a bribe to stay her impeding banishment that moved Alex to prepare another outstanding supper, but it is common knowledge full bellies are less bellicose.

Before dawn they weighed anchor and joined the line of ships filing through Beaufort channel to gain the Atlantic and the eighty mile run to Wilmington. Along the way they passed Camp Lejeune, a Marine Corps base, and it occurred to Elliot they must do something with garbage, but he was unwilling to learn what at the risk of being shot. The sea was flat, the weather mild and the convoy with its perpetual cloud of seagulls gave no indication this day was any different from any other of the preceding thirty-three.

By three in the afternoon, they curled around the coastline of Long Bay into the Cape Fear River downstream from Wilmington and joined as many ships going to port as leaving. Elliot was also perplexed by the large number moored on either side of the traffic channel, but his bewilderment was soon satisfied when officials in a state pier boat came alongside.

"Don't go upstream any farther. The port is shut down. Longshoremen strike."

"How long would you think it will go on?" Elliot asked.

"Your guess is as good as mine. It's in the middle of the third week and it's no closer to being settled than when it started. We're advising that you try another port, and in any case you can only stay tied up twenty-four hours before the fines start."

"You know any ports near here that will take my garbage?"

"Can't say I do, but somebody's going to be awful busy with loads of perishables if the refrigeration fails on any of these ships. Got to leave now. If you stay, pull up that barge real snug to your tug and make room for somebody else. Remember twenty-four hours and the fines start. See ya."

"Welcome to Wilmington," Elliot said to no one in particular, as though each word were an expletive, and added for the benefit of the others, "Let's stretch our legs ashore and see what the city offers."

Once again, the capacity of the putt-putt was tested but proved sufficiently sea-worthy to get them ashore. Alex perched in the bow facing the stern to watch Elliot navigate among the anchored vessels, while the middle seat was shared by Mac and Bones, the latter visibly in pain. When they tied up at the dock, it was agreed they'd return to the tug at eleven p.m. Elliot and Alex stood for a moment planning where they could meet and then find a restaurant before going separate ways to shop for themselves. As every city had a centrally located post office, Alex's choice won over Elliot's police station that might be anywhere. The two crewmen moved up the street at an uneven pace until they reached a corner where they stopped and Mac waved before they turned and disappeared.

The restaurant they chose was near the end of a cobblestone street that traced the river, now turning inky blue as the lights of the city went on. The place was softly lit and quiet, not the type of establishment sought by most stranded seamen swelling the city streets. The large wooden chairs were comfortable, the table was the generous size that does not crowd the settings and implies you are welcome to enjoy yourself as long as you want. Seated on the room's river side where the silhouette of the U.S. Battleship North Carolina was disappearing into the night, they shared a bottle of wine and dined on she-crab soup, chicken livers and grits with spoon bread. Their conversation became less guarded, Elliot admitting he'd called the Steele firm and had been directed to keep going, Alex disclosing she'd filed a long story with the *Times*. Both still cautious about revealing what might be too much, they talked mostly of their early years. The relationship was comfortable, making them almost late in returning to the putt-putt.

For half an hour they waited, seeking distraction by identifying stars and planets, but the diversion did not conceal their discomfort for long. As an hour passed and the night began to grow cold, Elliot suggested he take Alex to the tug and return to roam the town and check the police and the hospital. She quietly but firmly vetoed that proposal with the surprising declaration they were all in this together.

"Okay, let's see if the key is in its hiding place and I'll start the engine. What's this?" he said, unrolling a ball of paper that plugged the hole where the key lay. Elliot started to read:

Dear Skipper,

I'm sorry it had to happen this way 'cause you've always been more than fair, but I have to leave. After we left you this afternoon, Bones hurt so bad I talked him into going to the Emergency Room. They wanted him to stay overnight and have some tests and he said he would if I'd get him a donut and a postcard about the city to send to Mama. When I got back he was gone. Nobody saw him leave. He was awful scared of hospitals. I walked all over town, in all the stores, the hamburger joints. The police don't know where he is. I went to all the bars and the local AA place because he used to drink. I just got to find him, so I have to leave you and I'm real sorry 'cause you've always been good to us, but I have to do this for my brother.

Mac
P. S. Thank the lady for the dinners.
She's a good egg.

There was nothing to be said, nothing to do except return to the tug and try to sleep; nothing in the thoughts of either except feeling the brothers' suffering in being separated.

"Elliot," Alex whispered, "are you awake?"

"Yes. Have you slept at all?"

"No."

"At first light, I'll go ashore and look for them before we have to leave."

"They won't go with us no matter what, you know."

"I know, but I have to look."

Chapter 12

Alex woke at first light to the fog-muffled sound of the putt-putt taking Elliot ashore in search of Bones and Mac. All bunks empty but hers confirmed what her ears had suggested; she'd been left alone on the tug. His deliberately undetected departure was unsettling because it raised unanswerable questions in ever increasing numbers, depriving her of the warm comfort of returning to sleep. She believed he was not insensitive and undoubtedly realized his silent departure might cause some uneasiness, but as captain, he alone had been responsible for his crew while they were aboard, and as a decent man his concern extended beyond duty. Or was it a simple, mechanical response…you lose something, you find it?

She considered that for a moment then dismissed it as too simplistic an explanation for a complex person. He was a caring person, she'd observed it in his relations with Bones and Mac who were now in trouble, and he was trying to help. Had Elliot gone alone because if he found his crew, her presence might make Bones resist returning to the ship? Elliot's sense of self, she was sure, needed no chauvinistic platitude that this was man's work alone. Was it a reasonable deduction he was trying to immunize her from any future charge she'd contributed to the crew's defection? In reality his secretive departure probably had nothing to do with her, or at least it was a thoughtful gesture to not disturb her sleep. Lying in the bunk was an incubator for hatching embryonic ideas, aborted almost as soon as they were conceived. Hesitantly, she admitted she wanted to belong to this venture and her imagination was working overtime to assure there were no obstacles to her participation.

In what she regarded as a heroic measure, she decided to no longer gratify the adult version of make-believe and get up. Subscribing to her earlier recommendation to Elliot that cold water brings you fully awake, she endured the shock of a fifty degree shower, dressed and ate breakfast with a new perspective on her uncertainties. Her solution was so obvious she was annoyed at her failure to think of it sooner…she'd simply ask him and hopefully get a candid answer. Without realizing she was beginning to create Elliot's reply that it was her fault, she felt guilty and planned to leave the ship to prevent any conflict her presence might create.

The day, already unseasonably hot and humid, drew her to the deck to finish her coffee, but the stench of the barge tied alongside forced a retreat to the galley. A baseball cap, deck of cards and electricity-resistant gloves, remnants of the crew's occupancy, stirred up her recall of the hopelessness in Mac's note. For a while she kept busy washing dishes and cleaning the head, thinking these chores would distract her, but she was unable to forget Mac's heartbreaking vow to abandon everything to search for his brother, so lost to himself. When the memory wouldn't be suppressed, she committed to her journal all she could recollect of two pathetic derelicts.

She reread the journal entries that were the basis for the early newspaper articles on the garbage episode, followed by notes on her meetings with Camille, the Sanitation Department receptionist, and Jim Steele at his marine construction company headquarters. Unable to find bulletproof corroboration of Camille's allegations, there was no bridge to connect the original story with this endless voyage to nowhere. Without any conscious redirection on her part, the tenor of her notes became more appropriate for the development of a longer magazine piece, and when she recognized this change, it confirmed her mission was not metropolitan but national in scope.

By eleven a.m., she was written out and absentmindedly went back on deck where the fumes of garbage stewing in the sun left her gasping for breath. She found the pilothouse offered partial relief from the smell in exchange for the dead air of a confined space, but it was an ideal vantage point from which to monitor harbor activity with its parade of exiting ships outnumbering those entering, suggesting the settlement of the strike was even more remote than twenty-four hours earlier. Alex had never spent time in seaports; her limited observations of vessels were from a plane, making it impossible to appreciate the variety of designs that traveled the seas. For an indeterminate time, she read ships' names and guessed their origins from their national registration flags. The growing heat in the pilothouse detached her from concentrating on the ships and, without thinking, she peeled off her baggy top, leaving her in a bra. The crews of many passing ships communicated with pantomime, registering their disgust with the garbage by holding their noses while waving away the fumes, then applauding her scanty attire and beckoning Alex to come with them. Satisfied she'd seen enough ships for the rest of her life, she began studying the tug's controls and instruments. They looked complex and threatening without Elliot's mastering their coordination, and it annoyed her that his absence made her feel insecure. By way of regaining her concentration, she laid out the charts of their journey, tracing their course to Wilmington, surprised at how much she understood. Maybe she wasn't so dispensable after all.

By lunchtime Elliot had not returned, and with the three o'clock deadline approaching, she began to speculate on the amount they'd be fined. Correction, he'd be fined. It was not her fault. Conscious of her hands and nails while she ate, she concluded a little grooming would be the first order of business after lunch and then remembered she had no way of attending to the matter. Perhaps Elliot had some things; most men thought clippers were the ultimate in manicuring paraphernalia.

Where was he?

She thought of looking for Elliot's copy of *Moby Dick,* but not seeing it easily accessible, decided it would be an invasion of privacy to look among his belongings, not that he'd extended the same courtesy when he fished her out of the ocean. The way he went through her bag appeared to be preliminary to a strip search. And it didn't seem to bother him at all.

Looking to distance herself from the clock, Alex turned on the radio and dialed through endless agricultural reports and evangelistic preachers. Bored, she graduated to the more technical ship-to-shore telephone, hoping to call her office, but Elliot, either through an oversight or purposely trying to frustrate the female attraction to the telephone, had failed to teach her how to operate it.

He was a true enigma, unaware of the consternation he bred in others. How could this well educated, intellectually gifted man be satisfied towing a smelly millstone around indefinitely? It was inevitable she'd compare him with men she'd known, those from whom she'd been able to hide her identity and those who knew her family's importance. In both groups, some worked full time at trying to impress her, some their bosses, which when she thought about it was the same. Most were upwardly mobile mannequins hiding the real person from being discovered. She'd never met a man like Elliot, self-assured, unpretentious, reliable, provocative, irritating, resolute, puckish—she decided she'd described him much too favorably and added annoying. Right now, she was displeased with his prolonged absence, and she could only believe he'd decided to chuck the whole stupid project and take off, leaving her holding the tug, so to speak. If she believed that explanation, a direct contradiction to her earlier assessment was even a remote possibility, she should get off this sea going merry-go-round and return to New York.

It suddenly occurred to her she'd wasted the whole day thinking about him and not herself. It was selfish to maroon her this way and obvious two could have searched more places than one. Where would he look today that hadn't been explored last night? The only places Elliot hadn't mentioned were churches and whorehouses. Churches usually locked up at dark, and how long could a man survive in a whorehouse?

She'd wait till the harbor master came out to impose the fine and get him to put her ashore. But what if he arrested her and put her in jail until the fine was paid?

Now she began to doubt the value of her garbage investigation and fantasized she'd be the subject of ridicule and rebuke for wasting time and money. She'd quit the *Times* and work on a book, not a "Silent Spring" wakeup call but an insistent second alarm that the nation was still snoozing.

With only ten minutes left before three, it was time to get ready to leave. In the few minutes it took to stuff her belongings in a bag, she became aware of the mid-afternoon river traffic blaring discordant horns and whistles as the ships set their courses. One last look at the cabin and she went up on deck to come face-to-face with Elliot.

"Going somewhere? Trying to sneak away without paying the rent?" he asked, grinning at her.

"Where have you been? And stop smirking at me. Don't you realize the twenty-four hour grace period is up?"

"Government employees are always late. That's the first thing you must learn if you ever go to work."

"Don't joke with me. I'm mad as hell from sitting here all day wondering if you had any luck finding your crew."

"Not hide nor hair," Elliot replied. "They've truly dropped off the face of the earth. I rechecked all the places I went to last night and no one's seen them. Fast food, bars, movies, car rentals, train stations, bus lines, every place, police, even the banks and fire stations, post office, every place."

"How about shelters?"

"Yes, not there."

"AA meetings?"

"Not there."

"Churches?"

"Not there."

"Motels, YMCA?"

"Not there."

"Parks?"

"Not there. I've looked everywhere."

"There's one place you didn't mention."

"What's that?"

"Whorehouses."

"Yes, but I was going to spare you that embarrassment. Not there. When I realized it was no use to look further, I went round to the seamen's hall to recruit a replacement crew, but all the men are out on a sympathy strike to support the longshoremen. I'm stuck with no crew until they fly some men down from New York."

"I can crew," Alex said deliberately.

"Woman, you can't."

"Stop calling me 'woman.' You always do that when you don't know what else to say."

"All right, you can't replace Bones and Mac, and even if you could, you were going someplace."

"I've changed my mind, and right now I'm all you've got to help get this junk heap out of here," Alex said, growing more defiant.

"You may, just may, be able to help get us out of port, but you can't pilot this tug."

"Yes I can in open water. Teach me more. Remember, you started to."

"But that was nothing but steering. It takes time to run these things."

"Teach me, I'm a quick learner."

"Woman, I never knew such a quick talker."

"When we're at sea I can take the wheel while you nap in the pilothouse. And it was your idea to anchor at night. And stop calling me 'woman.'"

"As easy as that, eh?"

"Do you have a better plan?"

"When I saw you in the raft I should have waved and gone by."

"You'd be violating the sea codes."

"What sea codes?"

"The one that binds you to picking up helpless castaways."

"Who could ever think you're helpless?"

"Let's stop talking and figure out how to move this mess before you get a parking ticket."

"Wait a minute. I'm supposed to be the captain here. Now stop jabbering and listen to what needs to be done."

Having weighed anchor, the ease with which they positioned the barge to trail as they joined the flotilla moving downstream surprised Alex and Elliot. She attributed it to her lightning-like assimilation of seamanship and he, more realistically, noted how rapidly ships yielded their place in line to avoid the offensive cargo. Lethargic seamen on passing ships became animated, pretending to be overcome by the garbage and raised a white handkerchief flag in mock surrender. Alex never left Elliot's side, memorizing his skillful navigation of others' wakes and the changing tides. When they reached the mouth of the Cape Fear River and open ocean, the queue of vessels broke formation for individual courses. With the scattering of vessels, he relaxed his intense concentration, and Alex felt free to break her silence. When he read an instrument or adjusted a control, she'd ask him what that gadget was. Assuming a look of pained patience with her choice of nomenclature, he'd name the equipment and explain its function, and Alex would immediately memorize how it was used but discard the sea-jargon label. Earlier, when they prepared to leave Wilmington, he asked her to get a bar for the capstan to winch up the anchor in case the automatic lift didn't work.

"What's that?" she asked.

"It's a pole for that big, black knob with the holes in it."

"Why didn't you just say that?"

"Because capstan is its name. It's a derivative of Latin or French—I think. Now we have clear sailing, let's run through equipment and ship parts again."

"What for? Why not point or give the thingy a simple, descriptive name or a sensible pronunciation? For example, say front of top deck for forecastle, and it's silly to pronounce it 'folksil.' Who ever heard a urologist pronounce foreskin 'folkskin?'"

"That's ridiculous. Let's get back to name association again," he directed in an annoyingly didactic manner. "How do you ever expect to get licensed to pilot a ship if you can't use the proper terms?"

"I don't. I think seamen are an old boys' club and they concocted a silly vocabulary to exclude people. They should be reported for discrimination," Alex said, warming up to her protest.

"Capstan, which started you off on your high horse, is a very classical term."

"It's a dead word like Latin's a dead language."

"That's very enlightened. Now, kindly explain your expressions: thingy, thingamajig, thingamabob. Are they different forms of the same noun; good, better or best? And what about gizmo, whatchamacallit and doohickey?"

"Everyone knows they're transitional words. You use them until you're comfortable with a name that fits."

"You speak as though you majored in languages," he said, twitting her.

"Close, literature and creative writing."

"Ah! That explains everything. Would you like a turn at the whirligig?" he asked.

"You see how sensible that is?" she asked, reaching for the wheel.

They sailed in silence, savoring the serenity of the sea's solitude, grateful for the invigorating air of a waning afternoon, saddened there had been no definitive closure with Bones and Mac. There was no need to talk. Though not often understood or spoken, each felt their own or the other's frustration, disappointment, helplessness, pleasure, anticipation, excitement, anxiety, challenge, uncertainty, respect, satisfaction, puzzlement, reservation and need. They sailed into early evening's temperature contrasts of air and sea that enveloped them with tiny droplets, bathing their heads in a restorative baptism—stress washed away lively banter, heroics or devices of any kind. Turmoil and clatter, failure and discouragement became manageable memories as the past faded behind them, their voyage accompanied by the sea's rhythmic slap against the tug's bow to keep time for the throaty sound of the dependable engines. They sailed on till dark lowered and automatic running lights reminded them to seek a safe harbor for the night.

"Let's go on to Calabash," she suggested, "I've always wanted to see a town that had the name Jimmy Durante used to close his comedy shows—'Good night, Mrs. Calabash, wherever you are.'"

"I'll take the wheel now if you'll rustle up some grub," he said.

"Fair exchange. Where'd you learn that cowboy talk?"

"Two can play at linguistics," he said, gently letting her know he wasn't keeping the truce.

The menu consisted of canned hash, pineapple and instant coffee, a signal to Alex they'd eaten beyond the ingredients of her imaginative cooking. They dined in the semi-darkness of the pilothouse, he at the wheel while eating, she sitting in the shadows on a life jacket, studying his face lit only by the instruments' displays. She had never seen him without the beard which continued to grow untrimmed. Still unable to characterize his looks, she could without hesitation describe him as distinctly different. Once earlier she'd gone the route of trying to compare him to other men she'd known and failed.

He told her it would be late when they reached the channel into the Intercoastal Waterway leading to Calabash, and it would be best to anchor offshore. In the morning, they could refuel, restock the food supply and make a whirlwind tour of the metropolis of Calabash, population 1,325. She returned to the galley, washed their supper dishes and made a station-by-station check of the tug, ending at the stern. The hawser still held the barge secure, and the running lights intermittently flashed their warnings to other nocturnal travelers. Alex returned to the wheelhouse to report the inspection completed without detecting any irregularities.

"All's ship shape fore and aft, Skipper," she parodied, but her tone also indicated she wanted to be recognized as a crew member.

"Aye, aye, mate," Elliot replied, keeping the conceit alive. "We'll be putting in about fifteen minutes from now. See those lights over the spit of land? That should be Calabash, and tomorrow you can look for Jimmy Durante."

His estimated arrival time was accurate to the minute, and with relative ease they drew the barge alongside to stabilize it from swinging kite-like from the end of its tether. Once again the convoy sat offshore far enough not to abuse the welcome of the natives. After all, who could foretell the behavior of indigenes who named their place Calabash?

Alex, nudged from her sleep by ship horns, slipped on her baggy uniform and went out on deck to see a fleet of fishing boats clearing the channel from Calabash to the open sea. A gusty offshore wind chopped little white caps and scattered the stench, saving her from any insulting gestures from the exiting crews. As she watched, one trawler came alongside to learn how long the barge would be anchored there. When asked why, she was told the garbage diverted the gulls from searching the ocean to feed on tinker mackerel which were always chased by schools of sea bass and blues. Without the gulls, it was harder to find a catch. Within a few minutes, Elliot joined her and scanned the town harbor for a fuel depot. Estimating their tug drew no more water than the fishing boats, the depot should be easily accessible, and his tide information gave him a sufficient margin of error if he'd guessed wrong.

The economy of Calabash, little more than an ocean village, was fed on commercial shrimping and charter boat fishing. Alex and Elliot strolled the few streets before ending at the pier where they'd refueled, having encountered no off-season tourists among the locals who were pleasant but preoccupied. An abundance of small restaurants, mostly shuttered, suggested a seasonal influx of vacationers also contributed to the population's livelihood. Alex had almost given up on learning the origins of the village with the distinctive name when they were greeted by an ancient sailor, beached by age, presiding over the emptied waterfront. They responded to his greeting delivered in an almost unintelligible accent, and for the next half hour listened to his repertoire of anecdotal recollections. He immediately was attracted to Alex, and learning she was from New York, replied he'd never been farther north than Wilmington. A contest soon took place between the old man, who wanted to talk about nothing but New York, and Alex, who was unsuccessful in learning much about Calabash. Elliot at last broke in to end the conversational impasse by saying they had to catch the outgoing tide.

"You can't fool me, young feller, you just want her all to yourself," the old man challenged. When they said goodbye to the patriarch of Calabash, he handed Alex a crumpled tourist folder, saying, "I like you, young lady. You're a looker. Smart, too."

That evening in the galley at dinner, she entertained Elliot by reading the Calabash tourist folder to him. Paraphrasing the meandering text, Alex narrated a chronologically disjointed trace beginning in 1691 when the English Throne granted a Lord Proprietor a large, unspecified tract of land in which a village, later named Calabash, was settled. There was no other significant history mentioned, except indigo was grown for dyeing a fabric favored by the upper class. Today the small port harbored a substantial fishing business and boasted of unparalleled Calabash cuisine, although that was never described. There was an oblique inference to the locale being one of the few areas in the world that grew Calabash, gourd-like fruit which in its early stages could be eaten. But no Jimmy Durante. It was late when they finished supper and Georgetown, South Carolina was approximately eight hours away, so a layover offshore and an early morning start for the next incinerator prospects seemed wise.

At dawn the bright crimson sky lingered for a few minutes before turning a dirty, dark gray, prompting Alex to recite the familiar weather forecasting rhyme—

"Gray in the morning, red at night, sailor's delight.

Gray in the evening, red in the morning, sailors take warning."

Routinely, Elliot checked the radar weather and found only overcast along their course. Breakfast returned to event status with a delicious recipe created from the groceries purchased the day before. They weighed anchor, hopeful this might be their lucky day to reach a long sought destination. Halfway to Georgetown, a thick blanket of dark, rainless clouds hugged the coast, offering no hindrance to their afternoon arrival at the harbor's State Pier. Their reception, like few others, was gracious, but the town's enlightened citizens were fully occupied battling the urban blight of pollution from the local steel mill and paper company. Trying to environmentally process their own waste allowed no capacity to accept the haul from New York. Charleston, they were told, with its large paper processors and naval base might be better equipped to help Elliot.

With no reason to delay, they crossed Winyah Bay to the ocean and set the course for Charleston. The widespread clouds lowered to almost touch the water, and still there was no rain. Together, they ate a hasty meal in the pilothouse, and when Alex had washed the dishes and made her routine inspection of the boat, she returned to Elliot as rain swept in from the south. A slightly lower barometer and the radar reading showed the forming of a front far south pushing showers ahead of it.

"It looks like we're in for a soaking," Elliot told her. "Is everything lashed down tight? I think the winds will be picking up."

"It looked okay to me when I just checked them, but you may want to see for yourself."

"Take the wheel. You want anything from below?"

He was gone before she could answer, and the responsibility of piloting without him made her uneasy. Out of sight for a shorter time than she imagined, he suddenly appeared on the forward deck, making sure the anchor was fast. For a moment, she strayed off course, and the bow caught a wave sideways, spraying him. He looked up at her, warm and dry in the pilothouse, with an expression that unmistakably meant, 'you'll pay for that.' Then he was gone.

When he reappeared beside her, he'd changed his clothes and wore foul weather gear.

"Where's mine?" she asked.

"After the next wave," he replied, before pulling out a slicker and Southwester hat from inside his jacket. "If this gets heavy and rolls us around, you may find it better in the galley. By the way, do you get seasick?"

"I don't know. I guess we'll have to find out."

"If you have to vomit, open the passageway and do it on the rear deck. The sea will wash it away without taking you with it."

The night sky had closed in on the convoy, blocking vision beyond the prow, nullifying the running lights. Another reading on the radar showed the storm intensifying in power and size as it thundered northwest up the Florida coast for a Georgia landfall, probably the worst still to come. Elliot smiled at Alex, hoping to put her at ease as she braced herself against the chart table. She knew exactly what he was doing, and he knew she'd read him correctly.

"You wouldn't like to try out your rubber raft, would you?" Elliot's joke had the opposite affect intended and raised the tension level. The wind had picked up to a measured forty knots, throwing spray across the glass of the pilothouse before it guttered on the deck below and drained away.

Elliot reread the instruments and radar mapping. "Alex, this is going to be a nasty storm. It will reach the coast before we can, so that pretty much eliminates our chance of finding the protection of a harbor. We could turn around, but I don't think we can outrun it, and I don't want to head into it with the barge."

"So what do we do?"

"I think our best bet is to head out to sea and circle it."

"How far out to sea?"

"Between thirty-five and fifty miles," he told her, pointing at the charts.

"Let's do that. Maybe we'll get lucky and go all the way to Bermuda."

Elliot changed course in a long, gradual eastern arc to avoid getting whipped around by the barge at the end of the hawser. The new direction set the tug into a constant roll as waves battered its side. The seas, getting higher, threw masses of water across the deck. Creaks and groans registered the storm's abuse of the tug, and repeated shudders of the boat as it climbed to poise on the crest of a wave before crashing down into the trough were unnerving for Alex. Although the thermometer in the wheelhouse registered seventy degrees, she felt a deep-cored chill, even unrelieved by putting on her slicker.

"We're going to be all right," Elliot said.

"If we're going to be all right, why do you keep telling me that?"

"Because these are the only times you listen to me," Elliot twitted, thinking if he engaged her in repartee or even an argument, she'd pay less attention to the storm noises.

On they plowed, pitching through miles of turbulence. Elliot estimated they'd come fifteen miles since they turned east. Radar indicated another twenty-five miles, three and a half hours, before they'd reach calmer seas. Wind, registering at sixty-eight knots, almost hurricane levels, suddenly shifted, catching the stern of the tug on the way down a mountain of water to drive the bow in a forty-five degree angle before the vessel emerged, shaking off its watery captor.

"I didn't sign on for submarine duty," Elliot said.

"God, your jokes are terrible."

The wind grew in intensity till the radio mast shrieked like the banshees of Irish origin, warning of doom.

"If I ever get married," Alex said, "remind me not to take a cruise on our honeymoon."

"Now you're getting the hang of it," Elliot replied. "And remind me not to take my bride on a cruise."

For a while they tried to top each other with their quips, but the constant groans of the ship under stress pulled them back to the terrifying realization the vessel might be torn in two. Elliot led Alex through another review of the ship's controls and instruments and was surprised at how many she knew. At times questions and answers had to be yelled to be heard. When Elliot was convinced some new precautionary measures wouldn't frighten her anymore than the storm already had, he showed how to activate the mayday call for help signal and told her to put on a life jacket.

Minutes became an impossibly long measure of time, and one hour never seemed to surrender to the next. Elliot's fingers grew stiff on the wheel, and his eyes hurt from straining to detect something impossible to see. Every few minutes the motion of the waves brought the barge closer to the tug, causing a slack in the towline before the reverse action of the water walls spread them further apart, resulting in the tug being jerked back like a leashed attack dog. Elliot was sensitive to this dangerous tow but decided not to mention it to Alex, who had settled into the corner of the wheelhouse to prevent being knocked about. Elliot switched on the radar for another reading and found it inoperative, making him dependent on his compass and direct visual observations now extending no farther away than the ship's rails. On they sailed into the black violence, not knowing when it would end.

"Doesn't the shrill of that wind drive you crazy?" Alex asked from her dark corner.

"Of course it does," he replied, "but it's going to blow no matter what I think, so I know I'm all right as long as I can hear it."

"That's very philosophical."

"I'm a philosopher," he replied in a moment of rare intimacy.

She tried to return to silence to speculate on his confession, but the shrieking wind kept tearing at her defenses to undo her, and she had to talk to him or see him to contain her terror.

"How much longer?" she asked.

"About an hour," he lied. There was no point in telling her the radar wasn't working and he didn't know. If the time of catastrophe came, he would level with her because it was the only honest thing to do, no matter how hard it would be to see her suffer.

The crazed wind reached a decibel so high it was barely audible to the human ear. The barge, with a bigger mass than the tug, had become a pivot, jerking the motor vessel through a wide deviation from the compass course. The waves now rocked the tug so far to port and starboard Elliot could look down from the wheel, where he stood, at water on one side before rolling to look down on the other. They were shipping water and would capsize if he couldn't stabilize the ship by setting a different course. He knew Alex could not escape feeling the violent motion, but in her corner she was spared the shocking sight. As the storm blew through, it went from climax to climax, testing the endurance of the man and woman. Then without warning they entered calmer waters found in the eye of the hurricane, before being sucked back in to violence. As the wind swept back in with towering waves there was a horrendous screech followed by a sharp whine as the tug surged forward before settling down on a starboard course.

"My God! What's that?" Alex screamed.

"The tug's broken loose, but the cable has wrapped around the port propeller shaft," Elliot told her as he shut down the engine.

"What can we do?"

"You can take the wheel while I go under the boat and free the propeller."

"You can't do that in this storm."

"I think we've passed through the worst of it," he lied, "I can crab the tug on course for a while till we reach a better sea, unless you want to go around the world to the left for the rest of your life."

"Do you really trust me at the wheel?"

"You're all I've got, remember. Now, if you can get my scuba suit and tank and light and cable cutters out of that locker seat you've been warming, I'll be ready at the first break."

They sailed towards ever calming waters, always correcting for the failed engine to keep on course. Elliot's gamble to skirt the storm was paying off, and though the seas were still high, the violence was quickly draining away as the night passed.

"Okay, Mate," he said to Alex, hoping to rouse her plucky side, "it's time for you to take over. I'm going to head the ship directly into the waves to lower the roll even though it's off course. We'll fix that later. I'm shutting off the automatic steering so you can correct course without it if you need to. Take the wheel and see how it goes. Good."

"It pulls a lot to the port," Alex said.

"Can you hold it for twenty minutes? That's how much air I have."

"I think I can, but how can you keep from being swept away?"

"I'll tether myself to the stern. Now, if I'm not back in twenty-five minutes, hit that mayday alarm."

"Elliot, I don't want you to go. It's too dangerous."

"It's dangerous if I don't. How are your arms holding up?"

"Okay."

"Okay then, I'll see you shortly," he said as he padded out of the wheelhouse in the dark to the stern of the tug.

Now she was more alone than she'd ever been. There was no end to the sea, rolling in greasy gray hills and valleys scarcely distinguishable in the border between night and day—a time when form and perception are distorted beyond reliability. The isolation was enfeebling, the demands of survival overwhelming her resources. There was no one to call her name to prove she even existed. In a watery world six feet, sixty feet, six hundred feet or six light years away, someone struggled to rejoin her with herself so she could rejoin her world. This someone, this man worked against tremendous odds, limited oxygen and infinite ocean. This man she knew she could not live without.

The pull of currents on the rudder signaled her to keep a tighter grip on the wheel. The clock showed eighteen minutes had disappeared since he left the pilothouse. She glanced back at the stern of the tug but could not see where his tether was fastened. She glanced at the mayday alarm and wondered if she should turn it on. Maybe she could reset the automatic steering control and go back to look for him. Would she even see his underwater light? Could she get him to come up by jerking on the tether? The hell with the propeller, they could go around the world to the left together. She locked in the automatic steering and turned to go after him just as he entered the wheelhouse.

"Oh, Elliot, Elliot, I thought I'd lost you. Just when I found you, I thought I'd lost you," she cried, clutching him to her.

"How could you lose me? Remember, you told me you were all I had," he answered, his arms folding her to him.

Chapter 13

God smiled on all nature that Saturday morning following the great storm, bringing buds to blossom, wiping the cobalt blue sky cloudless, sweetening the air with the smell of newly watered earth. The sun rose to the accompaniment of birds testing their songs; a redemption of the elements recently gone awry, dew spread diamonds on the azaleas, and every grass blade of the newly laid sod stood at attention, framed by neatly swept, intricately patterned brick terraces and walks. Red, white and blue Japanese lanterns, strung strategically among the palms, hung like exotic fruit. A large marquee covered much of the acre of lawn between the house and the beach. Within the marquee, a wooden floor was readied for the pleasure of those who danced, and closer to the shore a temporary helicopter pad awaited arrivals. Twelve feet-high sheets of canvas on either side of the house reached to the water's edge to deny intrusion of the curious.

In the house, furniture was buffed once again, silver repolished. Cooks and caterers labored, florists arranged and rearranged, carpets were vacuumed, brasses burnished, lights tested, windows cleaned and it was not yet seven a.m. The owners had built their trophy house to take its place among a dozen others on the eastern side of the Isle of Palms, challenging the open ocean they faced. Twenty-four thousand square feet, lavishly furnished, were an architectural travesty of the low-country style favored by denizens of the deep South. But what the searching eye of a purist found lacking in tradition, the builder had endeavored to offset with size, and even the restraining hand of the lady of the house proved no match for her husband's zeal in the creation of his monument. Elevated by twenty-feet high concrete pillars to weather a hurricane's ocean surge, the grand edifice gave the appearance of being perched on ungainly birds' legs until coniferous trees and shrubs skillfully planted created the illusion the house had surmounted a forest. The structure rose three stories from the first floor's four-sided, apron-like veranda. A great hall swept up in the center of the house to roof level, and a wraparound balcony marking the second floor opened onto bedrooms, baths, an athletic equipment room, sauna and Jacuzzi. Space on the third floor held a ping-pong table, a billiard table, computers, television/movie equipment and storage. Surrounding the great hall on the first floor kitchens, pantries, a flower room and utility closets were situated to optimize service to the dining room, parlour, library, study and breakfast room. Communication with any interior room or outside parties was possible through devices concealed in the walls which swung into position when activated. On the ocean side veranda, a portion was glass-enclosed for the comfort of those who chose to observe avian and aquatic life in inclement weather. In times less festive than this evening's gala, one might exit from the veranda and descend a broad staircase to the space temporarily occupied by the marquee to a meticulously manicured croquet court, a game at which the master excelled but seldom won, remaining the perfect host.

The darkened bedroom, so silent as to be unoccupied, was the marital chamber of Jared and Mirnella Drayton, owners of the house. Jared Spicer, as he was named at birth, grew up in a small, isolated community accessible through the pine woods by a country road used to haul timber. Though at twenty his formal education was limited to a high school diploma, his quick intelligence and flawless timing carried him from operating a tree harvesting machine to a manager of field operations to agent that negotiated timber rights for a leading paper and pulp company. He quickly learned that a law degree would enhance the rewards of his negotiating skills, and with no second thoughts, committed himself to returning to school for seven years. Upon passing the bar, his former employer retained him to represent the company in a congressional hearing which lasted two years, much of the time spent in Washington. At the conclusion of the assignment, a prestigious law firm, retained by the paper company, offered him a position in the firm practicing general law, but Jared had seen the leverage exerted by lobbyists and chose that profitable but maligned specialty. It was not improbable that Jared would be approached by the new administration to accept a high level appointment which he would graciously decline, careful not to offend his benefactor, knowing he was more powerful in his existing role. He was a gregarious professional who guarded his private life to the extreme.

Jared had met Mirnella on a Charleston house tour where she and some other volunteers from the DAR were guiding tourists through historical mansions. At one point, Mirnella read something in a canned speech she'd been given, which Jared knew to be incorrect. When the tour was concluded, he approached her and suggested the script be rewritten for historical accuracy. He then quoted academically accepted data related to the error, which proved it could only have happened as he said. At first, she resented his correction and then realized she'd misplaced her irritation because it properly belonged on the DAR for their carelessness with facts. A few weeks later they met again at a charitable benefit attended by Charleston's most recognizable names, which evolved into a recitation of pedigrees, presumably intended to establish the Old Testament wasn't the only venue of the Chosen People. Convincing Mirnella they deserved better than the buffet offered at the reception, she and Jared had retired to a quiet restaurant and began a lasting relationship. Mirnella found reasons to visit Washington frequently and remove their relationship from the prying scrutiny of the South's wide web of relations and acquaintances. The general reaction to Mirnella's and Jared's marriage was a mixture of shock that the Drayton name would be diminished by Spicer, but the damage was not irreparable as Jared was rich, and the Southern gentry admired a man with lots of money as long as he didn't tell he'd made the money himself.

Jared slept the peaceful sleep of those who had arrived. Mirnella gracefully maintained the welcome of Old Charleston, the world in which she'd been raised but easily crossed over to charm the inhabitants of Jared's. It was a given that her flawless touch would produce the most memorable soiree since the antebellum days of the Holy City, as it was known. Why shouldn't he sleep in peace?

Mirnella came awake gradually, undisturbed by the little morning light that escaped into the bedroom of Jared's persistently, monotonous, atonal snoring. Nightly she fortified herself with an eye mask and ear plugs along with an assortment of emollients and a hair net. Impervious to external intrusions, Mirnella reviewed for the twentieth time the details of the gala she'd orchestrated for this evening. Attempting to project herself into the guests' reaction to the celebration, she started with their arrival. Driven to the front of the house, they'd be escorted into the great hall while their cars were parked at the nearby lot used for trips to the beach. More than four hundred guests would be honored by the presence of the Vice President of the United States as well as key representatives from both houses of Congress. A dedicated telephone line was already in place to instantly reach anyone in the world, and Secret Service men, who'd previously swept the property for dangerous devices, would pass back and forth a hundred yards offshore to prevent an ocean attack.

Mirnella decided not to disturb Jared for another hour after his long, sleepless, harrowing late-night trip from Washington. After several unsuccessful attempts to land at Myrtle Beach, Charleston and Savannah, the plane had flown into Charlotte, and Jared drove through the storm to Isle of Palms. As she arose from bed, the blinking light on the communication system registered the gardener wanted to be contacted. She found this unusual because the staff was instructed to disturb them in their bedroom only for emergencies.

Postponing her response to the gardener, she entered a shower that encircled the occupant with tiny streams of water from the ankles to any height desired. Stimulated by her increased circulation, she dried off, dressed and applied her make-up before answering the gardener's call.

"What is it?" she asked, about to remind him of the call rule when he broke in.

"Ma'am," he whispered like one who'd just seen a vision. "Look out at the beach."

She padded barefooted across the bedroom, carrying her shoes, careful not to wake Jared, and peeked between the slats of the venetian blinds.

"Jared," she screamed, her Charleston accent becoming more pronounced with stress. "There's a sea monster on our beach."

"A what?" Jared asked, still half asleep and frustrated by having misplaced his glasses.

"A huge sea monster, all covered with seaweed with a dark brown belly and a long tail that stretches up on our beach."

Jared stumbled from bed to the window and raised the shades, temporarily blinding himself. "My God, what is that? Call the police and tell them we have an emergency and to get here right away. Tell them we have something that doesn't belong here. I'll look for my shotgun."

Jared, still in his pajamas and unable to find his glasses, ran downstairs brandishing his shotgun and yelling for everyone to take cover. When he went out on the terrace to the backstairs, his line of sight to the beach was blocked by the marquee and he was forced to decide how much he'd risk for a better look at the thing. Deciding the day could only be saved with bold action, he hoisted and tightened the cord in his pajama bottoms and, with the shotgun at ready, crept along one outside wall of the marquee to a large palm.

A sudden movement behind the trunk startled him, and he almost shot the gardener.

"What the hell are you doing there?"

"I was spying for you," the gardener replied.

"Well, stay where I can see you and don't make any more sudden moves."

Jared stood his ground and squinted his myopic eyes to detect any movement by the thing, thinking, *Where the hell are the police? You can always find them during their donation drive for the Patrolmen's Benevolent League, but where in hell are they when you need them?*

"Jared Spicer, you be careful, you hear?" Mirnella called from their bedroom window, waving a red flag as though she were at a bullfight.

Contrary to Jared's orders, the gardener had fallen several paces behind his employer, leaving identification of the mysterious thing to someone more learned. After several uncertain minutes of blurred observation, Jared determined it was not a whale, as one that large had never been sighted; it couldn't be a Russian submarine on a reconnaissance mission because it was too near the shore, so it was most likely an old shipwreck washed up from the ocean floor by the storm. Of course, there was always the outside chance it was some type of evil axis vessel cleverly disguised to look like a shipwreck.

Jared called the gardener, still some distance behind, to come, take the shotgun and stand guard. He instructed him to fire one shot in the air if anything moved, and if it didn't stop moving to keep shooting at it. As the gardener took the gun, his eyes rolled to the back of his head, showing the whites, a reaction impossible to distinguish between pride in his new authority or terror from his lone vigil. Jared returned to his bedroom and dressed while alternately cursing the police delinquency and mentally calculating how much he'd reduce his year's contribution to the Patrolmen's Benevolent League.

"Stop or I'll shoot," Jared heard the gardener yell from below.

He rushed to his bedroom window just as the gardener fired a quick succession of shots and a cloud of seagulls rose from the mysterious thing on the beach. Within seconds, sirens announced several police vehicles carrying a SWAT team arrived. With a well coordinated flourish, the elite group disembarked and assumed positions for combat, disregarding Mirnella's pleas not to trample the plantings.

Jared, finally able to identify the sergeant's insignia partially hidden by the flak jacket, began a lengthy, disjointed description of his observations.

"Now, Mr. Spicer, you just let us do our job. First we'll send our probe man out to reconnoiter the situation and determine the danger, so I want all your people to stay inside away from the windows," the sergeant said, indicating the two dozen people who'd stopping working on the party preparation to witness the cause of the excitement.

"Sergeant, I've already been within fifty feet of the damn thing. It's very sluggish."

"Nevertheless, we need to send our probe man out to make an appraisal."

Just then a tall, lean man dressed in blue jeans and a flannel shirt wandered in. "Hello, Ruggles," he said to the sergeant. "I picked up your emergency notice on my police monitoring radio and thought I might be helpful."

"How many times have I told you that's illegal, Harrison?"

"And how many times has our marine bio-lab been helpful to you?"

"Can't you two stop arguing and do something about the thing on the beach?" Jared said, barely able to suppress his anger.

"I was just about to send a probe to the beach," the sergeant said.

"Mind if I join him?" Harrison asked, not waiting for an answer before leading the SWAT probe out the door.

"We won't be responsible for your safety," the sergeant called after him.

When the two men emerged from the marquee with the biologist still in the lead, he paused to survey the scene and then started for the water's edge.

"I'll cover you," the police probe in the flak jacket said.

After a close inspection, the biologist returned to Jared and the sergeant. "It's all right, perfectly harmless. It's a barge full of garbage," he reported.

"Perfectly harmless," the sergeant repeated to Jared, ready to dismiss the incident.

"No, it's not harmless. It's very harmful and I want you to get rid of it," Jared fumed. "The Vice President of the United States and four hundred guests are coming here tonight for a reception, and it's not harmless. You've got to get that out of here."

"Oh," the sergeant said in annoyance, "I wondered why the force was put on special stand-by and nobody gave us a reason. It's sure gonna wreck my poker game."

"Sergeant, doesn't the police department have a marine section that can move this?" Jared pleaded, throwing himself on the policeman's mercy.

"That's out of my jurisdiction. I'd have to check that out."

"There's no time to check, only to do," Jared yelled, returning to his belligerent style. "This mess has got to be moved."

"That's going to be some job to float that baby," Harrison volunteered in a mischievous summation.

"Sergeant, please can you call your chief and explain the problem. Tell him we need the police marine group to haul this barge away."

"They can't do it without an okay from the Harbormaster and the Southeastern Environmental Association," Harrison said. "The Harbormaster controls the movement of all commercial traffic, and the SEA has to authorize any handling of potentially toxic endangerment to the shore ecology."

"I think he's right, Mr. Spicer," the sergeant agreed, perceiving a bureaucratic impasse that would allow him to extricate his squad. "I guess there's nothing further we can do to be helpful. Parade rest," he called, commanding his men, who were supposed to be at attention, to break off lounging around and prepare for the next order. "Attention! Double time, march." And the police left without ever coming face-to-face with the perpetrator.

"Somebody get me a phone," Jared yelled to no one in particular.

"Well, I guess I'll be getting along," Harrison said. "Let me know how you make out."

"Where the hell is that phone?"

"Here ya are, Mr. Spicer, right along with a nice cup of coffee to calm your nerves," the gardener said, handing Jared a phone that plugged in to a sculpture by the marquee.

Why the hell can't the government be as efficient as the private sector, Jared complained to himself as he picked up the phone to find someone talking on the line. "Whoever is on the phone, hang up."

"Mr. Spicer, the cake for the party hasn't arrived yet and I'm trying to locate the pastry shop."

"There isn't going to be any party if you don't get off the line," Jared growled, about to call another city department when his wife set down a breakfast tray by his lawn chair.

"Here, dear, this will make you feel better."

"The only thing that will make me feel better is to get that barge out of here. It's beginning to stink." He picked up the phone and dialed the operator.

"May I help you?"

"Operator, get me the Harbormaster."

"What city?"

"Charleston, of course."

"This is your nationwide operator, you'll have to contact the local operator for that. I'll call them." There was an annoyingly long ringing before the phone on the other end was answered.

"May I help you," she inquired with the sameness of voice as the first. Jared wondered if the telephone company cloned its employees.

"Get me the Charleston Harbormaster."

"Do you have the number?"

"No, I don't have the number, that's why I called you."

"I'll switch you over to Information, they can give you the number."

"The Charleston Harbormaster's number is—"

"Wait a minute, I don't have anything to write it down with." In a moment, he found a paper napkin, wrote down the number and made the call. Jared heard a phone ringing at the other end of the line at least ten times before a recorded message announced, "You have reached the Harbormaster of Charleston, South Carolina, the Palmetto State. Port entry and exit must be authorized one week in advance. In the event of unexpected weekend arrivals, vessels must lay over in the outer harbor until Monday. Our service week runs from Monday through Friday, six a.m. to twelve midnight. In an emergency, call the police department—843-466-3267 or 843 Good Cop. Thank you."

Not one to be easily discouraged, Jared called the Southeastern Environmental Association, to be greeted with a phrase from George Gershwin's song "Summertime," sung by a basso profundo—

Summertime when the livin' is easy

Fish are jumpin'—

The music was abruptly cut off, to be replaced by an announcer who informed the listener the fish would not be jumping much longer because they were all being poisoned. The listener was further advised that no one would be in the office before Monday, as all were out monitoring environmental violators, adding that a contribution of fifty dollars or more entitled the donor to attend the annual Eastern Wildlife Conference free and watch a man wrestle an alligator.

Jared moved to the Coast Guard in his mental list. There had to be a warm body there; after all, weren't they sworn to vigilance 24/7? Jared decided to employ some different tactics to cut through the telephone minutia.

"Hello, operator, this is Jared Spicer from Washington, I want to speak to the Coast Guard's admiral in Charleston."

"Sir, you're not calling from Washington."

"I know I'm not calling from Washington. I said I was from Washington. Will you please stop wasting time and call him for me."

"Sir, we don't have an admiral listed for Charleston's Coast Guard. We have a list of departments and commands. I'll read a few to you."

"Disaster Response Command," Jared yelled after hearing a few of the choices. "That's it, and Search and Rescue Emergencies. They're the ones. Give me Search and Rescue first."

A live female voice announced, "Captain Vadin's office, may I help you?"

Jared, overjoyed he'd at last made contact with a real person, replied, "Oh! Can you ever help me," unaware the woman might think he may be propositioning her.

"Sir, would you state your business?"

"Now we're getting somewhere," Jared responded, making his intentions more questionable. "I have a load of garbage on my property which I need to get moved because the Vice President of the United States is coming for dinner."

"I don't think we can handle that. You see, we're responsible for the coast, like the name says, only up to high tide."

"But that's the point, this garbage is loaded on a barge that the storm washed up on my beach."

"I think you'll want to speak to the Disaster Response Command. I'll be happy to transfer you." With that the line went on hold while Captain Vadin's secretary happily transferred some deranged caller out of her life.

The duty officer at the Coast Guard's Disaster Response command was more concise but less helpful, explaining that because the garbage was intact and on the barge, it didn't constitute a threat. Jared put down the phone, muttering he hated stupid budget busting bureaucrats and would never again have anything to do with them if his livelihood didn't depend on it. All was not right with Jared's world. God was not smiling on 100 Ocean Drive, Isle of Palms, South Carolina. He spit out his cold coffee and did not savor the poached eggs turned to two solid plastic eyes witnessing his failure. He'd have to call off the reception, to notify the Vice President. It would cost the United States millions for an aborted photo-op; his law firm would be out thousands. Perhaps he should admit defeat right now and phone Bernice to have her stop everything at the Washington end; Bernice, the world's greatest secretary....

"Are you sure you want to do that, Mr. Spicer?" Bernice calmly asked Jared.

"I don't think I have any options left."

"Mr. Spicer, would you mind a dozen more people at the party?"

"What's that got to do with it?" Jared asked.

"Think about it. Everybody wants to have dinner with the Vice President of the United States. If we made that a prize, I'll bet we could get some department that would find a way to move that junk."

"You're solid gold, Bernice. Do it."

With the allure of an irresistible chance to dine with the Vice President, Bernice got the immediate attention of deputy directors and assistant managers of four federal agencies. Weekends, normally downtime in the government, department heads vanished and the minor inconvenience of a beached garbage barge would wait its turn for their deft resolution in the week or month ahead. But this was a potential crisis of national magnitude that could not wait for the absent superiors' return from Palm Beach, New York City or Las Vegas—this was why deputies and assistant managers were created. Between eleven and eleven-fifteen Saturday morning, representatives of Transportation, OSHA, EPA, the Secret Service and their emergency crews landed in Charleston, with their wives scheduled to follow later appropriately packed for attending a gala evening.

Bernice had worked the phones well, and she'd inspired uncommon zeal in those she'd recruited with the parting charge: "Remember, it's up to you whether or not the Vice President can attend the dinner to shake your hands."

An hour and a half passed since the Feds started their feasibility study. Endless measurements, calculations, tests for toxicity and methane emissions, buoyancy and weight estimates had resulted in several hypotheses suggesting even more solutions. The irrefutable discovery that no one challenged was the registration number on the barge, quickly traced to the Steele firm in New York by the EPA, which irritated the Secret Service. During the investigator's crossing and criss-crossing, Mirnella ran interference to preserve the plants while the gardener raked and re-raked the beach and placed lawn furniture barriers around the fragile flora. Heated discussion among the four agencies finally resulted in two proposals on which neither side would yield. The first envisioned covering the barge with the large canvas sheets presently standing on each side of the house and burning the methane gas vented from the contained garbage. The second, less radical and equally difficult to implement, required unloading the garbage bales onto small crafts and transporting them to some unspecified place. A deadlock immobilized the task force as the clock kept ticking.

Jared, nervously noting the tide had turned from its low and an hour had been wasted on self-serving, skewed intellectualizing, theorizing and hypothesizing, decided Bernice had placed too much trust on man's vanity and not enough on his need to dominate. Believing it was a long shot but his last chance, he sent an SOS to the Commodore of the Charleston Yacht Club, beseeching rescue. The Commodore, appropriately garbed in blue blazer and braided cap, earned by such moments of distress, immediately dispatched the club's motorboat squadron to the Isle of Palms and liberation. Some members interrupted their fishing, others waterskiing and still others the salutary benefits of sun and beverage. But like the Minutemen of

Concord, each responded to the alarm with fervor. One was heard to exclaim as they sped to their duty and he hoisted a beer, "This is what Dunkirk must have been like when they pulled the Limies out of France."

With an open bar by the marquee as an inducement to succeed, the boaters spun a spider web of rope from their crafts to the barge and made ready for the grand experiment.

Chapter 14

Long before dawn when the fury of the storm had blown past in a northwesterly direction and ocean mountains were reduced to large, gradual swells, Elliot headed the tug towards the South Carolina coast.

Alex, still in her life jacket, lay sprawled on the pilothouse deck, lodged against the pedestal holding the wheel. Saltwater-matted hair followed the contour of her left temple, cheek and jaw like a papier-mâché shell from which a sea urchin was emerging. White patches of crystallized spray, in no regular pattern, gave the appearance of a child's first experiment with make-up. Her baggy pants and top, made even more shapeless with the drenching rain, showed undried patches as yet unlightened by her body heat. The soundless rise and fall of steady breathing was the only evidence she'd escaped the night's violence to live in a sleep of exhaustion. Her appearance might draw sympathy for her ordeal, but the storm proved she was not paralyzed by terror.

Elliot, to keep from falling asleep at the wheel, invented a game of speculations about Alex in a question and answer format.

Q: Where did she get so much pluck?

A: Probably always tried to keep ahead of her brothers.

Q: How old is she?

A: Mid to late twenties.

Q: Had she ever been married?

A: Presently too independent for most men and certainly not old enough to panic and compromise with just anybody to not end up single.

Q: Where'd she get all that pluck?

A: Oh, I already answered that. I must be getting sleepy.

Q: How much does she weigh, and how tall is she?

A: About one hundred thirty pounds. Hard to tell in those bags she wears. Five feet eight.

Q: Where did she come from?

A: Can't tell from her accent, but then all Yanks sound the same.

Q: Should I teach her to run the tug by herself?

A: Maybe she already knows and is playing possum. She's a quick read, but I can probably trick her to find out. Sometime, I'll pretend to pass out and not come to. No, that's no good, she'd hit the mayday signal.

Q: Is she pretty?

A: I can't tell in that Halloween costume she calls clothes.

Q: How about cute?

A: I can't tell in that Halloween—oh, I already answered that.

Q: I wonder what she looks like with no clothes, no El—, no—

Elliot dozed off, his hands slipping away from the wheel, putting the tug into a sharp turn from its course. He recovered control of the wheel and gradually eased the boat back towards the west, but not without waking Alex.

"Did we just get hit by a wave, or was I dreaming we were still in the storm?" Alex asked.

"I fell asleep for a moment and took my hands off the wheel. Sorry to wake you."

Alex looked to the east at the faint rays of the sun still below the horizon. "You let me oversleep, by an hour," she said, confirming it with the large-faced clock. "You shouldn't have done that. You must be dead. I'm taking over now. Get some sleep."

Elliot showed her the charts and flipped on the radar to find it operative. "Wake me in an hour, Alex, and thanks for sticking it out last night."

He was asleep before she could reply, "Did I have any choice?"

She activated the automatic steering and watched the compass and course indicator closely to see if they remained synchronized. Satisfied they were holding the desired direction, she rummaged through a compartment of odds and ends and discovered an unopened packet of saltines. She was ravenous, gobbling up the contents without considering she'd crave water and slaking her thirst would accelerate the need to relieve herself, now unattended for several hours. So she went thirsty and searched for distractions.

The sun had escaped the horizon, warming the pilothouse as it mined millions of sparkling sea diamonds. How schizophrenic, this watery vastness that only hours earlier had threatened their lives and now appeased her with a new hospitable day. Last night had been terrorizing, worse than anything she'd ever experienced, but somehow she'd kept going to overcome her fear. And she'd also learned one could draw courage from another as Elliot had inspired her with the will to prevail. She glanced at him lying flat on his back, deep asleep and not snoring. He'd lied to her about snoring, she thought. She'd like a man who didn't snore. Another reading of the instruments confirmed they were on a direct course for Charleston, seventy-eight miles away. With visibility at maximum, the seas calming and Charleston seven hours distant, she'd let him sleep as long as he wanted.

His sense of self communicated confidence sufficient to engage the moment without bravado or the need to control others. Although his speech implied the authority many Americans attributed to English accents, there was another distinct quality that gave assurance he dealt only in truths. He made this adventure with its rejections and uncertainties, dangers and distress, discoveries and disappointments, chaos and peace the only place on earth for her to be right now. She'd come to uncover a plot and was discovering herself. She wondered if in the process of verifying his persona she'd also discover a stereotypical, strong silent type with nothing behind the façade. Unlikely if not impossible. He'd already exhibited sensitivity to others in such a straightforward manner it might be overlooked. Loyalty and determination beyond a doubt. He was manly and mannerly, intellectually curious, probably knowledgeable beyond the confines of rowing, tugs and garbage. So why did he continue on this voyage to nowhere? And why was she spending time profiling him? Was she falling in love?

The subject of her scrutiny stirred, yawned and rolled onto his side as though to prolong sleep before coming fully awake.

"Good morning. What time is it?" Elliot asked.

"Good morning. It's ten o'clock."

"And you broke your agreement by letting me sleep this late." He sat up, rubbed his eyes and then stood to look at the charts.

"Would you mind taking over for me? I'm about to burst," Alex said, leaving the pilothouse.

Yes, I see what she means, he thought to himself, hoping she'd return soon. When she returned to the wheelhouse, she had the fresh smell of having showered and shampooed. Her hair was tied in a ponytail that hung down to the hood of a clean sweat suit.

"Ah," he said, "I see you've washed your face and put on a new set of bags. You know you could be quite a pleasant looking woman if you didn't try so hard not to be."

"Thanks. I'll take that as a compliment. I wish I could say the same for you. By the way, respecting your nautical terms, the bilge looks fairly dry. The pumps must have been effective last night."

"If you're all together, I'll go down and see if I can get as pleasant looking as you." He descended the steps from the wheelhouse to the deck below in one leap. Alex was glad they'd returned to the banter, each comfortable enough after last night's impassioned embrace to resume their friendship without the awkwardness of having surrendered to the counterfeit lust of post-trauma survival. She mused on what either might have done if the storm had never struck them. But, of course, with no violence there would have been no ecstatic deliverance.

The rumblings in her stomach were a reminder she needed to eat and Elliot's extended absence was keeping her from making breakfast. *Sixteen hours between meals was too long,* she was complaining to herself, when the door to the pilothouse skidded open and Elliot entered balancing two plates of scrambled eggs, bacon, toast and two mugs of coffee on a large sheet-metal square.

"Voila!" he said. "I hope you like your eggs scrambled. The storm was pretty insistent on shaking them up in the can where they were stored in the refrigerator. I think I got most of the shells, but if you swallow any, just remember calcium is good for you."

"You cook better than I steer," she said, munching a piece of toast as she looked up at him from the locker by the wheel where she sat. She liked to watch his coordinated ease in piloting the tug. Most of the time he sat on the high stool with his hands lightly resting on the wheel, but in course corrections, making port or during choppy weather, he stood to better feel the tug and make immediate needed changes in direction or speed.

For the first time since they knew they'd survived the blow, as Elliot like to call it, she thought about the barge. "What do we do about your barge?"

"We look for it. I'm surprised some ship hasn't come across it and broadcast its whereabouts. My guess is the storm pushed it west and sooner or later it will be sighted and reported unless it sunk. In the meantime, we look for it."

For a while neither spoke of their thoughts.

"Elliot, what you did for me last night deserves much more than 'thank you', but the fact is nothing else in our language says it more completely. Thank you."

Elliot acknowledged the tribute without embarrassment or false humility. He gazed over the bow of the tug, detaching his observation of the sea, deliberating how he should tell Alex about last night's near fatality.

"Last night," he began, "got pretty bad. In fact, for a while I didn't think we were going to make it. When the barge began whipping us around, I thought we had about fifteen minutes left before we capsized. I was faced with the toughest decision I've ever had. One part of me, knowing and respecting you, was for telling you we probably were going to die. The other side told me I shouldn't tell you how desperate our condition was until it was almost all over. I chose the latter because I did not believe I had the right to take away your hope that somehow we'd be saved. When the barge broke loose, we were saved. I'm sure I'd do the same thing the next time, and I hope it was right with you."

"I would have done that for you," she said softly before going silent. In a return to the present, she asked, "What do you want to be when you grow up?"

He knew it was an ingenuous question with no suggestion he was postponing the responsibility of maturity. "I'm not sure I can answer that, but I can tell you what I want to be when I grow old, and strange as it sounds, this trip has given some form to a vague wish list. When I get old, I want to have a chair in the philosophy department of a top university, play championship checkers and wear hand-knitted woolen socks in the winter."

"Is there a woman in your old age?"

"Oh, yes. She knits my socks."

"And what do you do for her?"

"I write poetry of how lovely she is. Together we are in such harmony, one of us will often say what the other is thinking at the exact same moment."

"Will you be famous?"

"Definitely with her. After last night, maybe with you for a short time."

"Sometimes I think I want to be a top journalist with a major newspaper, and then I change my mind and want to chuck it, find a nice quiet place and write a book—at the moment about the environment."

"Why not both?" he asked.

"Because I keep discovering things are never as you expect them to be, which makes me think I'm not ready. I wonder if that will always be the case?"

"You'll notice it less if you look for the opportunity in change."

"I guess I agree with you to some extent because lately, as things have been turned upside down, I've begun to appreciate that the unexpected is what's real. I grew up with people who unconsciously had a plan for everything from baptism to school to debut, marriage, babies, grandchildren, right down to their funerals. Most were upset if the order was changed or they missed a step."

"They must have taken comfort they'd get to the last step right. My growing up has been different and maybe easier. Father wasn't there for me even when he was around, and Mum was in her own world, or worlds before her time, tracing ancestors. I was pretty much left to figure things out for myself."

"Do you have brothers and sisters?"

"No, do you?"

"Ditto. I always wondered why but for some reason never asked."

"Isn't it remarkable how two 'only' children turned out so wonderfully well?"

"Do you think others would agree?"

"It doesn't matter as long as we both think so."

"What is your father's business?"

"He's the ship captain of the Queen."

"Are you following him in that career?"

"My God, no. I'm on this tug to make some money, not for any other reason. Family succession has nothing to do with it."

"Were there other sailors in your family?"

"Depends on who you ask. Mum is sure she can trace us back to Noah and his ark. She's also sure the Swans descended from Sir Francis Drake. Must like the name associations. I'll have to admit she's pretty good, however. Once when I was at that smart-Alec stage—excuse me, no inferences were intended—I tried to refute her research and found she hit everything right on the nose. Tell me about your parents, if you'd like."

"Really not much to tell," Alex said, choosing her words carefully to conceal her family's affluence while remaining truthful. "They live on a farm in New York State near Lake Champlain."

"Cows?"

"Yes, cows and chickens," she replied without identifying they were prize Black Angus cattle and Cornish game hens. Seeking to abruptly change the subject, she asked, "Are you married?"

He turned from the wheel to laugh at her candor. "I wondered if you'd get around to that. Don't you remember last night after the storm I said, 'remind me not to go on a cruise on my honeymoon.' Never have, and no plans to. Have you noticed the sea is flattening out?"

"No, I hadn't."

"We've made good time. Should be in Charleston by about two-thirty."

"Aren't you going to ask me?" Alex asked.

"To marry you? I've only known you for a few weeks. Don't you think that's rushing things?"

"I mean if I'm married."

"The way I see it, if you were married and dreamed up an idiotic plan to get on this tug, then you must have done equally deranged things before. Therefore, you're single, recently divorced, or will be soon."

"Do you think I could get married?" she asked, seeking to learn, without asking him directly, if he was attracted to her.

"Oh, I suppose to some bungee diver, used car salesman or missionary."

"Why that strange assortment?" she asked.

"Because they don't care about risking their lives." Elliot turned on the radar to confirm his estimated land fall position. "We're coming to Folly Beach a little south of Charleston; we're ahead of schedule. Let's creep up the coast and enjoy our lunch as civilized people before heading into port."

"I'll fix a real southern meal while you practice your accent."

When she returned with Boston baked beans and frankfurters, he'd made no progress in speaking with a drawl and they agreed assimilation into the southern culture was unlikely. The unhurried passage along the coast, idyllically restorative, was interrupted by the ship-to-shore telephone.

"Hello," Elliot answered, his pique clearly registering with the caller.

"Elliot! Is that you?"

"I knew my day would be spoiled someway. Rich, what's going on? You still getting overpaid?"

"I've got good news and bad news. The good news is I've broken my wrist so you should be evenly matched to row against me. The bad news is your visa's expired and Immigration is looking for you. Better not go ashore anyplace before you get back to New York, or they'll ship your limey ass back to England. We don't care about you, but we want our tug back."

"You almost lost everything last night. We were hit by a killer storm and lost the barge. For a while, I thought the tug would capsize, but we finally pulled out."

"Are Bones and Mac okay?"

"I don't know. They jumped ship in Wilmington, North Carolina. I went looking for them, but they never turned up."

"You picked up a new crew in Wilmington?" Rich inquired.

"No, the port was down with a longshoremen strike and the able bodied seamen went out in support of them."

"Who's this 'we' you said rode out the storm with you?"

"Here, Rich, meet Alex. Alex, meet Rich," Elliot said, handing the phone to her.

"Hello, Rich!"

"Who the hell are you?" Rich asked, surprised to hear a woman's voice.

"I'm his first mate," she replied.

"Uh huh. I wouldn't be too sure of that. Maybe I can get some straight answers from you."

"I hope so," she said.

"Then tell me why he hasn't dumped the garbage yet."

"Nobody would take it. Of the seventeen ports the Sanitation Department listed as reception centers, none accept anything but local waste. Either the incinerators were shut down or the landfills' capacities were already reserved. We keep going from place to place trying to find a legal site to get rid of it, just as your father instructed Elliot to do."

"How come you know so much about this?"

"Because I'm the *Times* reporter who's followed this sham from the beginning."

"Don't tell him I asked you, but is he okay?" Rich inquired.

"Fine. Better as he goes along."

"Has he been sick?"

"No, just too serious."

"You take care of him. Now let me speak to him, please."

"Yes, Rich?" Elliot said.

"Elliot, I was serious about Immigration looking for you, and now that they can track the 'garbage man' as you're known, it will be easier to spot you."

"How did they locate me?"

"It seems you parked your barge on some big shot's beach on the Isle of Palms and it happens the V.P. of the U.S. is going to his house for dinner tonight. Naturally, Secret Service has swept the place for security, but there's no government or public service that can move the barge. When they found the registration number on the hull, maritime records listed our firm as owners, and they spotted your name on the crew listing. Now Immigration has registered you as an illegal, or as we say in polite circles, persona non grata."

"That's downright inhospitable. If they deport me, how will you get the tug back?"

"We'll have to recruit a crew to substitute for some of our regulars who we'll send to pick up the boat. Otherwise it goes into storage till the rush of our spring business is over, which means lost revenue."

"Have any objection to my staying on till I find a site to unload and return to New York? Maybe then I can work something out."

"Fine with me. If the old man has any objections, he can get back to you. Now we know for sure where to find you. In the meantime, will you pick up your garbage so the V.P. can have a nice shore dinner? Goodbye, Elliot. Goodbye, Alex."

"Goodbye, Rich," they said in unison and headed for the Isle of Palms at full speed.

It was two forty-five, three quarters of an hour before the flood tide would reach its high and shrink back with the pull of the moon. Closing on a point of land that marked the end of Sullivan's Island and the beginning of the Isle of Palms, the sound of a swarm of agitated mechanical hornets filled the air. Growing closer, one could detect the origin of the pitch, intensity and varying volume of this ear-numbing drone, and an onsite inspection of its source disclosed a wondrous assembly of powerboats of all sizes and configuration. Common cause had bound man and machine in a web of ropes to the massive garbage barge to remove its offending presence before the arrival of the Vice President of the United States and four hundred guests.

The rescue attempt was now in its third hour with no encouragement of success. Considerable time had been wasted in the initial, hasty formation of the boats. Often one was so close to another that at full power it sprayed the neighbor crew or created troughs in which other boats rolled helplessly. Several at full power dipped low enough to take on water in the stern until the bow had been counterweighted. One large, sleek boat, designed for professional racing, broke the tow line and its two oversized, supercharged engines hurled the missile with such force an occupant fell backwards into the ocean, still clutching his gin and tonic. Several times other tow lines snapped with the twang of a broken violin string, a problem not remedied until the Commodore coordinated the boats' application of power with a series of colored flares he shot high in the air. So intense was the rescue effort, nobody had yet raised the question of what to do with the barge if they moved it. But the unyielding object of their efforts saved them that embarrassment, and if any in the growing crowd of spectators, composed of government employees, caterers, neighbors and curiosity seekers was a miracle worker, he chose silence to perpetuate the spectacle.

Inevitably, when there's a buck to be made, vendors and bookies show up to work the crowd. Only the time constraints of printing T-shirts with a representation of the event discouraged the vendors, but the bookies diligently took bets on which boat would be the next to break a tow line, run out of gas or retire from the hopeless struggle. The sweepstakes offering was an elaborate design predicting the barge's removal within a given time. The odds soared to 100 to 1. And in the midst of this mounting confusion, the Commodore tirelessly circulated among the club members, rallying them for a sustained exertion.

It was this carnival atmosphere which Alex and Elliot entered on Saturday, 3:10 p.m.—peak high tide. At first unnoticed, they drew within a thousand yards of the occupied squadron, when a great cheer arose from the onshore spectators. Immediately, the motorboat engines dropped to idle and the crafts' bells, whistles and horns joined in a thanksgiving for salvation. A launch, sporting the Yacht Club Ensign, broke from the fleet and came to join the tug. Elliot cut power as the launch came alongside and a distinguished looking, gray-haired man, in dress appropriate to his rank, introduced himself.

"Good afternoon, Sir. I'm William Randolph, Commodore of the Charleston Yacht Club. And you, Sir?"

"I'm Elliot Swan, skipper of the tug."

"Do I detect a bit of an accent from our sister country? Your appearance is very fortuitous. As you've no doubt observed, we've been unsuccessful in trying to move that barge off a gentleman's beach."

"Is the hitch to the barge intact?"

"Three hundred feet of it."

"And secured to the barge?"

"Firmly."

"How deep is the water one hundred feet from the mean, high tide line?"

"I'd judge twelve to fourteen feet. The shore drops off quite abruptly."

"We'll clear that," Elliot said. "I'll move in about two hundred feet from the barge, and if one of your friends can fish the free end of the tow line out of the water for me, I'll tie up and give it a try."

The squadron was now positioned one half on each side of the barge with the tug in the middle to pull the haul straight out from the beach. With a series of the Commodore's flares, all engines were gradually moved to full power, and the barge with a large groan slipped off the watery shelf where it had rested and was afloat. Cheers from the shore acknowledged the success and the crowd began to disperse; yacht club members, sunburned and half drunk, detached from the barge. Immediately, an army of landscapers descended on 100 Ocean Highway to return it to its pristine excellence. God again smiled on the Spicers.

On the tug's way to deeper water, the Commodore intercepted Alex and Elliot with an invitation for them to anchor and go ashore for a proper thank you from the grateful property owners. Remembering Rich's warning, Elliot courteously declined. "After all, Commodore, I only came to pick up my own garbage. By the way, does Charleston have a facility for burning this load?"

"No, Sir, but I've heard if it's big enough, Texas will take anything."

Chapter 15

Alex and Elliot agreed, with no schedule to meet, mid-afternoon was not the time to start another leg of their journey. Unable to go ashore, Elliot decided to take advantage of Charleston's offshore refueling and calm water for a post-storm inspection of the tug. Alex saw no point in just sitting around when she could explore the Holy City, as early Charlestonian worshippers, ignorant of Jerusalem's iconic status, characterized their settlement. With no hesitation, she lowered the putt-putt and confidently announced she would land *there*, pointing to a small, sandy beach pressed between the Battery Promenade and the yacht club. A few simple instructions on the putt-putt's operation, which she mastered quickly, prepared Alex in Elliot's words, which he delivered with a wink, for her maiden voyage.

Having spent an hour to refuel and inspect the tug and seeing no sign of Alex, Elliot, feeling restless, recalibrated the instruments, made minor adjustments on the engine and, anticipating more idle time, put on his diving gear to inspect the propeller jammed by the barge's tether. Satisfied no damage had been done, he swam around the hull checking for potential malfunctions then climbed back on the deck confident the boat was completely operative.

That woman, as he thought of her when he was feeling authoritative, had not returned.

Before they'd dropped anchor in the channel, he'd considered telling her if she chose to go no farther, this was a good place for her to leave the tug. It was uncertain whether he could recruit a replacement crew in Charleston, and he did like having her around. For a few more minutes he kept busy with unnecessary chores before going below to shower and change his clothes, then decided against it until the putt-putt had been hoisted and made secure. Still fidgety, he found his copy of *Moby Dick,* neglected for days, and tried to find the page where he'd left off. Captain Ahab's obsession with the 'White Whale' distracted him until he suddenly realized Alex had been gone three hours.

From the optimum visibility of the pilothouse, he scanned the coast all along the waterfront. Sailboats, earlier skidding across the Cooper River mouth, had departed for their moorings in West Ashley, leaving the undisturbed sea flat and glassy in the failing light. He waited and watched, then thinking she might be disoriented, switched on the tug lights.

As though a broken communication connection had been repaired, he heard the faintest coughing of the putt-putt's engine even before he could see her in the twilight. As the dinghy drew nearer, the cough of the reliable motor turned to a chug, chug, chug that bounced across the water's stillness to him.

Like an anxious parent discovering one's child is safe, his worry turned to irritation at her for being thoughtless before realizing he was being stupid. She was an adult. She'd set herself adrift in the Atlantic in a less stable craft, and she was smart. Perhaps too confident, but plenty smart.

"Hey landlubber, don't you know you can get run down with no lights?" he called as she came within hailing distance. "You were gone so long I thought you'd jumped ship, beginning to give me an inferiority complex."

As the putt-putt came within range of the tug's lights, he saw it was filled with an assortment of bags, boxes and packages.

"Whew," he whistled in astonishment, while silently chiding himself for being so upset by her absence when he should have known she was shopping.

She ignored his male reaction to her female industry. "I'll help you hoist the putt-putt as soon as we finish here."

When the contents of the putt-putt had been transferred to the galley and the dinghy secured, Elliot sat silent, his eyes never leaving her as she emptied and stored four bags of groceries. Six unopened packages on the table held the attention of both, his curiosity and suspicion prompting her to tease him a while longer.

"What?" she asked in a sharper tone than intended.

"Aren't you going to open the others?"

"I'm not sure. You remind me of a strict teacher that never approved of anything I did, even before I did it."

"Come on, we've both had a long day. I'll make a simple dinner and then we can get a good night's sleep," he said, trying to repair whatever damage he might have done.

"That's the thing. I thought we'd had such a bad week, with Bones and Mac taking off, and the storm and you learning you might be deported—I thought we should forget all that and have a wonderful dinner, a ship's party, some fun for change. So, Mister Curious, after I got ashore and filed my story with the newspaper—incidentally, they're running this as a weekly feature—I looked for and found a wonderful upscale restaurant that puts a complete meal together to take home. It looks delicious, and we only have to pop it in the oven. We have hors d'oeuvres and a paper tablecloth and napkins, not paper towels, real napkins, and I got a bottle of French wine."

"Alex, you're a miracle. I won't spoil the ambiance now, but you did all the work so let me repay you."

"Nope. It's our party but my treat," she said as she unpacked the dinner from three of the remaining bags.

"I'm still curious about these other packages."

"This is the best part. I bought you a decent looking sport shirt, appropriate for informal dining in the sub-tropical zone. Here, unwrap it and see what you think."

"You don't like the way I dress?" he joked, pointing to the dirty work clothes he'd not yet changed. "Okay, if you insist." He scrubbed his hands on his pants before carefully opening the package she'd handed him. The shirt was aquamarine linen, full in the arms, caught at the cuffs with two breast flap pockets; a garment to be noticed because of its understated excellence. "I can't wear this on a dirty tug, it's much too elegant."

"You can for tonight."

"If you say so. You're the boss." He leaned forward and kissed her on the check. "Thanks."

"Remember now, you said I was the boss. Why don't you clean up and put on the shirt while I get the dinner ready for the oven. Then you can set the table, put out the pâté and pop the wine while I take my turn."

"Yes, boss," he muttered on his way to the shower, carrying his new shirt at arm's length from his dirty work clothes. When he finished bathing, he examined his beard, seriously considering shaving, but decided to stick to his plan of growing it until he found a home for the garbage. Shiny clean, hair combed, and dressed in clean blue jeans and the new shirt, he presented himself for inspection.

"Not bad, not bad at all," Alex allowed. "Whoever said clothes didn't make the man?"

He pretended to lunge at her as she grabbed her three packages and hurried from the galley. Elliot arranged and replaced the table setting more precisely on the cloth by the napkins, unwrapped the pâté and crackers, but left the wine to chill, supposing her sense of the passage of time might be as vague when she dressed as when she shopped.

Thinking she'd had ample time, he called, "The candles will be stubs and we'll have to eat this delicious smelling feast in fluorescent light pretty soon," and then she came into the galley.

"Holy mackerel, holy mackerel," he said, unable to draw on his English fluency to adequately express Alex's affect on him. "Walk around a bit and say something so I know it's you."

"Can I assume you prefer these to my working clothes?"

"Wow!" he said, expanding his vocabulary. He leaned against the table, the wine bottle clutched in his hand, and feasted his eye. Her flowing blonde hair, no longer in a ponytail, fell in gentle waves to her shoulders. A light tan accentuated her radiant complexion, wide-set eyes softened to green in the candlelight, full lips slightly parted in a smile for being appreciated, made her uncommonly beautiful. Her light blue, low cut blouse and fitted, unbleached linen pants left no doubt she was generously endowed. She went barefoot as a sign of temporary extravagance.

"The candles are burning low, we should start our feast," she said.

He poured the French wine into two jelly jars, handed her one and raised the other in a toast. "Here's to us."

Both drank a portion and then sat silent, perhaps wondering what that toast meant. Elliot was the first to speak.

"Alex, first, I don't want you to think because I agreed you were the boss tonight you'll be in charge tomorrow. Oh no. At the stroke of midnight, Elliot, the captain of his destiny, resumes control," he declared, burlesquing the seriousness of his lecture. "It's back to normal, Captain Elliot Swan at the helm."

Alex hung her head, pretending she'd been properly admonished, and they both burst out laughing over their silliness.

Elliot poured more wine and offered Alex pâté. "You must have some before I eat all of it."

She rechecked the quirky oven and predicted dinner would be ready soon.

"Alex, what would you have done if I'd changed course and missed you?"

"Didn't we discuss this before?"

"Yes. I guess I'm asking myself, which is rather stupid, because if I hadn't intercepted you in the raft, I'd never have known you were there to begin with; so how could either of us have known we'd missed the other?"

"Is this the philosopher or the wine talking?"

"I suppose both. I've never subscribed to the predestination purists, but I do believe it is no coincidence when two people meet and know it was intended."

"We'd better eat or the cook will get drunk," Alex said, in part to end a conversation she was unsure about pursuing. The meal was as delicious as the restaurant had claimed, as successful as Alex hoped. Elliot ate like a man possessed, sitting back when he'd finished to assess the wreckage of the culinary receptacles piled high in the sink.

"You certainly know good food," he said, reliving the experience of a gourmet dinner. "And I particularly appreciate there are only jelly jars to wash. It's much too pretty a night to stay here. Let's sit on deck. I'll be with you as soon as I bag our throwaways."

It was a sweater-weather night, too cool for Alex's new clothes, so Elliot in a moment of couturier ingenuity substituted a clean bath towel for a stole. They sat and looked at a moonless night, all the better for Elliot's identification of constellations. Toward the east, the low-lying silhouette of Fort Sumter broke the rim of the horizon; northwest up the Cooper River, lights on the girders revealed the architectural design of two cantilever bridges connecting Charleston with Mount Pleasant. Alex invented her own version of 'Steeple Chase' for Elliot by describing her route through the city in relation to the church spires poking above the three story limitation enforced by the historical society. She rated it among the most beautiful cities in America, and her brief exposure to those she presumed were natives, as she saw them leaving residences, impressed her as being polite but remote. She told Elliot she'd been saddened he'd not seen the city and offered to be his guide if he ever wanted to return when his visa was reinstated, which led to the question of where he'd go if this Jason-like voyage ever ended.

"My plans are to, or I should say I'd prefer to, take a philosophy doctorate at Columbia and then join the faculty at one of the top universities in the U.S. if they let me back in."

"Any plans to go back to England?" she asked.

"It appears I'll be going back whether I like it or not. Would you like to visit me?"

"As long as I don't have to attend teas in one of those horrid hats the queen wears. And if the U.S. won't readmit you, what about school?"

"I suppose Cambridge or Oxford, maybe a German university."

"You know, Elliot, this sounds silly, but sometimes I don't want this journey to end," she said.

"There's an old expression that when the wine is in, the wit is out."

"No, I mean it. I realize I've never had an adventure before, and I get the feeling the longer it goes on, the better it will get."

"It will be different in the morning when Captain Swan is the boss."

"I'm serious. I think what we're doing is real. Can you imagine what it would be like to live a fake life, like those people in the house where we found the barge? I'll bet they never knew before what happened to garbage, or gave a damn, let alone smelled it."

"You are a most curious woman, but I'm getting to like you. I don't understand you, but I like you."

"Oh yes, you do understand me, Elliot Swan. You just couldn't say you like me all by itself."

"It's almost midnight. I think we should turn in before I put on my captain's suit and get domineering. Oh, there's something I almost forgot," he said, drawing her to him as she rose from her seat. "It was a great party, Alex. Thanks." He folded her into his arms and kissed her on the lips.

Sunday was a continuing sunny apology for the storm two days before. Carolina mornings in the spring can be glorious, and this one was among the best. A light but steady breeze enticed early sailors to set their boats to weaving, intersecting patterns across the bay even before the Holy City's bells reminded its people this was the Lord's Day. Excursion ferries plowed between City Dock and Fort Sumter, delivering bleached sightseers and recovering sunburned tourists. The wind turned the palm trees along the Battery into sighing instruments; grim-faced joggers and walkers intent on their rounds seemed indifferent to this ear's delight.

Alex, with her purchased breakfast brioches, had planned well for them to descend gradually from the high of their gourmet dinner. They took their food to the place on deck they'd occupied the previous evening, comfortable in their new relationship, comfortable with long silences; their minds, in tandem or together, skipped along the previous weeks to this moment. They seemed to have consciously dismissed the inevitability they'd weigh anchor and move to another stage not guaranteed to be as good as right now.

"How about you? Do you want to sail to England, sell your garbage, get another visa and come back here?" she fantasized.

"Or run the barge aground on Fort Sumter and get even with them for starting your Civil War?"

"Or take the barge back to the house on the Isle of Palms and tell them they gave us the wrong garbage?"

"We can play this game on the way to Savannah, so we should clean up our breakfast dishes and leave," Elliot said.

"How far is it?" she asked.

"About ninety miles. We could stop at Beaufort on the way, that's about fifty miles, but Sunday's they're probably not accepting waste."

"It would be fun to see Beaufort, but you're the captain, I guess," she said.

"I hope I never again get marooned with a mate as insolent as you."

"Don't worry. You won't."

Mid-afternoon they dropped anchor off Fripp Island, a gated community for the very rich whites, cheek and jowl with St. Helena's Island, one of the few remaining bastions of the Gullah blacks. Even from the tug, the contrast in topography was apparent to the naked eye. At one of the estates on Fripp, Sunday afternoon festivities were fully underway, a tea dance orchestra, as it was popularly known, pumped out golden oldies of the 50s and 60s, the mixture of instruments and voices bouncing off the water's sounding board to violate the peace of a pleasant afternoon.

"Let's go ashore at St. Helena's," Elliot suggested. "I'm tired of being cooped up on this tug."

"Do you think we should? I have terrible visions of you being scooped up by Immigration."

"It's Sunday. The government doesn't work on Sunday and particularly in an out of the way place like this. I'll wear a hat and sunglasses. We can take the putt-putt to one of those little coves," he said, pointing to the chart, "Spend an hour and be back for supper."

"Oh, Elliot. I don't feel good about it." Having learned she rarely won any points arguing when his mind was already made up, she tried to persuade him by caricaturing the risky venture. "If you insist, but remember if we get stopped, just act natural and I'll tell them you're my idiot brother."

They found their little cove, providing one of South Carolina's countless boat landings, tied up the putt-putt and walked down a dusty country lane to a small village. At a crossroads a rough wooden sign, fast deteriorating in the Carolina weather of blistering sun and torrential rains, advised anyone interested that the 'Gullah' settlement was a half mile away. They traveled the half mile through a sparsely wooded area without seeing a person and had they been driving might have missed the half-dozen buildings, partially hidden among the live oaks, that housed a church, school, art gallery/gift shop and dormitories. Unlike times past, most of the black families were no longer concentrated in or near the compound. Elliot and Alex stopped to read a historical sign which described the importation of black slaves to work the sea island and tidewater plantations in the early days of the southern colonies. Contrary to popular belief that 'Gullah' was derived from Angola, it was more probably associated with the Gola tribe in Africa from which slaves came. The Gullah language, with few cases, genders, tenses and numbers, has been described as the worst English spoken in the world. Writing Gullah required transcribing many words phonetically, illustrated by a statement given by a witness in a court case, i. e., "Me herre dem; dem blan fuh yerre we; yez yerre yandeh semkah yerre yuh." Translated into English, it roughly meant, "I heard them; they obliged to hear us; ears hear yonder same as hear here." There was an extensive bibliography on the Gullah culture.

In one of the small, bleached wooden buildings, indifferently identified as the art gallery/gift shop, they met a black man of unusual significance. A gifted painter, eloquent conversationalist and broad intellect, he had chosen to stay with his people and share their struggle to succeed rather than abandon his heritage for the certain rewards of an outside world that beckoned him. His surname was Denmark, the great-great-great-great-grandson of the black free man,

Denmark Vessey, who led the unsuccessful Charleston slave rebellion in the mid-nineteenth century which cost him his life. As the conversation with Denmark developed, Elliot mentioned they had recently been in North Carolina's Beaufort, which he correctly pronounced 'Bowfort', but had yet to visit South Carolina's town of the same name which he also pronounced 'Bowfort.' Denmark gently informed Elliot that Beaufort, South Carolina was pronounced 'Bewfort' not 'Bowfort', but he couldn't for the life of him say why.

Alex felt good lazily walking around with Elliot, although more than once she looked over her shoulder, startled by some imagined stalker. Elliot, unconcerned about his illegal alien status or willing to risk it for a few glorious hours in this bucolic indolence, was invigorated by the release from being ship-bound. When the day's warmth began to lower with the sun, they returned to the putt-putt and the security of the ocean's deportation immunity. As they neared the tug and the offshore sounds of the party's endurance, a helicopter, at low altitude, swooped over Fripp Island's pine groves, hovered over the party site, presumably photographing the rich and famous, then banked and slid over the water to inspect Alex and Elliot. After several low level passes, the aircraft returned to the course from which it had appeared and flew out of sight.

"Alex, are you sure you don't owe money to that chopper crew that put you down back at Virginia?"

"They're not after me. They want the law breaker on this boat."

"Do you think?"

"No. It was probably some magazine or newspaper taking pictures of a party they couldn't crash."

"Have you ever thought about what it would be like to be really wealthy?"

"Lots of times."

"I mean to be really wealthy."

"For example?" she asked.

"Imagine never having to clean another loo or shop for groceries or buy a car on the installment plan or—"

"You aren't even near well off."

"I know, I'm just warming up. What would it be like to go to England tomorrow afternoon just for tea, or own one of these sea island mansions and visit it only once a year because you're always in Paris or New York or Newport or Hong Kong?"

"Even the very wealthy have to stay home occasionally to count their money," Alex added.

"And, of course, you'd never need to go to the stores because the stores would come to you, and an accountant would pay all your bills. You'd never even know you'd spent any money."

"Or take out the garbage," she joked, "you could have a butler who'd choose your wine for you."

"The Steeles have a butler, but I don't think they're very wealthy, certainly well off, but not very wealthy," Elliot said. "Rich and his father work. I don't suppose they have to, but it's an old family business and they probably don't want somebody else mucking it up, but I don't think they're very wealthy. What do you think most wealthy people do with themselves? What would you do if you were really wealthy?"

"Just what I'm doing now," she replied. "Some sit on boards of companies and schools and other non-profit institutions, charities, museums, opera companies, symphony orchestras. When you think about it, there are many worthwhile organizations that need prominent people."

"And their money," Elliot added.

"And their money," Alex agreed.

"They must keep seeing the same people over and over again. Quite boring, I would think."

"Some people feel more comfortable not breaking new ground."

"Not for me," he said. "I want as many experiences in my life as I can crowd in."

"Elliot, why are you fascinated with money?"

"Because we never had much. Lots of respect in the community but not much money. This is my first full time employment and I'm a garbage man. Not very impressive, would you say?"

"It's temporary, Elliot. It's to pay for Columbia."

"What if it's not enough to get me through?"

"You could get a loan. I could lend you some money till you get your degree."

"Oh no. I'm not going to live off my girlfriend."

"You'd pay me back when you got a professorship."

"That's so generous. I love you for it, but I can't live off your salary. You'd probably give up things you need to subsidize me. Thanks, I just can't do that."

"Think about it," she said, giving notice the subject was still open for discussion. "In the meantime, we should think about supper."

When they finished eating and went on deck for their coffee, he said, "In the morning, I think we should learn if 'Bewfort' practices southern hospitality and takes garbage."

"Aye, aye," she replied, and they looked for shooting starts before going to their separate bunks.

The deep water approach to Beaufort afforded an excellent view of the grand, late eighteenth century, low country houses facing the ocean from thirty-six feet above mean high tide. A half mile further along the shore old stone and brick commercial buildings marking the business section made a graceful arc as though to prevent several acres of small wooden houses behind from tumbling into the water. No industrial structure insulted the visible tranquility of the town, and no one Elliot could ask without leaving the tug knew of a reception center for waste. Next port, Savannah, Georgia.

"Have you been to Savannah?" he asked.

She wagged her head from side to side, unable to say 'no' with pins in her mouth, preparing to sew a tear in her sweats.

"I only know it was founded by a general named Oglethorpe who laid out the town in a series of squares and all traffic goes counter-clockwise."

"You're a veritable encyclopedia. Where did you learn this?"

"On a TV game show. It's described as a beautiful city. I'd like to go ashore and see it."

"That doesn't make any sense. If you're caught, everything you've done so far has been a big waste."

"Including you?" he asked.

"I'm not talking about us, but that could be a dramatic way to end or at least stall a relationship," she answered.

"I'm just irritated about having no luck getting this job done. Uh oh, here comes that helicopter we saw yesterday."

The aircraft dropped from its altitude of one thousand feet, ideal for patrolling large areas without sacrificing good visual contact, to the tug's height to get a close up of Elliot and Alex. A man sitting next to the pilot slid open a door and waved to direct their attention to him and then began taking photographs. The helicopter bore no identification except registration numbers. It circled the tug twice, the cameraman all the time taking pictures, before it skidded to the back of the barge, presumably to record its serial numbers, then disappeared.

"What do you make of that?" Elliot asked.

"It appeared they were more interested in photographing us, especially me, than a simple recording of a huge load of garbage."

"That makes sense, but it's not much of a compliment to you. Did you recognize him?"

"Never saw him or the pilot before."

"Maybe your newspaper is worried about you and wants to be sure you're all right, so they have a local lens keeping track of you."

A marked increase in vessels traveling north in open ocean routes or up the intercoastal waterway confirmed the spring migration of temporarily displaced Yankees as surely as the seasonal transience of birds. While the sun arced higher, announcing winter's inevitable but reluctant retreat to polar origins, a succession of pleasure crafts passed in review, displaying women covered by little more than their tans, conspicuous as figureheads. They wore their exposure as members of the 'have hads' in contrast to the paler members of the sorority, the 'have not hads.' The tableau did not go unnoticed by either Elliot or Alex, the former regarding it as a welcome relief from the continuous frustrations of his employment, the latter viewing the exhibition as a blatant disregard for the good name of sexy. But it did remind Alex she should get a bathing suit at the next port of call.

Savannah lay on the Savannah River ten miles northwest from its entrance to the Atlantic. The city enjoyed a deep-water port, and a considerable tonnage of diverse shipments passed in and out of its harbor annually. River traffic was lively but more orderly than the Cape Fear passage to Wilmington. Georgia's port facilities, sensibly located and clearly marked, simplified Elliot's job of finding the Disposal Waste Reception Center and taking his place in a long line of dissimilar vessels on the same errand. He watched the unloading of several ships at the head of the line and properly concluded the handlers would not get to his load until the next morning.

"Let's have supper aboard the boat and sneak ashore for a look at Savannah as soon as it gets dark," he suggested to Alex.

"I think you're crazy, but I've learned there's no point in arguing with you. But for God's sake don't talk to anyone; they'll pick up your accent right away."

"All right," he grumbled, pretending she'd taken all the fun out of their adventure.

Once ashore, purchasing a bathing suit before the shops closed was Alex's highest priority. Elliot hesitantly followed her cue, settling for khaki shorts after rejecting a countless array of exotic designer creations which, one by one, she held up for his inspection. They then departed for the residential section to walk square by square, inspecting the early nineteenth century architecture which both agreed reminded them of Boston's Beacon Hill. Although there was probably a greater chance of Elliot being detected in Savannah than Beaufort, Alex nevertheless felt fewer moments of panic when they were unexpectedly approached on the street. On their way back to the putt-putt, they encountered a policeman, a block away, speaking to pedestrians. A quick detour took them across the street but within hearing of the conversations, revealing the policeman was collecting for the Policemen's Retirement Fund.

The next morning, unseasonably hot and steamy even for Savannah, made the galley and pilothouse too oppressive to occupy while the tug lay motionless waiting to unload the garbage. Estimating it would be at least two hours till they were directed to tie up at the service pier, Elliot decided to clean up some of the trash left by the storm. He stripped to the waist and began soap-stoning the deck, soon to be joined by Alex in her newly acquired bathing suit, asking how she could help. He unpacked the sea hose and demonstrated how to wash away the soap stoning residue through the scuppers and over the side of the ship. Declaring anyone could do something that simple, she picked up the hose and waited for him to signal her to wash down a section.

"Now," he urged, "before the slime hardens in the heat."

She directed the nozzle at the deck and turned the water pressure valve on full. Unprepared for the force, Alex lost control of the hose which snaked the nozzle to point directly at Elliot. He stood immobilized, water gushing down from his head, hair and beard matted and tangled, his pants an unrecognizable, sodden, clinging mass. He leapt toward her to avoid the water stream, the soap stone mop held as though brandishing a weapon, while she kneeled to regain control of the hose in apparent subservience, all perfectly coordinated with the arrival of the photographer in the helicopter taking pictures of the episode.

Chapter 16

It was late morning before the tug was signaled to position the barge for unloading at the waste reception dock.

Weeks of wandering from delays to rejections, without any hint of assurance the effort would ultimately be rewarded, had depleted the exhilaration he'd anticipated when success seemed at hand. Now he was only minutes away from telephoning Steele to report the mission was completed. Had he known that Savannah wasn't another bogus name on the Sanitation Commissioner's list, he'd have come directly here, made the drop, returned to New York and left for England within the visa's allotted time. Now he was an illegal alien, officially restricted from setting foot on U.S. soil. It could have been so easy. So easy, but not so good with Alex—the unpredictable, irrepressible, gutsy, flippant, headstrong (no, headstrong was too harsh), determined, self-sufficient, elegant and smashing-looking. Alex was probably the reason he no longer found satisfaction in accomplishing the assignment.

Roused from his musing, the Reception Center's P.A. system directed him to make fast at the dock and come ashore to file discharge applications, identification of tug and barge owner, master of the vessel, crew and verification the garbage load was being removed in Savannah. Still not totally returned from his reverie, he left the pilothouse to go ashore.

"You can't do that, Elliot. If you step on that dock with all those port officials, you're a goner."

"What will we do? We can't just sit here."

"Tell them you've broken your leg and ask them to send somebody aboard. I'll wrap your leg in a sheet and prop it on a chair."

"Master of the tug, please come ashore and attend to your paper work," the Reception Center called.

"I can't," Elliot replied on the bull horn. "I've broken my leg."

"We'll come aboard and carry you to the office."

"Oh, you can't do that. I also have an infectious disease. I'll send my first mate to fetch the papers and we'll fill them out here."

"We can't do that. As captain, you have to be photographed and submit a resume. How come your mate doesn't have the disease?"

"She's very germ resistant. Just hand her the papers at arm's length so she doesn't touch you."

"What's the name of this infection?"

"It's a, it's primus lacka aqua. Can we please get on with it? I'm getting very tired."

"Perhaps we should call Immigration."

"Don't do that. Their moon suits have proven to be ineffective. Just unload me and I'll go away without bothering anybody else."

"I don't think we can process your waste under the circumstances," the Reception Center told Elliot.

By now a crowd was gathering at the dock, and crews of other ships waiting for service followed with interest the exchange between Elliot and the faceless public announcement voice. Elliot decided to try another approach.

"I beg of you, please take the load so I can return to New York at top speed to see my dying mother."

"I suppose she has the primus what d'ya call it, too."

"No, she's just old—one hundred and one and hanging on to see her only child before she goes to meet her maker." Elliot threw in a little religious touch, hoping to find a Baptist in the Reception Center office.

"We're sorry you're having so many problems, but you may be posing a threat to public health. You'll have to leave. We're already behind schedule. We'll cast off your lines. Pull away into the river traffic slowly and leave the harbor. Good luck."

With Alex spotting obstacles on his blind side, Elliot made a spectacular reverse in their course and headed downriver towards the Atlantic Ocean. The reality of the garbage's permanence seemed indisputable. He should have known the prospect of dumping the load seemed too good to be true; and it was. Alex was right, he had his own White Whale, but unlike *Moby Dick's* Captain Ahab, this monster was relentlessly pursuing him.

"If this keeps up, we'll run out of American real estate," he said.

"Don't get discouraged, we still have the Gulf Coast, and then there's Central America and—"

"Now I know why I keep you around. You make the ridiculous seem rational."

"Speaking of ridiculous, did you hear what you were saying at the Reception Center? Not quite up to Shakespeare's Falstaff, but I'd pay to hear that ad libbing and to clear up why you keep me around. It's because I'm cheap labor. I work for nothing."

"If you're not happy here you should get back to New York before they replace you with a real reporter."

"I think it's time you taught me how to take this cruise ship into port because I have a feeling something dreadful is going to happen to you."

And on and on they bantered, partly because they wanted to ease each other's disappointment over Savannah, but mostly because they were happy to be falling in love.

While checking the charts for the next leg of the journey, Alex observed the Intercoastal Waterway could be entered near the mouth of the Savannah River. Southbound traffic was so light this route would not impede their progress to Brunswick or Jacksonville, Florida. The waterway passed between the Georgia coastline and a string of sea islands including Ossabow, St. Catherine's, Sapelo, Little St. Simons, St. Simons and Jeykll, which were romantically known as the Golden Chain. Alex let slip she'd once visited the Sea Island resort on St. Simon's, a very chic compound, but repaired the damage by adding "as a babysitter, of course." To further distract Elliot from her potential faux pas, she told him she'd read that St. Catherine's, the second island they'd pass, had been the rice plantation of Button Gwinette, a Georgian statesman, whose only signature known to exist was on the Declaration of Independence. In the 1940s, St. Catherine's was acquired by a New Yorker who made his fortune on five cent mints. After his death, the island became a preserve for exotic animals.

The seventy-five mile trip from Savannah to Brunswick restored their perspective; the peacefulness of undeveloped shore, the slap on the water of fish breaking the surface to catch a low-flying bug, white egrets walking awkwardly on the mud flats as though their legs were in splints but becoming all grace when airborne. As the sun set, they chose an anchorage on an inlet that curved out of the waterway to bend around Brunswick.

Huge slashes of reds, oranges and purples streaked across the western sky; a slight breeze swept all insects away from the tug, but in the sheltered side of the cove fireflies and birds made their presence known with intermittent pinpricks of light and night music.

Day gave way to night. The tug and its tow were positioned and stabilized away from the traffic of other vessels. Hatches secured, night lights switched on, loose gear stowed. Elliot and Alex had done this all before, each anticipating the other's moves so there was no need to talk. Occasionally when they were coiling lines, their arms would intertwine or in the confines of a narrow gangway they'd press against each other long enough to feel the other's warmth before their eyes met and they parted.

Supper was simple and leisurely, lingering to listen to the subtle sounds of the dark. When they'd eaten, Elliot stacked the dishes in precise, graduated order before Alex gently bathed each in a blanket of scented, lustrous bubbles, completing her ritual with an immersion in clear water before they emerged bare and purified. One by one, Elliot carefully dried the diverse shapes and sizes and laid them in their place. When their rite of communion was accomplished, Alex went out onto the moonless deck to celebrate her thoughts. Elliot followed to stand behind her, wrapping his hard arms around her shoulders, his face buried in her fragrant hair. No words were spoken. In a brief moment, releasing them from an agonizingly long wait, they turned and entered the cabin, a faint light from the pilothouse separating them from the shadows. Elliot folded her in his arms and kissed her hungrily as he pulled her sweatshirt up to her shoulders.

She backed away from him to pull the garment over her head and stepped out of her sweat pants to reveal her nakedness.

"My God, how I want you," Elliot groaned as he stripped.

"Where?" she asked.

"I'll put our bunk mattresses down here."

"Hurry."

They lay next to each other, he exploring the plains of her body with his open hand as a sculptor perfects his art. As he touched her, little animal sounds escaped her lips until she cried out in pleasure, "Now."

He entered her and they were lost to each other.

"And then I bought some Brunswick stew for supper. The recipe originated here as you might guess and it has chicken, onions, tomatoes, cloves, peppers, lima beans, corn, Worcestershire sauce and I suppose anything else they found lying around. It tasted so good when I sampled it I couldn't resist," Alex said the next day as she helped Elliot hoist and secure the putt-putt on her return from visiting the coastal town.

"You're getting to be a real 'take-out queen.' I don't know how you find these restaurants, but so far your choices have been excellent. How much do I owe you?"

"Not a sou. I'm on an expense account, remember? I felt so righteous filing my story I went right out and spent some of the paper's money. Besides, I'm living rent free."

"When am I going to read this saga?"

"When it's finished. Unlike *Moby Dick*, I don't know how it's going to turn out."

"Tell me about Brunswick."

"It's a town that seems unable to make up its mind about what it wants to be and therefore is not a typical anything; part fishing, part lumbering, part manufacturing and so on. Everyone seemed to know about the barge parked out here in the cove."

"Any sign of disposal facilities?"

"The town's elevation is near sea level which prevents landfills, and they haul local trash only to an inland incinerator at another city."

"Thanks for the information. I'll cross that off the list later. Let's be on our way to Jacksonville with a quick look at the harbor at St. Mary's on the border."

As the charts showed the Intercoastal Waterway to be quite circuitous, they abandoned it for the open ocean and swifter passage. Few pleasure crafts left the protection of the inland route, but large coastal tonnage and trans-Atlantic ships were often sighted though not close enough to draw the passengers' or crews' reaction to the seagull-covered garbage. This day, as those preceding, registered ever higher temperatures as the tug moved towards lower latitudes. Alex, responding to the warming days, suddenly appeared in the pilothouse in her newly purchased bikini, receiving the traditional whistle from Elliot and his apology that they were in water too deep to anchor, preventing him from showing his appreciation. She replied she now understood why ships were given female names—a subliminal admission men subconsciously compared sailing to their inamorates.

"Come here and be my compass," he said, drawing her to him for a kiss, tender but lusty. "Why do you stay on this aimless, uncomfortable trek?"

"Because I can't leave you. Do you remember the night of the storm when I left the pilothouse to find you or save you just as you came out from under the boat? I was terrified that you'd been tangled up in the line on the propeller or couldn't get back on the tug, about to be swept away; but I had to save you. I could not let you be lost to me."

He held her tight against him and tenderly kissed her forehead. They sailed in silence, losing track of time.

When they returned to less important matters, Elliot asked her if the newspaper was getting impatient with her absence.

"I don't think so," she replied. "They still accept my phone calls, and they've run my story as a series, but the editing has shifted the emphasis from possible political shenanigans to the marathon voyage of the garbage."

"Are names mentioned?" he asked.

"Only yours. The skipper had to be identified to give the account credibility, real stuff, not fiction."

"How is it your name isn't used?"

"Well, it appears in the byline but not the narrative. Nobody reads the byline, and I thought the narrative should be told in third person to preserve its integrity," she said, trying to get off the subject.

"Why is it I always know when not to believe you?"

"We've probably been together way too long. Perhaps I should stop seeing you."

"Unless you're a trans-Atlantic swimmer, that sounds like an idle threat," Elliot replied.

"But you should think of what's best for you. In the beginning, you were a real folk hero until your visa lapsed. Now you're a public enemy number one/folk hero, depending on the age of my readers. Are we going to check out St. Mary's?"

"Probably should, it might be your only chance to see its beautiful downtown."

Elliot was overjoyed to discover St. Mary's wasn't on the Sanitation Department's list. Fortune welcomed the garbage with open arms, the town held a parade to celebrate the honor of being the recipient of a fine Northern Gesture amid fireworks and honking horns, and he and Alex tearfully set course to return home.

"Wakeup, Elliot, you're having a dream," Alex said from the wheel.

"Where are we?"

"Just outside of St. Mary's."

"They're going to take the garbage. They're going to—oh, no, it was a stupid dream."

"I was about to wake you up so we could make port."

Elliot uncoiled himself from the top of a locker and sat rubbing the sleep from his eyes. "How long was I asleep?"

"About two hours. Maybe you better stand by and guide me through a landing procedure till you're fully awake."

"What a good idea," he replied, standing behind her and surrounding her with his arms.

"As I used to tell my dates when I was a teenager, 'keep both hands on the wheel'."

In a half-hour, they reentered the Intercoastal Waterway to join the parade of private vessels bound for St. Mary's harbor. Realization usually less than anticipation was certainly not in the same league as Elliot's dream. A quick scan with the binoculars convinced them it would be a waste of time to moor and inquire about disposal facilities in a harbor jammed full of pleasure boats.

"Do you dream much?" she asked as they reset their course for Jacksonville.

"I dream, but I don't know how much 'much' is."

"Every night?"

"No, less than that. How often do you dream?"

"A lot until I met you. I mean, men were not in my dreams all the time, but with you I don't seem to need dreams for whatever reason people have them. Every night I think about you for a long time before going to sleep and that does it. Many of my dreams used to be about being unprepared for an exam, no matter how much I planned, and some of that carried over into my job."

"My dreams seem to come, strangely enough, when I'm not highly focused on a project. For example, this afternoon was some sort of fantasy about the garbage that came out of the blue, and I've never been more relaxed about the whole thing. Occasionally I have a dream about my grandfather or a friend. Both have died and I'm certain in my dream they've come to tell me something. When I wake up, I know they've told it to me but I can't remember what it was. Jung has done a lot of research on dreams, particularly those with theological overtones, or undertones. I never can remember which it is. If I ever get back to dry land, I mean to look into that."

"Do you enjoy reading?"

"Very much," he answered, "but I haven't had much time since I left New York. I'm less than halfway through *Moby Dick,* and if I don't get back to it soon, I'll have to start all over. Obviously you're a reader as well as a writer. What other than newspapers?"

"Shakespeare, Henry James, Jane Austen, Truman Capote, Eliot."

"George Eliot, or me?"

"Neither, T. S., the 'Cocktail Party' Eliot. Andre Gide, Bryon. And you?"

"I favor nonfiction, especially histories. I suppose it's a mutated gene I inherited from my genealogical mother. I was reading the John Adams papers before I started this trip, but they were published in four volumes and I thought I might lose one on the tug, so I brought *Moby Dick*, a single volume and truly profound work on social and psychological positions."

"Do you like it?"

"I don't think I like it, but the demand on me to read it is too great to give it up. What's the most puzzling book you've ever read?"

"The Bible. There are so many levels on which one can read it, I'm never sure I get it right. Would you like me to read *Moby Dick* aloud while you're piloting this leg of the trip?"

"I'd like that."

They reached the entrance to Jacksonville's harbor in the early evening, a time at which they frequently arrived at their destinations. The large, land-protected port was filled with U.S. Naval, commercial and private vessels arriving, docking and departing along the miles of channel's piers which from the air must have looked like an open zipper.

Too late to hunt for the elusive disposal facility, they went to a less congested stretch of St. Johns River and secured for the night. The warmth of the water surrounding their mooring softened the air, and an offshore wind carried the river traffic noises away to a barely audible hum. They ate supper on deck, leaning against the pilothouse, shoeless, close enough to compare the length of their legs. The tug rocked gently with the wakes from passing ships, and the fore and aft warning lights of the barge bobbed in a recurrent cycle of twos. Dew began to bathe them with feather touches, but they stayed on deck and made a game out of guessing what the buildings were that showed only in silhouette against the Florida sky. He tried to tease her into betting on their identities, but she turned him down on the basis that in tomorrow's daylight, they still couldn't be sure without going ashore.

"Do you ever have the feeling we've known each other before?" he asked.

"You mean like deja vu or in another life?" she asked.

"Not exactly. More like in this life but in separate circumstances, as though some power had altered your consciousness. Every now and then I look at you and I feel sure you're in so many of my experiences but know that can't be. It's impossible for me to sort it out, but I know it's real."

"Have you ever felt this way before?"

"Never. I've been what you might call an even keel bloke, very much aware of what's going on and realistic about my status. No extrasensory perception. What you see is what you get because it's real. No 'ifs' because there are endless 'ifs.' None of this adequately expresses my attachment to you, but it's not to be ignored."

"When I was eighteen, a great aunt told me I was an old soul. You can imagine how I reacted to that. When I was twenty-two, I saw my great aunt again just before she died, and I asked her how she could tell I was an old soul. She said because she was an old soul and as I grew older, I'd come to recognize others. We've talked about this before, but on the night of the storm I knew I'd found you and I knew we'd met before. I would have done anything not to lose you, even though I may see you the next time around."

They sat still as lovers often do, feeling not thinking, fulfilled, losing all sense of the outside world. When they returned to the present, they heard the faint music of a beach club orchestra. He rose and offered his hand, bringing her up before him to slowly encircle her waist, holding her in a slow dance. When the music stopped, she led him into the cabin, undressing him slowly and deliberately, before she guided his hands to explore her body as she helped him remove her clothing, lingering over each garment. When they lay together, she took control of their lovemaking, sending tremors through his body until she consummated the adventure.

Both awoke to the sounds of a freighter's shrill whistle and throaty motor as it wallowed its way to sea. Elliot, first out of bed, opened the hatch a few inches to survey a slice of busy river traffic though the sun had yet to rise.

"Good morning, darling," Alex said, pecking his cheek on the way to the shower.

"Good day to you, sweet love," he replied, picking up the two mattress makeshift bed and stowing it on the bunks. When he turned to the counter wedged between the stove and the sink, all the breakfast fixings were in reach, which allowed him to get the meal ready while viewing the port side of the world through the dinner plate-sized glass aperture. It had never before occurred to him, but now looking in daylight at the buildings they tried to identify last night gave him the feeling he was inside a giant camera peering out through the lens. Last night had been special, as the previous week had been—an ever-growing friendship and a promise of lasting love.

"All yours," she said, emerging from the shower, her face slightly shiny from washing, her hair still damp but beginning to curl as it dried.

"When you go ashore today, you should buy some lighter clothes. You're going to roast in those sweats, not that I don't find them stylish or anything."

He washed and came to breakfast in the shorts she'd bought him, thankful not to be limited to winter shirts and pants. She was always showing him kindnesses, and being a prisoner of the ship unable to do things for her nagged at him. He sat across the galley table from her as she ate, his gaze never leaving this woman he adored. She looked up to find his eyes fixed on her with tenderness that made her shy.

"What?" she said, unable to think of anything else, like one who suddenly surprises others making love.

"You know, I never noticed it before, but you're cross-eyed," he replied.

"Only with voyeurs." She rose, went round the table and sat in his lap. "I love you, Elliot Swan."

"I love you, too, little girl, but you mustn't bother the captain when he's on an errand," he said, standing up and sliding Alex off his lap as he slapped her rump.

Chapter 17

In half an hour they finished their housekeeping and departed on other errands, Alex in the putt-putt to go ashore and shop in the grocery store, Elliot to refuel and scan the harbor for the waste disposal facilities before returning to the previous night's mooring site. Once back at their rendezvous, he returned to reading *Moby Dick,* picking up where Alex left off, but the noise of the heavy river traffic broke his concentration, reminding him his mission was still to be accomplished. In the middle of summing up his journey to date, an activity he frequently engaged in of late, the ship-to-shore phone signaled.

"Elliot, this is Rich."

"Hello, Rich, how are you?"

"Fine, but more to the point, how are you doing?"

"We're in Jacksonville, Florida. That list Sanitation gave me is a complete bust. I've also tried ports you never heard of, and none will take this load, so I just keep looking as your father asked me to. Do you want me to take the stuff back to New York?"

"God, not now. That's the last thing you should do, not with the publicity you're getting."

"What are you talking about?"

"You don't know?" Rich said in surprise. "You haven't seen the latest edition of *National Exposure*?"

"National what?"

"*National Exposure*. It's a scandal tabloid sold at grocery store check-out counters. There's a front page picture of you looking as though you're going to beat the hell out of that Appleyard woman."

"You're crazy."

"And the headline reads, 'Publishing Heiress Held Love Slave.' Now, listen to the story. 'Alexandra Appleyard, heiress to the *Times* publishing empire, apparently held captive by illegal alien Elliot

Swan, is pictured here on a filthy garbage boat and believed to be forced to do menial tasks or risk a beating. The incident in this photograph occurred in Savannah, Georgia, and prompts the question: Is there white slavery at work here?' Do you want me to read on?" Rich asked.

"No, that's more than enough," Elliot replied. "Now I think I know why the helicopter with the photographer kept dogging us. Those bastards. If I were a citizen, I'd sue."

"You wouldn't win," Rich said, "everything they print is innuendo. How do you think they put the story together?"

"Remember, the progress of the garbage barge has been monitored since it left New York, so they pretty much knew what our next port would be. Although Alex never disclosed her identity as a crew member in the articles that ran in the *Times*, her name appeared in the byline. Somebody must have put two and two together and then added some sleuthing to unearth the family's connection. One day near Fripp Island, South Carolina, a photographer in a helicopter was snooping around a big outdoor party and, when he left the scene, took low level pictures of us and the serial numbers on the barge. Then the next day, he snapped us washing down the deck in Savannah. Bingo! Incidentally, I was just playing angry because she squirted me with the sea hose."

"But she looks almost naked in the picture," Rich said.

"She almost was. She had a bikini on."

"Oh, one more thing. The Appleyards have contacted my father, and it wasn't a social call. You'll probably hear from them. Keep me posted, and good luck."

Almost as soon as he finished speaking with Rich, Elliot heard the putt-putt, but he was in no hurry to welcome the woman who'd deceived him by hiding her identity. He remained in the pilothouse, watching the outboard draw near, furious with himself for being so easily manipulated. When the smaller craft tapped the larger boat's hull, he went down to the main deck to confront Alex. She looked up from the outboard to see an angry man and then sought to regain her composure, unloading the groceries by herself, but couldn't lift the heavy packages. Elliot jumped onto the putt-putt, pitched the grocery bags onto the deck above, and almost before she could climb up to join him, he started hoisting the putt-putt to its davits.

"You're certainly a pleasure to come back to," she said.

"Rich called. Anything else you didn't tell me?"

"You think I had something to do with getting this published?" she replied, pulling a copy of *National Exposure* from a grocery bag.

"Directly or indirectly, yes; you choose. Which do you want to deal with?"

"Let's try directly first. I had no idea what that helicopter was doing. Just as you hadn't," Alex said.

"I'll reserve judgment on that answer till later. Let's try indirectly."

"Likewise."

"Come on, Alex. You can't expect me to fall again for that line you gave me about the paper letting you set up that sea rescue and living on a tug with three men without pressure from your family. No employer in his right mind would take such a risk with being sued."

"My news chief gave me permission to follow the garbage story from day one when I went to the Sanitation Department. I'll admit my pick up from the raft was my idea, but when I checked in and filed my story, the chief always knew I was all right. He never knew until the damn scandal sheet did this story who I was, and I wanted it that way because I wanted to make it on my own. You think I would have set this up and ruined my cover and enjoyed the staff at the paper bowing and scraping to me; 'Yes, Ms. Appleyard, No, Ms. Appleyard.' I guess you don't know me as well as I thought you did. The Appleyard name hasn't been connected with day-to-day operations of the *Times* for more than two generations. Now that's out, who knows how damaging that will be."

"But that's beside the point of your phony story that you were investigating political intrigue when all the time you were on a lark trying to become an environmental journalist. You should have left the boat a long time ago and gone back to the paper before they replaced you with a real reporter."

"That's dirty, Elliot. You're hitting below the belt."

"You're right. I withdraw that remark."

"Maybe I'll join Greenpeace," she said, her mind wandering off the quarrel.

"They'll have to change their name to Green War."

"Very funny."

"Well, how about that story you were a baby sitter at the Sea Island Resort and that's how you know so much about all the islands we passed coming down. I'll bet you know every swank resort and town on the Atlantic Coast."

"For instance?" she asked.

"Charleston. That's how you found the best stores and restaurants so easily. Been there before?"

"Yes."

"Savannah?"

"Yes."

"St. Catherine's?"

"Yes."

"We know about Sea Island on St. Simon's, don't we?"

"Don't be such a poop," she said.

"You're getting vulgar."

"I always get vulgar when I'm mad."

"More correctly, when you're being found out. I'm just trying to get some perspective here. Jacksonville?"

"Yes."

"Palm Beach?"

"Yes, but I was never in Calabash before."

"Maybe you'd like to convince me you leveled about your family living on a farm. You made it sound like a farm-farm, not the northern branch of the Kentucky Derby."

"I never lied to you about that or anything else. Just because you didn't ask if they bred race horses or Black Angus or Cornish Rock game hens doesn't make me a liar."

"No, but pretty deceitful. That's just one step away from lying."

"Foul," she yelled.

"Withdrawn."

"You're using legal language as though I were on trial, which of course I am. These were things along with the family money I didn't discuss with you or anyone else because I was afraid it would make a difference in our relationship, and then I met you and liked you, never knowing it would get serious, thinking I'd go back to my career and no one would be the wiser. I've already lost my career," she added sadly.

"You don't need a career. You don't need anything because you have it all; all the money in the world, and most of all, you don't need me."

"Why do you always get so macho when money's discussed?"

For a while they stayed silent, glowering at the canned goods from the grocery bags as they rolled around the deck.

"Maybe you should leave the tug now we're in port," Elliot said in low, measured words.

"There's no way I'm getting off the tug until this garbage is environmentally processed. You're not the only one who has an investment in this crap."

"You're getting vulgar again."

"I meant to."

"I could physically remove you, you know."

"With your record of being an abusive illegal alien? I don't think so. I'd scream my lungs out and they'd have you in jail before I fixed my lipstick."

"You wouldn't."

"I would."

"And another thing," he said, beginning to lose ground, "You're the reason I lost two crew members."

"You know that isn't true. One was ill. Now who's playing fast and loose with the truth?"

Elliot, feeling he'd made a tactical blunder, stooped to recover the groceries from the deck. Alex followed his example of picking up the spilled food and went into the galley. In the compact galley, they stored the food, trying not to be near each other, but it was impossible for each not to impede the other, causing profuse apologies. While trying to unentangle in one episode, the ship-to-shore phone rang.

"Hello, Mr. Steele. How are you?" Elliot asked, turning on the speaker phone as requested.

"Fine, thank you, Elliot. I know Rich has already told you of the embarrassing *National Exposure* incident, so I'll get right to the point. Ms. Appleyard will have to leave the tug and I'll fly two crew members down to help you out."

"That's what I suggested, but she won't leave the tug."

"What do you mean, she won't leave the tug?"

"Just that," Alex cut into the conversation with a matter-of-fact tone. "I'm not getting off this tug until we properly unload the stuff."

There was a long pause on the New York end and then some conversation too muffled for Alex and Elliot to understand.

"I would hesitate to do this, Ms. Appleyard, but I can order Mr. Swan to physically remove you."

"But he won't do that, Mr. Steele, because I would scream and it would be confirming the allegation already out there that he's an abusive, illegal alien."

There was another pause and more indecipherable chit-chat.

"This is Jack Appleyard speaking, Mr. Swan. Are you mistreating my daughter, Mr. Swan?"

"No, sir, I'm treating her better than she deserves. She could do with a good spanking."

"You're the one who needs to be spanked. You're acting like a spoiled child," Alex said. "I'm just fine, Daddy, don't worry. I'm better than I've ever been."

"Why don't you come home now, dear?" Alex's mother said. "I'm so worried something will happen. Everyone's asking about you, come home and everything will be forgotten. We'll have a nice party for you. Are you eating properly?"

"Not now, Mother. Elliot and I are in the middle of a fight," Alex said.

Another muffled conversational huddle in New York followed before Jim Steele, acting as spokesperson, said, "Elliot, what do you propose to do with the garbage?"

"Keep looking till I find its home unless you want me to dump it in the ocean."

"You do that, Elliot Swan, and I'll report you to the authorities," Alex said.

"Well, I guess we better keep looking. We're charging New York City less for our towing services than an EPA fine. Good luck."

"Goodbye, Mother, Daddy."

"Goodbye, Alexandra dear," her parents said in unison. "And Alexandra, the next time you're photographed, try to wear more clothes," her mother added.

Elliot shut down the phone communication then looked at Alex.

"I guess the enemy of my enemy is my friend," she said.

"Whatever that means," Elliot replied.

Since Elliot returned from refueling, the tug had been at anchor more than two hours. The daytime volume of Jacksonville's port activity was so great that a ship lying idle at its mooring soon drew the attention of the harbormaster. His responsibility for keeping the commercial channels free of presence without purpose endowed him with considerable authority, which he exercised only when his skillful persuasion came up short. As he sat in the state pier's newly constructed control tower, a raised, glass-enclosed box offering optimum vision of his domain similar to an airport's control tower, he felt proud his innovation for port monitoring was the first in the country. He'd finished his second cup of coffee and a first-to-last-page review of the current issue of *National Exposure* when he noted a tug, tied to a barge piled high with contents too far away to identify, was still at anchor.

Finding no application for port entry of such vessels among his meticulously organized records, he assigned his deputy to take his place observing the port from the tower, descended to his launch and set out for the trespasser. When he neared the object of his investigation, he discovered the barge was loaded with garbage feeding hundreds of gulls and supporting some form of vegetation in its early stages.

"Ahoy," he called, enforcing his authority with the naval vernacular.

Elliot, annoyed at being diverted from his brooding, stuck his head out from the pilothouse and yelled, "What do you want?" Recovering from his misdirected irritation, he weakly said, "Sorry. What may I do for you?"

"I'm the Jacksonville harbormaster, and I want to know what you're doing here."

"I'm here to get rid of this garbage. Could you please direct me to the disposal pier?"

"Do you have an appointment? I don't remember seeing your application in the records. Where you from?"

"I'm out of New York and I was never told I had to file an application. Why don't I do that right now?"

"Not so fast. How do I know you're from where you say you are?"

"Just check the tug and barge registrations," Elliot said.

"Then you must wait for your application to be approved after we confirm your origin."

"Can't we do that right now as long as I'm here?"

"After that, you'll have to wait in line for your turn. And let me give you a little tip, English," the harbormaster said with a hint of fatherly discipline. "There's no point in going through all this because we can't process your load, anyway."

"Why not?" Elliot asked, his voice rising in frustration.

"Because your junk is bailed and we don't have the equipment to cut all those bail straps and we sure as hell are not going to do that by hand."

Elliot turned towards the cabin and screamed, "All hands on deck. Come on, Mate. As long as you're on this boat, you're expected to work. Hurry now, we're leaving port."

Alex, who'd listened to this whole exchange with some amusement, went out on deck and was immediately spotted by the harbormaster.

"Aren't you the one on the cover of *National Exposure?*" the harbormaster asked.

"No," Alex said. "That was either the second or third Mate. We're sisters. Triplets. We all look alike."

Elliot was all business, raising the anchor and entering the harbor channel to the sea almost before the harbormaster was out of sight. The port, stretching about ten miles from city center to the ocean, was clogged with traffic thwarting Elliot's attempt to make a hasty retreat from a bad morning.

"We'll resume our schedule of four hours on, four hours off, and with these longer days, sail from dawn to dusk to get this trip over," he informed Alex. "In good weather I'll sleep on deck by the pilothouse in case of an emergency when you have the wheel. Any questions?"

"Not for now," Alex said, wisely allowing him to play the role that the captain's word was law—for the moment. She hadn't noticed until now how the accumulative stress from near calamities was beginning to overtake him. As she added up the successive incidents he'd experienced from the beginning of the trip, she realized few had been carefree days—continuous rejections at the ports, Bones and Mac jumping ship, the near-fatal storm, the loss of the barge, his visa expiration and now the *National Exposure* ballyhoo. That was more than enough for anybody.

"We can reach St. Augustine this afternoon, so we'll have a look there and then moor for the night on our way to Daytona Beach. And another thing, I'll get my own meals." Elliot's obvious attempt to distance himself from dealing with the business of his relationship with Alex needed a declaration of independence for no one but himself. She would wait and let him work through this assessment of where he wanted to go.

When she took the wheel, he went below and heated up a tasteless can of spaghetti left over from the stores laid in before Alex started doing the shopping. He stretched out on a bunk, got up, read a few pages of *Moby Dick* before he lay down again. *Why the hell didn't she tell me upfront who she was? She did. Why is she so determined to stay on the boat till the garbage is done with? She said because she wanted her articles in the paper to make a public object lesson on officials' environmental irresponsibility. Why didn't I believe her earlier? Because no ordinary woman gets set adrift in the ocean. But she's no ordinary woman. Think of how she rode out the storm;*

remember she was gutsy enough to go looking for me under the boat. Would she do that for anybody or just me? Probably for anybody because she didn't love me then. Why am I still angry at her for not telling me about her family owning the Times? Why didn't I believe she was protecting her job with anonymity? Okay, that makes sense, but what about her fortune? Maybe she thought that would affect our relationship. Has it? I'm not sure. Why don't you ask her? I can't do that now.

Elliot heard Alex blow the whistle signaling her duty was over. He climbed to the wheelhouse to check the charts with her for positioning before she went below for a nap.

She was restless. Things were too unsettled. Feelings, hers and his, possibly agitated out of proportion to the harm done by the tabloid. The public revelation of her identity and the absurd implication of their decadence were two separate issues that needed to be dealt with as such. The disclosure of her lineage forced her to assign a value to her self-worth, which she might have been avoiding with concealment. The issue now, admittedly, was not whether she could continue to work at the *Times*, but if she was good enough to work at the *Times* and could tell the difference between the two. Although Elliot seemed to understand she hid her identity to preserve objective judgment of her work, he acted as though his importance in the relationship was depreciated with the disclosure of her family's wealth. She drew comfort from the progress she was making in sorting things out and wondered how Elliot was doing on his obstacle course.

As they neared St. Augustine, she finished her nap and went up to the pilothouse to find Elliot stern-faced, totally absorbed in sailing although they were on a flat sea. "Could we stop at St. Augustine long enough for me to pick up some things? I know you said we couldn't make Daytona Beach by dark, so we'd have to moor somewhere along the way. I won't be long."

"I thought you did your shopping this morning in Jacksonville."

"I did, but I forgot some things. Personal things."

"Okay. I'll moor right off the peninsula where these two rivers join the Intercoastal Waterway. If they make me move, call me on the ship-to-shore phone and I'll let you know where I am."

When she'd gone ashore before, he'd never mentioned the possibility of moving to a new location. For a moment, she panicked and almost considered canceling the trip ashore, fearing he might leave, and in the next instant, hated herself for not trusting him.

What was happening to her, she wondered. She'd once trusted him with her life and now suffered doubts. As though to compensate for her loss of confidence in their relationship, she left her pocketbook minus her credit card where he'd easily see it and let down the putt-putt.

In less than two hours she returned, clutching a bag in each hand as she climbed onto the deck. He acknowledged her with a silent nod and weighed anchor as she, with considerable effort, single-handedly raised and secured the putt-putt.

Now underway with clear sailing until dusk, Elliot called from the pilothouse to the galley to suggest Alex might want to eat her supper before relieving him at the wheel. Alex said she was not hungry and would take over her duty in fifteen minutes as scheduled.

Fifteen miles down the coast, a fast moving bank of clouds swept over ocean only a short while into her turn at the wheel. Her first instinct was to call Elliot on the intercom for relief, but she checked that impulse, deciding that unless the seas became rougher and dangerous, she'd wait the storm out. As quickly as the squall came up, it blew out, and Alex was rewarded with a bright rainbow arcing up ahead to connect ocean and land.

At the first sign of fading light, he returned to the wheelhouse to select a site for mooring, and when the tug and barge were made fast for the night, they descended to the galley like strangers whose entire acquaintance had consisted of a ride in an elevator.

Elliot, not impatient for another supper of tasteless canned spaghetti, yielded the galley to her for the preparation of supper. Alex, relying on a mixture of memory, guesses and luck, concocted an aromatic fish and vegetable chowder in a quantity for two, declaring she didn't know how to reduce the recipe by half.

"I'll only have to throw it out if you don't want it," she explained, giving him an excuse to save her from being wasteful.

"I'll take care of the dishes," he told her. "I dirtied some, too."

After supper and dishes were done, they sat opposite each other at the table, he updating the ship's log and she rolling a ball from a skein of yarn held by the back of a chair. He cautiously peeked at her, and she pretended not to see him. When she dropped the ball of yarn, by accident or on purpose, and it rolled across the floor, he bent to retrieve it.

"What's this?" he asked.

"Just one of the personal things I picked up in town. I decided by the time you grow old, I better know how to knit socks."

"You certainly are no ordinary woman," he said out loud, very aware she would know he'd already decided that.

There was an awkward pause while she let him find an impersonal subject for conversation.

"What's St. Augustine like?" he asked.

"It's old," she replied. "The oldest European settlement in the United States, 1565."

"Beautiful?"

"Quaint. The city was burned down three different times but some old buildings, seventeenth century I believe, remain. The history of its sovereignty affiliations is fascinating because it was founded by Spaniards, ceded to the English in 1763, receded to Spain in 1783 and ceded to the U.S. in 1819. Legend has it that this was the site of Ponce de Leon's Fountain of Youth."

There was another pause in the conversation, suggesting Elliot had stalled on reentry.

Knowing he was groping for the ideal lead that evaded him, she said, "We need to talk."

"About what?"

"I need to talk about me, you need to talk about you. We need to talk about us," she answered. "Since I brought it up, I'll start. What are you so angry about?"

"All right, you asked for it. I'm mad at myself because I didn't believe you when you first came aboard—your name, the job, your reason for wanting to come along on this garbage haul. And I'm twice as mad because I later did believe you and was taken in by the way you spoke your mind and acted on your convictions. You were a self-starter who at the first try caught a fish and persuaded me to teach you to pilot the tug. Your independence, no, self-reliance, really impressed me, and I began to believe you and trust in everything you said. I see now I may have looked the other way when I had any suspicions. When the storm hit us, you never quit, and I'll always admire you for that. Then I realized how important you were to my life. I trusted you in everything, and I began to fall in love. Some parts of me had been closed, and I never knew that before you. Giving up being in charge was a new experience for me, made me uneasy at first, but loving you was better. The story in the scandal sheet about your identity and the family's money made me feel betrayed, that you hadn't trusted me to really tell all. Now I'm still mixed up about the money part. I'm not sure if it would make me less of a man in any life we had together, so part of me may be punishing you for something you never did, and I'm mad as hell at myself for that."

"We seem to be okay on everything except my family's money, and I want to emphasize it's my family's," Alex said. "So let me get to that right off. You might never think this, but I have a real problem with my family's money, too. Even though they tried to bring me up without it affecting me, it has. Since I was a child, I had the best toys, the best birthday parties, clothes, schools, vacations, everything. They tried to teach me money doesn't need to matter, but it does, and I'm still trying to disprove that. When I was eleven, I mucked out our horse stalls; by thirteen I could cook and serve a five-course dinner. My last two summer vacations, when I was in boarding school, I worked at an inner city day camp. College summer jobs included reading proofs for a suburban newspaper and being grunt at a New York fashion magazine. I was taught to appreciate, be responsible and productive, but the money issue is never far away, and I feel if I drop my guard, it will bury me. In the last couple of years, my dates suddenly became different people when they learned of the family's wealth. I discovered money makes one treat people differently, too. So, it's not just others who change, it's me as well. I wanted to delay telling you until I was sure it wouldn't change us, to be sure the Elliot Swan I'd fallen in love with wouldn't be a different man. But I blew it and I'm sorry."

"I guess we were both concentrating on problems that didn't exist until we made them up," he said. "I'm as sorry as can be because I must have hurt you and I never wanted to."

"Do you feel we have a reason to save this love?"

"More than ever," he said, finding his wonderful smile lost for a day.

"So what do we do next?" she asked.

"Keep talking. Do you think I could fetch my mattress out of the pilothouse?"

Chapter 18

She was awakened by the motion of the tug as it rose and fell in a partial perpendicular course over the swells. The rising sun, still low enough to make a full, direct entry into the cabin portholes, flooded the space as Alex had never noticed it before. She rolled over to look at the indentations in the mattress next to hers where Elliot had slept. She touched his pillow as she might stroke his forehead and was thankful for reconciliation; more than that, much more than that; indebted to whomever guards lovers for the survival of two whose passions overtook them but could not break their bond.

When she'd washed and dressed, she took their breakfast to the pilothouse to find Elliot tracking a school of porpoises.

"Good morning," she said, going to kiss him.

"Good morning, love. We're on our way to Daytona Beach—about six hours away," he said, taking the cup of coffee she offered him. "See the porpoises? They've been running alongside since we started."

"They're so playful, almost makes you want to get in the water with them."

"There was a story, supposedly true, that Aristotle Onassis was entertaining some people on his yacht in the Mediterranean when a guest accidentally dropped her dinner plate into a school waiting for food scraps. One of the porpoises caught the plate on its snout and juggled it for several minutes. When Onassis saw this amused the guests, he ordered his steward to bring a set of plates on deck for all to play catch with the porpoises."

"I don't believe you." Alex laughed and drew near for a kiss. "Do you realize you took my half of the bed last night?"

"Oh yes. That's the half I wanted," he replied with a smile, helping himself to another piece of toast. He studied it for a moment and added, "I never knew it could be so much fun to look over burnt toast at someone special."

"I never before in my life burned toast," Alex replied.

"That only shows how easily you can be distracted."

In less than half an hour, they'd be off the coast of Daytona Beach. Alex, now at the wheel, traced with Elliot the nearly ruler-straight coastline and the quarter-mile wide parallel strip offshore that opened to Port Orange, the ocean access to Daytona Beach. When they drew near their destinations, sea traffic consisting mostly of non-commercial vessels picked up, suggesting there was an outside chance a trash reception facility might accompany a waste discharge center required by so many boats.

Waved out of the port within minutes and with no need to go ashore for supplies, the incident was noted in the log and they set course for Titusville, an afternoon's sail away. They moored en route for the night, ate supper then went to bed, planning for an early start. For a while they lay in bed listening to night sounds. Somewhere, a good distance away, the horn of a ship made its presence known to anyone interested.

"Alex, may I ask you something?" he said and without waiting for her response went on. "Why don't you simply accept the reality your family is wealthy and someday you may be too? Why try to hide from it? You know you can't. You must know you are an extraordinary person, rich or not. You're certainly smart enough to know when someone defers to you because of your money; they'll probably never understand you, and you're probably better off without them."

"I wish it were that easy. Think of how the tabloid disclosure affected you."

"Score! I know I wasn't a great test case. I'm still trying to sort out why I acted as I did. I told myself it was because you didn't trust me and that was partly right, but it was mostly because I couldn't compete with such wealth and I was afraid if I tried, I'd lose. But I'm learning my misunderstandings don't get straightened out if I don't talk them through."

"And I've learned I can never love or be loved if I duck the tough questions and answers."

They grew silent, knowing there would be other times to explore risky matters, but they were finished for now.

"Good night, Alex dear. Do you think we'll ever get rid of the garbage?" he asked.

"Oh yes," she replied.

In two days and one hundred plus miles of sailing from Titusville to Melbourne and Fort Pierce harbors, no facilities could or would accept the garbage. If the mission was a failure, they at least found some consolation in the weather and watching the southeastern coast of the United States pass in an endless panorama. Scores of resorts, retirement complexes, tournament fishing sites and government installations blurred in a disorganized mass, with only NASA's Space Center in a distinct locale. At one point, Elliot remarked he'd never looked at so much and seen so little.

"Do you want to keep up this futile voyage?" he asked Alex.

"Sure, we have the entire Gulf Coast of Florida left before we go on to Alabama, Louisiana and then Texas."

"Seriously, Alex, at some point we have to say enough is enough."

"But that still doesn't get rid of the junk, and you have a deal with Jim Steele. Tell you what. Let's stop at Palm Beach and—"

Elliot interrupted her with, "They don't know what garbage is in Palm Beach. Even I know that."

"Let me finish. We'll stop at Palm Beach and stock up on food. I'll file my story and come back and cook us a nice dinner. Then we can talk about it."

Palm Beach, an ambience still to be reckoned with, was in the 1970s more a state of mind than today's vulgar ne plus ultra of conspicuous consumption. The achievement of a residential address acceptable to the establishment's arbiter of manners conveys a prized cachet to heads of households and domestic staffs as well. Thus, Barney Mulligan and Monique Christophe had reason to take pride in being employed by a certain Wall Street type whose marauding sorties were unknown to most and forgiven by a stylish few titillated by knowing a twentieth century pirate. Barney Mulligan, an extroverted, blue-eyed, blond Irishman, was a compelling figure in his precisely-pressed, navy blue, chauffeur's uniform, glistening black shoes and shiny, patent leather, visored cap. An automobile mechanic before ascending to a more prestigious employment, he maintained the household's vehicles at peak performance. Barney was also a ladies' man whose dalliances were seldom discouraged by the hour or venue. Before long, he'd earned the confidence of his employer to act as his factotum on trips to New York where appetites he was unaware of were awakened.

Monique Christophe from Haiti arrived in the United States a year or two after Barney was hired by the Wall Streeter and began work as a maid at the same address. Her limited English belied she was street smart and gifted with a keen intuition, allowing her to exploit the commonplace. As she grew out of her teens to beautiful, voluptuous womanhood, Barney planned another seduction, which over time he was surprised to learn she'd deftly turned into a courtship proceeding at her pace.

Frustrated by his failure to scale the battlement with a frontal attack, Barney changed to underground tactics by enthusiastically agreeing to teach Monique English and in turn learn to speak Creole. Linguistically, the enterprise was a limited success, both finding entrenched generic pronunciations impossible to overcome; however, Barney's wandering eye became confined to only taking respectful measure of one subject. Barney's having told her as much gave both the comfort of accomplishment, yet the tension of denying their sexual drives was never absent. One Sunday afternoon, having helped the boss and his wife board a plane for New York, Barney returned to find the house vacant except for Monique in the steamy laundry room washing the bed clothes of several weekend guests. For a moment he stood in the doorway of the laundry unnoticed by Monique as she emptied and refilled the washing machines. Her thin dress, plastered against her hips and breasts by the humidity, epitomized animal sensuality with every motion. She straightened from her work to wipe a loose strand of hair from her face, opened the top buttons of her dress to cool her body and then saw Barney. At once it was a foregone conclusion they would collide in a primal ritual, abandoning all the manners they'd practiced for so long. In a continuous motion he swept Monique up onto the folding counter and mounted her while she stripped him of his clothing. For three hours they drove their bodies, then fell apart to sleep and never again lie together.

In nine months, Monique delivered Jesus Christophe Mulligan, a boy with a middle name for his mother, a surname for his father and a given name for the only character Barney could recall from his childhood Catholicism. For three years, Monique and Barney relied on their friendship to keep watch over their son. Then one day in halting English, she told Barney what he already knew—they'd never be in love. He kissed his son, said goodbye to Monique and Jesus Christophe, and left, promising to send monthly expense money which he faithfully honored.

From early childhood, Jesus Christophe showed an inclination towards mechanical objects and disassembled many to learn how they worked; reassembling them was most often unsuccessful but never discouraged him from continuing to satisfy his curiosity. Those experiments that didn't threaten life or limb of mother or son were viewed as the child's precociousness, and the failures were considered an inheritance from his father.

By ten, Jesus Christophe had discovered the wonders of the boatyards where rich and famous, ignorant of things done manually, entrusted with blind faith boats worth millions of dollars to those they rarely saw. In Jesus Christophe's mid-teens, his café au lait coloring, soulful eyes and mile-wide smile disarmed young and old alike, perhaps predicting he'd also inherit Barney's delivery of malarkey but with a West Indian accent. On his eighteenth birthday, Jesus Christophe received a present from his father...the last of Barney's checks and the parent's final communication. Mother and son understood this was Barney's way of saying he'd fulfilled his obligation and the boy was old enough now to take care of his mother and himself.

As college was no longer an option, Jesus Christophe enrolled in a trade school and extended the hours of his part-time job while Monique continued to work at the Wall Streeter's mansion. When the time came for Jesus Christophe to choose specialized courses at the trade school, he elected combustion engines with emphasis on vessels' diesel power plants. Intelligent, quick, industrious and knowledgeable in marine engines, he was found in demand by many of the regional marinas, but he only sought employment at and was hired by the upper scale yards in Palm Beach.

It took no time for him to discover the fleet of Palm Beach, sea-going pleasure boats was owned more for pleasure than going to sea. The marina was often filled with yachts of all descriptions at anchor, arranged by the wind in precise order to display their desirability much like an automobile showroom featured its most exotic models to tantalize lesser folks. The boats, however, did not go unoccupied, for those wearied with entertaining in the opulence of their shoreline residence could easily transport their festivities to a yacht. These adoptive vessels, if anchored on the perimeter of the flotilla, were often the site of skeet shooting contests and assignations. It is no wonder then that Jesus Christophe, a charming, good-looking and non-violent shipwright, would be sought by some to cuckold their husbands.

Still single at thirty-five and living in the apartment he and his mother had occupied before Monique moved back to Haiti, his salary had advanced to provide his mother's retirement and a comfortable bachelor's existence. Occasionally he thought if he didn't marry he might also go to live in Haiti when he neared retirement and help an impoverished people in their struggle for survival. At this stage in his life, he was not lacking in female companionship, but he realized he was isolating himself from a potential soul-mate with the easy satisfaction of paramours. But this dilemma was resolved one day, perhaps not in the way Jesus Christophe would have chosen, but with unmistakable finality.

The Monday afternoon was warm but not humid when Jesus Christophe was dispatched to a yacht anchored a half-mile off the Palm Beach shore. He arrived to find no one aboard but the owner's wife taking a sunbath. Within a few minutes, he'd made the necessary adjustments to the engine and came up on deck to find it empty but heard her call him from inside the lounge. Temporarily blinded by the sun, Jesus Christophe did not at first see her standing at the bar in the corner. Then, as his eyes adjusted, she turned naked, holding out a drink to him. She told him she was out there all by herself until the next afternoon and was lonely. There was little other conversation until he took her and they both fell asleep, shortly to be awakened by the voices of several men coming aboard.

"Honey," one called, "I'm back early. Did you get the engine fixed? Honey, where are you? We're going to shoot some skeet off the after deck."

"My God," the wife said, "Hal's back, you've got to go."

Jesus Christophe was pulling on his pants when the husband entered the lounge.

"You son of a bitch," the husband yelled at Jesus Christophe. "I'll fix you so you don't rape anymore women. I'll blow your balls off with my shotgun."

As the husband turned to get his gun, Jesus Christophe ran into him, knocking him down. By the time he'd recovered, Jesus Christophe had dived off the yacht and was swimming at full speed out to sea. Volley after volley of bird shot spattered the water as the shooter, all the time screaming oaths, tried to find the right range.

Jesus Christophe, now out of shotgun range from the yacht, heard the men arguing over following him with the motorboat and shooting him or chasing him out to sea till he drowned from exhaustion. Several times the motorboat engine coughed from flooding before it kicked in and their search began. Jesus Christophe changed direction and swam furiously farther from the shore as the men, now shouting their disagreements, kept changing the course. He was now nearly a mile offshore when a second outboard, making putt-putt sounds, cut across about three hundred yards in front of him to head towards a tug pulling a barge loaded with garbage. Jesus Christophe floated for a moment to catch his breath and saw the husband's boat making slow, large arcs as they expanded their hunt. He turned to swim away from the men and directly towards the two vessels now stopped to take a woman and the motorboat aboard.

In one last effort, Jesus Christophe reached the barge, climbed on and hid behind a bale of garbage. He lay gasping, taking great gulps of air, his lungs burning, fighting off stomach cramps and nausea, then he passed out. As his body returned to normal, a heavy sleep settled on him. When he first awoke, disoriented by the stench and rolling motion, his impression was that of a bad dream, a lynching or worse awaiting if captured, then the reality he'd found sanctuary in a heap of garbage. He disentangled himself from trash he'd piled around him, becoming aware that the barge was moving at a moderate speed. Cautiously, he stuck his head out of the hole that hid him to discover in the early morning light he was out at sea with no land in sight.

Chapter 19

On an early morning embarkment to a destination unknown, they again ate breakfast in the pilothouse, indulging in melon, proscuitto, croissants, blackberry preserves and coffee, a tribute to Alex's creative shopping to break the monotony of most sea fare.

"By the way," he said, "what were the men in the motorboat doing yesterday?"

"They said they'd lost something and were circling, hoping to find it. One acted as though he'd been drinking."

"Palm Beach is certainly impressive-looking from the sea. I've heard so much about it, I'm sorry I couldn't go ashore," he remarked.

"They surely know how to overcharge everything. I felt held up with the prices they get for food. At home, I could have bought twice as much for what I paid in the gourmet market I visited. I saw no supermarkets, everything is gourmet here. I hate the way all that money is wasted just to keep up."

"That's the way, Alex. Give 'em hell," he said.

"I mean it," she said, getting incensed in reliving the experience.

"I know you do," Elliot replied, drawing her to him for a hug. "I'm glad you remembered to call me from the store so I could give you the tug's new position. The harbor people bordered on being nasty about my mooring long enough for you to get back to the tug."

"I'll bet the natives have such an exalted view of themselves, they believe the Gulf Stream current was raised above the surrounding ocean level in their honor."

"You have to admit that's pretty extraordinary. I would never have believed it if I hadn't seen it," Elliot replied.

Another tourist-poster-perfect day accompanied their journey; dazzling blue sky, whispering soft winds and miniature white caps breaking on a jade sea temporarily diverted them from thoughts of their weary business. When the tug rolled at just the right angle, the couple could see flashes of light reflected from the windows of buildings along the distant shore, like semaphores guiding the way.

"Where shall we stop today, Alex? I'm in no hurry to reach Miami; I've seen enough of it on TV."

"Let's pull in closer to the coast and if anything looks promising; we can land and inquire."

"It just occurred to me, I've been going at this thing in the wrong way."

"How's that?"

"Why didn't I think of this sooner? You should make the contacts with the port authorities in person. How can they refuse a beautiful woman?"

"That's sexist, but it might work."

"Let's give it a try," Elliot said as he steered towards Delray Beach.

The day only got better, and the prospect of being turned down by Delray's authorities almost convinced them to skip the town. When they pulled in toward the shore, seeking signs of their objective, even from three miles out they could see traffic jams of pleasure boats and the wall-to-wall tanned bodies confirming this was an all-play-and-no-work community—leftovers from Palm Beach, Alex called it.

"So much for Delray," Alex said as they swung out to sea.

There was a third party, undetected but equally disappointed the barge didn't make port or come close enough to swim for it. Jesus Christophe was hot, thirsty and smelly. He'd not eaten since lunch the previous day, and even his unslaked thirst seemed petty compared to the stinking hideout's insult to his high standards for personal hygiene. It was inconceivable any skipper would haul a load of garbage along the coast behind him on a pleasure cruise. Whatever the skipper's reason for port hopping, Jesus Christophe would stay alert to take the first opportunity for jumping ship. Yesterday's exertion had exhausted him, sleeping as though drugged till morning, so he had no idea if the tug sailed all night or anchored offshore. He'd peeked from his hole a couple of times to see the woman who boarded the tug yesterday and caught several glimpses of what appeared to be the only man, whose voice he'd heard. Hearing no other voices, he assumed there were only two aboard and therefore they sailed only during daylight hours.

It was clear that he could not return to Palm Beach under any circumstances. The marina would be madder than hell at him for jeopardizing a customer's business and leaving the company's outboard at the yacht he'd gone to repair. They'd probably hold back mailing his pay, and he'd need a P.O. box so that mad man with the shotgun didn't trace him. His girlfriend could pick up his clothes at the apartment he'd sublet and have his car till things were straightened out. For now he had to find some way to get ashore.

"We never finished our talk about what we should do when the East Coast real estate runs out," Alex reminded him.

"You're right and that's probably because I haven't any new ideas. It's been about two months since I left New York and there's nothing to show for it," Elliot replied, getting serious.

"What would you think of slowing down to creep along the coast and scout out every city and town till we reach the Keys and if we haven't hit the jackpot by then, call the Steele Company?"

"It's possible by now the city has its EPA-approved incinerator working and they'll take the junk back. It never occurred to me before because money's never been raised by trash depots, but maybe we're paying too little to have anyone take this stuff off our hands. We probably should discuss it with Jim Steele. This crazy trip must end someplace worthwhile."

"Oh, it hasn't been a total loss," Alex said with a wicked smile.

In silent accord with Alex's suggestion, Elliot cut back the tug's speed to crawl along the coast, viewing an endless succession of seaside homes and resorts but no indication of a trash depot. Water traffic, heavier than usual, cautioned them it would be prudent to find a place to moor for the night as locations were becoming fewer and farther apart. They chose an anchorage two miles out from Boca Raton, a Spanish-named shore town which Alex had heard meant 'Mouth of the Mouse.' Edified by this revelation, Elliot remarked the phrase was so difficult to say quickly in a tongue-twister contest and visually disagreeable to contemplate, any foreign language offered a better name.

At the other end of the tether, that connector of tug and barge, there was one who found no amusement in his domain of five hundred tons of garbage or any other circumstances of his existence. A cautious surveillance of his surroundings when the vessels dropped anchors convinced Jesus Christophe he was again too far from shore to swim out of his predicament and a more creative strategy for survival and escape was imperative.

Jesus Christophe, a deliberate and cunning man of unusual intelligence as well as sex drive, rarely dropped his guard, except with women, which until yesterday had not been life threatening. That catalytic incident had accelerated a series of experienced hardships and grave perils threatening his life and limb. Denying the urgency of his body's demands, he carefully planned the first step towards liberation. Late at night he would slip into the ocean to wash away as much garbage stench as possible from his clothes and body. Then he'd board the tug moored adjacent to the barge and make sure there was no one on deck before entering the galley. He prayed it would be unlocked and didn't squeak from the salt air. Familiar with many tugs' interiors, he assumed the couple's berths were separated from the galley. If the bunk cabin was part of the galley, he'd be forced to carry out his mid-night requisitioning while they slept nearby or go hungry. As his hunger grew, his appetite for risk increased and he knew there was no turning back. Although he was famished, he'd be careful, very careful, taking only small quantities of any given food to make the shrinkage less detectable and if time allowed, squirt dish soap all over him so he could later wash away the residual stink.

It was a perfect night for a robbery, moonless, the constant slapping of waves against the hull an inducement to sleep and a cover for foot pads. Elliot and Alex, following the protocols of most Americans, left the galley unlocked. Fortune favored Jesus Christophe because the sleeping quarters were separate from the galley, although the bulkhead between the two was open, revealing the couple lying on mattresses spread at the foot of the bunks. Jean Christophe quickly found the stores, selected those that needed no preparation and demonstrated monumental restraint in limiting his pilfering. A couple of times one of the sleepers' breathing cadence changed, as though signaling wakefulness, freezing Jesus Christophe in his tracks until the steady rhythm returned. Bundling the loot in his shirt, the night visitor left the galley after flooding his thirst and silently withdrew under the cover of night.

He was ravenous but forced himself to eat slowly, knowing digestion worked better on an empty stomach if food wasn't gulped. With hunger and thirst at least temporarily satisfied, Jesus Christophe turned his attention to longer term considerations. Somehow he must learn where the barge was being taken. From his hurried inspection in daylight, the stuff was baled with no consideration given to vegetable/animal matter, plastics, glass, metal or paper. The surface of the mass had either been eaten away by gulls or shrunken by dehydration, exposing the more solid ingredients. Bottles, pipes, toasters, bicycle wheels, shoes, batteries, buckets, a washing machine, radios, towels all scrambled together in a thirty-feet high, surrealistic sculpture. Jesus Christophe reflected for a minute on people who discarded so many of these objects before they were worn out.

"Darling," Alex called to Elliot in the shower, "if you're in no rush to get under way, let's have breakfast here in the galley."

"Good idea," Elliot said, entering the galley wrapped in a towel. "It's pretty smelly in here. I was sure we anchored upwind from the barge. I wonder if the wind shifted during the night. Temperature changes can cause a hundred and eighty degree swing, you know."

Elliot stuck his head out the hatch and reported the pennant was blowing away from the pole in the same direction as the previous evening. He dressed, made a cursory inspection of the tug and returned to the galley.

"Have you been snacking?" Alex asked him.

"No, why?"

"I could swear we had six croissants and two melons left from yesterday's breakfast, and now there are only three croissants and half a melon. You sure you don't eat in your sleep like some people walk in their sleep?"

"How about you? Are you pregnant and eating for two?"

"No, you silly man. Sit down and let's eat."

Close inspection of Oakland Park, like Pompano Beach, Deerfield Beach and Boca Raton before it, disclosed a monotony of disappointment. This heavily populated strip of Florida was punctuated with golf courses relieving the myriad of buildings shouldering their way to the sea, but there was no sign of relief for Elliot's wandering. Fort Lauderdale, often called the Venice of the South because of its canals and foot bridges, was port of call for multiple international shipping lines, but its extensive harbor facilities did not include garbage processing. Another day had been wasted in this futile search, adding one more failing mark to the log.

Heavy ocean traffic and the time dictated a mid-afternoon mooring with Miami, the next day's destination. Two to three miles off shore they dropped anchor, careful to be upwind from the barge, watched the sun's shadows change the profiles of the coast before withdrawing to the galley to take turns reading *Moby Dick* aloud to each other. Elliot admitted his loss of patience with their endeavor, which was not as traumatic as Captain Ahab losing a leg, but it might be damn close. They no longer talked of what their individual lives would be like when the voyage was completed, but what they would do together.

Concealed by a hollow in his putrid sanctuary, Jesus Christophe was being revisited by hunger and thirst, bedfellows of a plaguing uncertainty in his future. Still apprehensive about being caught if he reached land, he invented different disguises to change his physical identity, but there was no perfect solution to avoid detection from records other than going underground as an undocumented alien. Maybe Miami's large population of Cuban refugees would absorb him until he invented a new persona. Although his preparations for freedom consumed most of his time not invaded by thought of food, drink and bathing, he was aware of his continuing ambivalence about carrying out his schemes for escape. As the coupled tug and barge again lay too far out to reach land except by boat, Jesus Christophe, now growing desperate, decided to make a run for it late that night in the putt-putt. He convinced himself he would not be stealing but only borrowing the boat and would tell one of the marinas it had slipped its mooring and belonged to the tug out there.

Suppertime that evening was particularly tormenting for Jesus Christophe as the aroma of hearty food carried downwind to him from the tug's galley. By nine p.m., he was restless, by ten agitated and then the lights in the galley went out, giving him hope the couple would soon be asleep.

Although uncertain if he'd waited long enough for night's first deep sleep to have its full effect on the couple, he made his move, noiselessly pulling himself onto the tug's deck. A quick scan of the tug assured him he was alone as he hurried to the putt-putt, hanging secure on davits above the water. Scrambling into the small craft, he prepared to lower it but discovered the key to the engine was not in the ignition. Temporarily foiled, the idea that crossing the starter wires might solve the problem became unrealistic when he saw there were no tools in the small boat to open the engine's casing. All seemed hopeless, knowing he must return to the barge and wait another day for another opportunity, but the nagging hunger and thirst repossessed him. He would have to steal more food.

It was another moonless night, with no contrasts of light and shadows to expose his thievery, but such darkness also decreased his visibility to locate things and increased perils and opportunities in equal but opposite proportions. Whether carelessness or decreased visual acuity was the undoing of Jesus Christophe will never be known; the result was the same.

He entered the galley to hear the regular breathing of the sleeping couple, felt his way along the counter to the bread box and took half a loaf. Next he found a can of tuna fish with an opening tab attached to the lid and was about to add a bottle of beer to his loot when he accidentally knocked a spoon from the drain board onto the floor. Jesus Christophe froze as he heard the breathing of one sleeper change in restlessness.

Then the woman whispered, "Elliot, wake up, wake up."

"What is it?" the sleepy male voice asked.

"Did you hear that noise?" she asked.

"No. Go back to sleep. You're probably dreaming."

Silence followed, but the new tempo of the woman's breathing indicated only the man had gone back to sleep. As Jesus Christophe backed from the sink to leave the galley, there was a crunching noise as he stepped on the fallen spoon.

"Elliot," the woman said, "There's another noise, something's in here."

"Meow," Jesus Christophe volunteered, unable to think of anything else to do.

"That's only a cat," Elliot said.

"We don't have a cat," Alex replied with some irritation.

"My God, we don't," Elliot said, jumping up from the floor, brandishing the copy of *Moby Dick*, the only assault object available, as Alex turned on the cabin lights.

"Please, Mister, I didn't mean any harm," said Jesus Christophe, cowering against the bulkhead. "I just wanted something to eat. See. Here, I'll put it back and be out of here in a flash."

"Don't leave or I'll crown you," Elliot threatened, waving *Moby Dick* in the air. "Where did you come from?"

"From that garbage barge."

"Don't try to fool me. Who are you?"

"Jesus Christophe."

"Now I've heard about all the foolishness I want to hear. Who the hell are you?"

"Honestly, Mister, I'm Jesus Christophe."

"And the next thing you're going to tell me is you walked here."

"No, Mister, I swam."

"You swam? From where?"

"When you were anchored outside Palm Beach, I swam out to the barge."

"For God's sakes, why?"

"To get away from a bunch of men who wanted to kill me."

"Why did they want to kill you?"

"For getting too sociable with one of their women. I swam out to your barge to get away from them, and then you took off before I could get off and none of your anchorages were close enough to shore for me to swim back, so I've been living in the garbage."

"Yes, you do smell disgusting."

"Ask him if he came in the cabin last night and took the croissants and melons," Alex said as though she didn't have immediate access to cross examine Jesus Christophe.

"You say your name is Jesus Christophe?"

"Not really, it's Jesus Christophe Mulligan, but I hardly ever use the last name since my father left home thirty years ago."

"You know, Alex, this whole trip is like a dream. I pull people out of the ocean with unbelievable stories, with unreal names and I never get to where I'm going."

"Where are you going, Mister?"

"To all the ports along Florida's coast till I get rid of that garbage. Wait a minute, I'm asking the questions here. How do I know you're not a drug dealer or a murderer or some other criminal?"

"Because if I wanted to steal the tug, I could have knocked you both out last night, dumped you in the ocean and taken off with the tug."

"But you don't know anything about tugs."

"Oh yes, Mister, I've been working in marinas for years and I studied marine diesels in trade school. And, by the way, I can tell your engine is running a little rough and needs to be checked."

"I can't stand that smell anymore," Alex said, "You're going to make me sick. Jump in the ocean and wash away as much as you can, then come back and take a shower. I'll wash your clothes and you can wrap up in a blanket until they dry."

"Oh Missy, you're a very kind lady," Jesus Christophe said, heading out of the cabin happy at the prospect of being clean.

"Don't you think you're showing just a little too much compassion?" Elliot asked. "We don't even know he's not a killer."

"He doesn't give us many choices. I could pilot the tug and you might overpower him then throw him overboard when he's least expecting it. We could make him go back to the barge, pull close to land and let him swim in if the sharks don't get him or—" and she paused to emphasize what she believed was most practical and humane, "or we can let him get clean and fed. He'll probably be more open if we treat him kindly; and think about it, where can he go in a blanket?"

"What are we going to do with him the rest of the night?" Elliot asked, not convinced Jesus Christophe could be so easily immobilized.

"Let him sleep on deck. There are no keys in the pilothouse to start the tug, and we'll lock the cabin so he can't get in," Alex replied. "Could you go back to sleep now you're so awake? I know I can't."

"I guess you're right, but don't get close enough for him to grab you, and hide the kitchen knives," Elliot counseled just before Jesus Christophe came into the cabin.

"I'm sorry to get your deck wet," Jesus Christophe apologized, "I'll clean it up as soon as I get showered."

"He's a neat devil," Elliot remarked. "I'll give him that."

"Ssh, he can hear you."

"Here are my clothes, Missy," Jesus Christophe called as he held them through an opening in the shower curtain to Alex.

"They really do stink," Alex said, loading them into the washing machine.

Wrapped in a blanket with a certain regal dignity, Jesus Christophe devoured in great mouthfuls the food Alex put before him.

"You'd better slow down, Jesus Christophe, or you'll be sick."

"Thank you, Missy. You are very kind and I would like to repay you when I get settled."

"Will you return to Palm Beach?"

"No. I can never do that. The crazy man searching for me in the harbor would kill me. You know they always blame the man for fooling around with a woman, but she wanted it so bad she made the first move," Jesus Christophe confessed, sensing he'd found a sympathetic ear.

"Well, we won't go into that," Alex replied. "Where were you heading when you boarded the barge?"

"I hadn't even thought about it. I only wanted to get away from the husband with the shotgun."

"And where do you think you'll go from here?"

"I'm not sure. Maybe Miami. Probably a port city because boats are all I know about to make a living. You've been as nice to me as anyone ever been, Missy. I'll be off the boat at first chance so I don't trouble you and your Mister no more. Now I know I kept you awake too long already. I'll sleep on deck if you don't mind so you can go back to bed. You can lock me out, you know, if you and Mister is concerned. So I'll say good night to you, Missy and Mister."

"Good night, Jesus Christophe," Alex said.

"Jesus Christophe," Elliot began, "I, well, I find that name a bit awkward. Is there something else we could call you?"

"Call me J.C. if you like, Mister," he said, leaving the cabin to sleep by the pilothouse.

When J.C. had gone, Alex snuggled close to Elliot and asked, "Do you think I was running away when you pulled me out of the ocean? I was wondering if I was afraid I'd be caught by the entanglements of all that money chasing me the same way J.C. was trying to escape the men who were out to get him."

"Don't you think that's a Freudian stretch?"

"Perhaps, but I can really relate to J.C."

"That's probably because you are both waterlogged."

Alex punched Elliot in the ribs and said, "You're an impossible misanthrope. Good night, darling."

"Time for breakfast," Alex called to J.C. sitting on a hatch watching the gulls flock over the barge. "Come in and put on your clean clothes and we'll eat."

"Good morning, Missy. Good morning, Mister," J. C. said and bowed his head over the plate as he had last night before beginning to eat. His eyes showed his satisfaction with the meal, but he didn't speak until he finished eating.

"Thank you, Missy." Then he turned his attention to Elliot. "Mister, what do you plan to do with that garbage?"

"You asked me that last night, and I don't have a better answer this morning. Keep looking for a processing facility."

"You may be a long time looking," J.C. replied, "That's mixed junk, and I don't know of any port on the coast that takes throwaways of everything all jumbled up. The Sanitation or Public Works used to separate the stuff, but they stopped and the public has to do that job now and if it isn't separated, they won't take it. I hear they get so much plastic and paper, it's swamping the recycling plants."

"You seem to know a lot about the problem," Elliot said.

"Mister, it just makes common sense, everything is done up in fancy packages that you just throw away. When I first started at the boatyard, if I needed a tool I'd pick one out from where they were hanging on a nail in the wall in the hardware store. Now it comes in a hard plastic package wrapped in a cardboard box. No wonder the dumps are filled up."

"I agree, it seems stupid the way safety packages have gone from medicines to hammers," Elliot replied.

"And another thing, everybody's got to have the newest and an extra one. In Palm Beach, I never saw anything thrown away because it was worn out, and nothing broken ever gets fixed. Just get a new one."

"How is knowing this going to solve my problem?" Elliot asked, unable to see the relevance of J.C.'s discourse.

"If you think about it, the world's richest countries are to blame, especially us. Third world countries do without or find new uses for stuff we throw away. In a Palm Beach store I saw a beautiful basket made from used wire. For two days I sat in your garbage and thought about not being caught by the man with the gun or how hungry I was getting. To take my mind away, I began looking at the reusables sticking out of the garbage…bottles, tools, rubber boots, radios, brushes, plastics, tin cans. You name it, some stuff third world countries might use, poor countries like Haiti, where my mother lives. That got me to wondering, why don't Mister go to one of these poor countries?"

"That's an idea, J.C. That's worth thinking about. And you know we'll pay fifty dollars a ton or twenty-five thousand dollars for the whole load."

"For that they'll take all the junk whether or not they can reuse any of it," J.C. said, "I guarantee it."

"Now about you. If I can get rid of the load at any Atlantic port, you leave too. If I don't, I'll try the islands, Haiti included."

"You got a deal, Mister. I also want to pay you back for everything so far. If you pull into the first boatyard we see, I'll be sure your engine is okay."

"Deal?" Elliot asked.

"Deal," J.C. confirmed.

Chapter 20

A little later when Alex and Elliot were alone in the pilothouse looking for a boatyard in the Miami area, he said, "I'm feeling better about J.C., but I wonder if he really knows marine diesels as much as he claims."

"How are you going to find out?"

"I think I'll stop at the first big yard and have them check the engine while J.C. and I watch. If they tell me something needs adjustment or repair and it agrees with what J.C. has already diagnosed, there's a good chance he knows what he's doing."

"Are you going to put him off the boat if he's wrong?" Alex asked.

"No. I made a deal with him that he must leave only if we get rid of the garbage before we reach the Keys."

"You're a fair man, Captain," Alex teased. "I listened carefully to you two talking, and I'd say you're both getting to know each other."

"He certainly makes up for his limited education with above-average intelligence, and I'm less wary about him being dangerous. The idea that one of the islands would take the load is worth considering."

"Why not try to phone his mother and see if Haiti is interested? J.C. probably knows how to reach her, and she can check out the locals."

"Sometimes you're so logical you astound me," he said.

Boats entering and departing from coastal harbors to sail Elliot's course were so numerous he was forced to continually adjust engine power and in this process, he heard a noise unnoticeable before.

"What's that whine?" he called to J.C. polishing bright-ware around the pilothouse.

"That's what I mentioned to you earlier. We should check it out at the next big boatyard."

A few miles further a large, busy commercial yard dominating a marina offered the expertise they wanted. When docked, Alex left to file her story with the *Times* and shop for provisions. By mid-afternoon, the yard mechanic had diagnosed and adjusted the engine exactly as J.C. would have done, Alex's expedition was successfully completed, and they were ready to leave. Elliot received the gloomy news there was no garbage reception center in the greater metropolitan area, and their cargo was subject to the all-too-familiar derision from several groups of tacky Miami natives as they prepared to leave the yard.

J. C., keeping quiet about his engine diagnosis being questioned, dismissed the slight with Elliot's sincere apology.

"I'm sorry I didn't trust your judgment, but I had to be sure I could believe you. I can understand if I insulted you and you wish to get off the tug while we're still in port, but I'd like you to stay."

"Maybe this is how we become good friends," J.C. replied. "I'd like to stay with our original agreement so we can all decide what to do when we reach Key Largo."

"There are only a couple more possibilities such as Coral Gables for offloading the garbage," Elliot reminded J.C.

"I think it would be wise to try and contact my mother right now so we know our chances in Haiti."

"Let's do it," Elliot said, letting J.C. take over the ship-to-shore phone.

The moon was rising as they dropped anchor off Key Largo, the largest vertebra of Florida's spinal column reaching into the Gulf of

Mexico. One hundred miles of elevated concrete, designated Highway One, clung to near sea-level isles, providing a lifeline along a gentle curve from Miami to Key West. To the casual observer, a few miles offshore, the phenomenon of parallax created the illusion cars traveling along this route were airborne.

They now reached the time and place to commit to one of two courses—a voyage to Haiti, offering the possibility of at last being freed of their onerous burden subject to the caprices of strangers, or the alternative route which lay along the western coast of Florida and states bordering the Gulf of Mexico's coast where prospects seemed no greater than the ports they'd already investigated. J.C., anxious about Elliot's decision, never tried to influence the outcome, although this week's events forced him to consider if he was a drifter. Would returning to his Haitian roots help him start over? But before the magic of metamorphosis empowered J.C. to exchange an old environment for a new, other matters needed attention, not the least of which was Haiti's willingness to accept the garbage and Jim Steele's approval for Elliot to travel there.

First things first, thought Elliot as he started the laborious process of seeking Haiti's official approval to unload their cargo. Reaching Monique, J.C.'s mother, on the island's antiquated telephone system took monumental patience. After several unsuccessful attempts, son and mother were connected and, consistent with the West Indian temperament, a lengthy conversation ensued dedicated to a detailed report of the status and welfare of countless relatives. At last the subject of garbage disposal was addressed, which Monique promised to bring to the attention of the town's fathers and get their response at once. Unreliable communications and entrenched Haitian bureaucracy conspired to test the Anglo-Saxon interpretation of 'immediately', but an agreement by both parties finally filtered through Monique's interpretation, and the tug's departure, subject to Jim Steele's blessing, would soon be underway. Although Elliot cautioned J.C. the trip could be delayed or canceled, the latter couldn't repress his excitement and encouraged Elliot and Alex to learn to dance the limbo which he continually demonstrated in preparation for Haiti's welcoming festivities. The phone conversation with Jim Steele was friendly but directed towards a factual report on the port-by-port experiences.

When he had all the information required to make a decision, Steele expressed gratitude for Elliot's perseverance and concluded saying, "I'm not a gambling man, but you've gone this far; let's try a little farther in view of Haiti's approval. And if they end up refusing the load, go dump it on Castro on your way home."

"We're going to Haiti," Elliot announced, and J.C. was so happy he limboed until his back nearly touched the deck.

The island of Cuba, approximately seven hundred and fifty miles long, lay at its nearest point ninety miles from Florida. Its varied topography, stretching from northwest to southeast, offered multiple opportunities in agriculture and natural resources. Its history has been marked with turbulence since Columbus first went ashore. On their course to Haiti, Elliot set the compass at one-hundred sixty-five degrees over open ocean to make landfall at Caibarian, a small village on Cuba's northeastern coast. This first leg of the voyage was about two hundred miles along the Great Bahama Banks before entering the Old Bahama Channel to hug the island's coast for another three-hundred eighty-miles to a point near Guantanamo at Cuba's easternmost tip. From there, the course would take them one hundred miles across the Windward Passage to Haiti.

Now confident that J.C. was trustworthy and had a vested interest in reaching Haiti, Elliot allowed him to pilot the tug in daylight hours. This arrangement gave Elliot periods to rest and skipper the tug later into the night, which he calculated might get them to their destination in six days. The passage along Cuba's northern coast was as pleasant and leisurely as a trip on any Caribbean cruise ship. The air, now golden but softened by each day's brief early morning shower, was conducive to congeniality and optimism. Traffic was occasional, but those aboard the tug were rarely distracted from the panorama of a tropical country passing by.

On the evening of the sixth day out of Key Largo as they rounded Cuba's easternmost shore to enter the Windward Passage, a fog thickened, convincing them to take shelter in a remote cove and postpone the crossing to Haiti till the next day.

After dropping anchor and setting the warning lights on the tug and barge, they ate another of Alex's creative suppers, half from the sea, half from the ship's stores. The anticipation of reaching Haiti within a day induced a state of euphoria in the trio. Elliot, as he handed each a bottle of beer, stated it was against his principles to drink with passengers or crew, but this one exception was justified. J.C. replied that this time tomorrow Elliot would be drinking native rum.

Being near his origins stimulated J.C. to play Haitian host, proudly recounting the wonders of his Motherland. Haiti, he explained, meant 'mountainous land' in the language of indigenous Arawak Indians. Once safe haven for pirates, the island gave way to French planters, and later rebellious slaves defeated British, French and Spanish armies to create the world's first Negro Republic. Near Cap de Paix, where the tug would make landfall, the historic fortress Citadel was located, attracting thousands of tourists annually. And like every country in need of a legend, there was one for Haiti: Henri Christophe, a waiter who became a king.

When asked if he was a descendant, J.C. answered, "Everyone in Haiti is named Christophe."

Occasionally the trio grew silent, transported to another world by the spectral night or the haunting call of a mist-muffled fog horn. J.C., sensing the drama of the mood, related tales passed down by his mother of voodoo and occult powers in this alien society they were soon to enter.

"Ahoy, there! Standby to be boarded," the voice bellowed through the dense fog.

Elliot tried to shake off the deep sleep such weather induced, unsure if this nautical hail was the conclusion of a dream energized by J.C.'s stories or if everything, including J.C., was fiction.

Then Elliot heard J.C. call out from the pilothouse where he'd slept, "Just a minute, sir, I'll call the Captain."

Elliot, now fully conscious, pulled on his pants and went up on deck to find a U.S. Navy cutter fifty feet off his port side.

"What do you want?" Elliot inquired.

"We're coming aboard for a search."

"A search for what?" Elliot persisted.

"Illegal and toxic materials," the deck officer replied. "Catch this line and secure us to your bow."

With a dramatic flourish, an arrogant junior officer jumped aboard to confront Elliot and J.C. as Alex came from the cabin to join them.

"Do you want to tell me what this is all about?" Elliot asked.

"Who am I addressing?" the lieutenant demanded without answering Elliot. "Where's your skipper?"

"I'm the skipper, Elliot Swan. Now tell me what this unwarranted intrusion of our privacy is all about or get off the boat."

The lieutenant seemed temporarily bewildered that anyone would challenge the authority of the U.S. Navy and apparently decided a more civil approach would expedite his assignment. "You have breached security and entered restricted waters around Guantanamo Naval Base, which automatically classifies you as a level one risk."

"Are you telling me a tug pulling a load of garbage that moors in a cover on a foggy night to get out of the sea lanes is a threat to your service? Come on now, lieutenant. The U.S. Navy can do better than that."

"Nevertheless, I'm commandeering your vessels and taking you into custody for a move into a designated safe area for a property search. Bosun Ruggles, you and Dilly come aboard and make sure Mr. Swan follows the cutter to Fail Safe Area Zero."

Boarding the tug, Ruggles hitched up his belt to pat the forty-five automatic pistol strapped to his waist to indicate he was prepared for any deviation from the lieutenant's orders. Dilly confined Alex and

J.C. to the cabin and the cutter, tug and barge formed a bizarre procession to Fail Safe Area Zero. Alex sensed the only way to appeal to their jailers during this trip to an undisclosed destination was to kill them with femininity and kindness. When the coffee was brewed, she put on her tightest sweater and pants and minced her way on deck.

"I thought I told you to stay in the cabin," Dilly said, his eyes contradicting his voice as they grew large with appreciation.

"I hope you don't mind, sir, but it's so cold and damp out here, a nice hot cup of coffee might taste good," Alex breathed her words heavily for extra effect.

"That's mighty nice of you, ma'am, but you should go back inside."

"Wouldn't your partner in the pilothouse like some? Maybe I could take a thermos full up to him. And as long as I was going up there, it couldn't hurt to take two cups so my skipper can have his morning coffee."

"Well, I guess that would be all right, but you'll have to stay in the cabin as soon as you're finished."

Admiral Titus Norwyn Thomas, a man of uncomplicated deliberation, reduced his modus operandi to a few simple axioms— show up, always volunteer, take cold baths, never look back and if you catch 'em, kill 'em. Graduating in the bottom ten percent of his class at the Academy, he advanced in rank at a relentless pace, rewarded by incompetent seniors for the substandard execution of his duties. As a pleb, his classmates called him Ty until they were subjected to his circumlocution, at first misconstrued as unusual enlightenment, but tiring at last they awarded him the nickname 'Windy'. Later still when he assumed command of junior officers in fear of his withering critiques, he was secretly referred to as 'Typhoon' Thomas. His command, unable to predict his idiosyncrasies, kept everything straight and simple, Spic and Span. It was no wonder, then, that the lieutenant, who apprehended the tug and barge, was following to the letter his Admiral's directive to let nothing other than fish into the waters around Guantanamo's Naval Base.

As the sun burned off the fog to announce a glorious day, the cutter, tug and barge presented a curious spectacle of contrasts ranging from spit and polish to abandoned filth. Fortunately, the procession faced the wind and was spared insult to its collective olfactory nerve.

Admiral 'Typhoon' Thomas pushed back from the breakfast table, to which he'd welcomed members of the Senate Appropriations Committee, and enjoyed a Cuban cigar with his guests. The august federal delegation had arrived only the night before, landing just as the fog closed down the airport. It was budget preparation time again, that annual period signaling legislators to awaken to their responsibilities and depart on a junket in the name of 'on-site reconnaissance'. It was, of course, the intention of many of these senators to return to the rigors of Washington fully energized by a restorative stop at Jamaica, the Bahamas or Florida, but for the present, they were savoring the power they exercised over the military by granting or withholding some defense project.

On this trip they'd gathered to review Admiral Thomas's security strategy. The morning's agenda scheduled a visual presentation in the briefing room to be followed by a fast water tour of some key areas surrounding the base. On signal given by the Admiral, copies of the plans for the morning's activities were passed to the committee members and they scattered from the breakfast table to do whatever people do before a meeting. They assembled again fifteen minutes later and were briefed with a variety of graphics for an hour and one half. The meeting was concluding with procedures established for intercepting any potential security risk in the ocean bordering the Naval Base, when an aide bent close to Admiral Thomas to inform him two suspicious vessels had entered restricted waters and were now being escorted by a cutter to Fail Safe Area Zero for search and interrogation. Seizing this as a fortuitous opportunity, the Admiral announced to the committee an incident had occurred for which this program now under discussion had been designed. He hoped seeing firsthand procedures for dealing with potential threats would justify his request for an additional appropriation.

Within the hour, the Admiral's high speed launch was provided with lunch and libations and the on-site reconnaissance was underway. Admiral Thomas stood most of the trip at the bow of the launch like a Viking icon describing the many accomplishments on the base despite underfunding, but most of his rhetoric was lost to the wind or the tranquilizing Bloody Marys. At last the bosun announced he'd picked up the silhouette of three vessels on the horizon. The Admiral called for full speed ahead and instructed Sparks, the communication man, to contact the cutter now identifiable.

Upon receiving the message, the lieutenant on the cutter ordered all hands on deck to stand by for a rendezvous with the Admiral's party. Now within a mile of the object of their mission, the Admiral ordered his helmsman to reduce speed and approach the convoy five hundred yards across the bow of the cutter and, maintaining that distance, slowly circle to the trio. When the Admiral abandoned the binoculars for naked eye surveillance of the trio, he noted the last vessel bore a white, covered mound which suddenly was animated into thousands of seagulls. Ordering a closer inspection, the launch moved downwind from the barge and a gust of hot, humid, choking air swept over the investigating group. There was an eruption of coughing and spitting before a half dozen white handkerchiefs masked the faces of the legislators, signifying surrender to the garbage enemy.

The Admiral's fury building to storm form broke over the helmsman. "Get this craft windward of that swamp at full speed."

The order was obeyed with such a violent turn of the rudder at full power, the senators thought it might capsize and shifted their attention from poker to life vests.

"Sparks," the Admiral bellowed, "are we still connected to the cutter?"

"Yes, sir."

"Give me that phone," the Admiral barked, impatiently grabbing it. "Now hear this. This is Admiral Thomas speaking. Get the officer in charge of the patrolling cutter on this communication, pronto." For a few minutes, Thomas tapped the mouthpiece in irritation before his victim was located. "Are you the officer in charge of this screw up?" There was a brief pause. "What's your name?" Another pause. "Well, Lieutenant, as of now, you are relieved of your command of that cutter. Turn your suspect loose and make it clear it was your mistake and return to the base immediately." Pause. "Of course you should take your two sailors off the tug before you return. And another thing, tell the duty officer I said to assign you to the base garbage disposal for a month. Maybe you'll learn the difference between a dirty bomb and a dirty pile of garbage."

Chapter 21

"Land ho, off the port bow or whatever you're supposed to say," Alex reported, taking one hand off the wheel to indicate the direction of the sighting, still below the horizon for Elliot and J.C. on the deck below the pilothouse.

"That should be the point near Mole Saint Nicholas," J.C. replied. "See if you can find that on your charts. It's about thirty miles west of our destination."

"Oh, yes, here it is. I'll change our direction two or three degrees north and skim along the coast to Port de Paix."

"We should make landfall about sunset. Let's moor offshore for the night and put into the harbor with good light in the morning. You'll be home tomorrow, J.C.," Elliot said.

"I'm so impatient I could almost swim there."

"I'll bet you could. With sharks chasing, you'll set a new record for speed swimming. Are there protected coves for anchoring, J.C.?"

"There must be. In the seventeen hundreds, pirates made La Tortue and the northern coast their hideouts."

With the end of the voyage in sight, expectations special to each occupied their thoughts. J.C. recollected his last visit several years back when he was dazzled by his mother's youthful looks and vitality. It was improbable she'd remained unchanged, but how much older would she look? Would he recognize his myriad of relatives and be able to attach the right name to each? Could he still recall enough Creole to speak with many who had no other language? There would be much work to unload and separate the reusables before disposing of the worthless trash. With that done, Alex and Elliot, whom he counted as good friends, would return to New York City, and he'd be forced to decide whether to stay at Port de Paix or move on in search of another life, becoming a drifter forever. And then there was the immediate prize of twenty-five thousand dollars. Who could the townspeople trust to manage this money for their benefit?

When all had gone to bed, Alex lay awake, thoughts ricocheting off her consciousness. Her unexplainable hunch that Port de Paix would be the final resting place of the garbage that had dogged them for two months did not come without extracting a price of uncertainty about Elliot's and her future. Would Elliot be deported with no recourse for returning to the States and end their relationship? Wait a minute, she'd started down that road once before, and he'd assured her, at least she'd thought so at the moment, that he loved her and they'd work out any immigration misunderstanding. Was she raising realistic deterrents they might encounter, or was she surfacing her own doubts about taking on a long-term commitment? She lost her way in her searching and skidded back to start over.

Elliot was caught between false optimism that Port de Paix would accept the garbage and the haunting probability some unforeseen dilemma would return him to useless wandering. He searched for a more rational outcome and realized he had never before found the unpredictable future so unsettling. He sensed the presence of his life's love beside him and considered how long he could expect her to stay on this failing mission. He recounted the days, as accurately as he could, since he'd left New York City to do a four-day errand. It was the stuff of fantasies and fables. If asked whether the passing weeks were productive, he'd answer no; if rewarding, a resounding yes. This woman beside him who he wanted forever was his personal destination. He suddenly knew he must tell her this often, in fact, right now. He listened to her breathing, not the slow, long, easy breaths of sleep but those measured by wakefulness.

"Alex," he whispered.

"Yes," she answered softly.

"I've been lying here thinking how much I love you. I couldn't wait to tell you."

"I'm glad you did. Always tell me, no matter what."

"My life would not mean much without you. I never want us to be apart," he said.

"No, never be apart," she replied, "Now sleep well, my darling."

All three aboard the tug awoke to the music of a typical West Indian band, squeaky and off key but of unquestionable tempo. The tune, drifting out from the dock at Port de Paix, was a spirited attempt at 'God Bless America,' intended to convey an enthusiastic welcome from the town's citizenry. Alex, Elliot and J.C. simultaneously arose to dress, breakfast and weigh anchor to draw into shore, lest the Haitians think Americans ill-mannered and unappreciative of the hospitable greeting. Closer to land, the incoming visitors saw the crowd in the town plaza, numbering several hundreds, was dressed for fiesta anticipating a minor miracle with the arrival of one of theirs— Jesus Christophe. Dozens of small fishing boats met the tug to accompany it to the dock, and a man in one sailboat with colorful bunting on the mast signifying someone of authority shouted reassurances the water was deep enough for the American vessels. In a few minutes, the tug and barge lashed together tied up at the dock, causing the crowd to cheer in gratitude despite the offensive odor.

With the gangplank in place, a party of three came aboard to establish the authority that ran Port de Paix. The leader of the delegation was an unpleasant looking, middle-aged, corpulent man whose muscles of earlier years were now covered with fat. He was stuffed into riding breeches, black leather boots and a linen shirt with a red sash running over his left shoulder and secured by a black leather belt. A wide-brimmed, planter-style straw hat set to the level of his eyebrows shaded a swarthy complexion and cold, dark eyes. He was an unmistakable bully.

His left flanker, a small man appearing diminutive even in the presence of someone only an inch taller than he, chewed nervously on his lip and continually reseated a peaked hat, several sizes too large, with the same sweep of his hand employed to return his wire-rimmed glasses to the bridge of his nose. He wore a makeshift khaki uniform laden with medals dangling on colorful ribbons from his left breast. His face was expressionless, having frozen from many years of capitulation, and his deference to the big man required no verbalization.

The third man, oldest of the three, sported a wispy, gray handlebar mustache that twitched from the involuntary action of the man's tic. His baggy, pajama-like garb and faded green espadrilles would have dismissed him as a simple peasant had it not been for the rakish coal-scuttle style pith helmet, in the manner of the Bengal Landers, atop his bony head. He carried a highly polished ebony staff as a symbol of his office. With an almost imperceptible gesture of his hand, the hulk commanded silence from those assembled on the dock and the band's musical tribute ended in disarray to rival the mournful voices of bagpipes with the air going out of them.

Addressing Alex, Elliot and J.C. in broken English, he introduced himself as DuBois, holding office in some unintelligible department of the town's government, deliberately ignored his lackeys and embraced each of the Port's newly arrived guests with a sweaty hug. He then proclaimed the day was an official fiesta and the celebration would begin following a short service in the church across the plaza. A gaunt, dispirited priest robed in a long monastic cassock stepped forward, blessed the garbage and, to the cheers of the crowd, padded away in his oversized sandals, vestments dragging in the dust. The band struck up a discordant melody familiar only to the natives, and everyone moved towards the church. J.C., unable to pick out his mother from the chattering, swarming mass, was about to become concerned for her welfare when she suddenly emerged from under a large, lemon-colored parasol, as though wearing a halo.

"Mama!" he yelled, leaping down the gangplank. "Mama Monique," he repeated, picking her up and twirling her around, all the time hugging and kissing. He finally put her down, holding her at arms' length to gaze at a beautiful woman looking young enough to be his sister. "Mama, Mama, it's so good to see you."

"Aren't you going to introduce me?" Monique asked, reminding her son of good manners.

"Of course. Forgive me. I got so excited."

"Don't worry, we weren't going to charge you for the boat ride," Alex said.

"You see my friends have a good sense of humor. This is Alex and this is Elliot," J.C. said.

"How do you do?" Monique said in her most careful English.

"My friends brought me here."

"I can see that, but why didn't you fly?"

"It's a long, complicated story, not for fiesta day. We'll save that for another time," J.C. procrastinated, hoping his mother would not remember to bring up the subject later but knowing she would.

"Would you like to celebrate fiesta with us? You're the reason for this happy occasion," Monique said.

"We'd like that but—" Elliot hesitated, "but I have strict orders to guard the tug at all times and can't go ashore."

"That's too bad. There are so many wonderful things to see in Haiti and fiesta is one of the best." Monique turned to J.C. to remind him they must hurry off to church but extended her invitation once more. "Are you sure you can't come to this service commemorating a gift from heaven? The people in Port de Paix are very trustworthy, and if anyone were to jeopardize our good fortune, Sister Felice would work her voodoo and they'd be doomed for life."

"Elliot, it would be a shame for you and Alex to miss the festivities. The people will protect you from any harm and there are no Immigration people in this part of the island," J.C. said.

"Come on, Elliot, let's do it," Alex urged. "The whole carnival's in our honor and nobody will know or care your visa has expired. They won't even know you're English if you let me do all the talking, no matter how difficult that is for you."

So the procession of Monique and J.C. under the halo parasol and Elliot and Alex arm-in-arm went to church.

Before the massive doors of the primitive church, beautiful in its simplicity and absence of ornate icons, people milled about greeting and gossiping with friends and relatives as though they'd not seen each other a day or two earlier. As Alex climbed the stairs to enter the narthex, she realized she had no hat.

"I can't go in. I have no head covering," she said.

"Now you expect me to get you into heaven," Elliot said, untying the red bandana around his neck for a scarf, concurrently with the communicants, presumably temporarily talked out, sweeping into the church.

An hour later, when the priest must have concluded those souls not already saved were beyond redemption and exhausted his list of saints deserving homage, the congregants began a musical chant of low notes reminiscent of its African roots and filed from the darkened sanctuary to the blinding sunlight to dance, sing, eat and drink into the night. Eight simple, wooden chairs, the only seating in the plaza, were arranged in a row for the honored guests' comfort as they observed the spectacle. The priest established a line of demarcation and DuBois, with a lackey on each side, sat in the three seats to the cleric's left. On the other side of this human boundary, Monique, J.C. and Alex took their places in order with Elliot at the end to avoid any inquisitors not deflected by Alex.

Partially isolated, Elliot spent most of his time searching beyond the casual observation of a spectator at an entertainment. He found the people passionate but respectful of each other, childlike in their interaction and unjustifiably optimistic. Seemingly not depressed by the statistics, Haitian longevity that averaged less than forty years and the country's poverty among the worst in the world, the people still lived a spirited life. Elliot dropped his eyes from the joyous, animated faces to see not only children but adults shoeless and most wearing patched and badly matched garments.

He watched the attention paid to J.C. by scores grateful for his return to Port de Paix with a cargo that was an unexpected piece of good fortune. They stood in line to thank him, and some of the giggling young women urged each other to hug him instead of shaking his hand. Monique, entranced with this adulation, sat quietly absorbing and storing future memories and occasionally uttering 'hallelujah'. The priest, as the hours went by, seemed to be disappearing as though absorbed by the fabric of his robe or worn away by the energies of his flock expressing unrestrained revelry that by his standards bordered on transgression. From time to time as he shifted in his hard chair, Elliot caught glimpses of DuBois and his flunkies withdrawn from the people's conviviality, uneasy and sullen. Whispered inquires through Alex to J.C. to Monique provided hints the fiesta had released the people's pent-up desires for a return to more freedom, which had gradually eroded under four terms of DuBois's administration. Now DuBois sensed a threat to his authority from the Americans and J.C., their puppet.

Several times just as the revelers seemed to weary, they got a second wind and the lively music sent hundreds of bodies swirling around the plaza. As the tempo increased, several couples spun out of the group and presented themselves as partners to the honored guests for the next round. The priest, regarding such pleasures as too temporal, stayed mummified while DuBois and his henchmen remained aloof from the dancers' invitations who, undaunted by these refusals, presented themselves to Monique, J.C., Alex and Elliot, hopeful for a more cordial reception.

"We must accept their invitations to dance," Monique said discreetly in English, "or it will be an insult."

Alex stepped forward to choose a fat, grinning partner, and Monique, J.C. and Elliot followed her lead. Elliot, paired with a wide-eyed teenager who continually laughed at his clumsiness, looked desperately for Alex to save him, but she circled the floor away from him with the surprisingly graceful fat man. Mercifully, one of Monique's numerous nephews, smitten with Elliot's young partner, asked and was granted permission to dance with the teenager. A tall, skinny, boisterous woman twice J.C.'s age selected him to explore some wild gyrations, presumably West Indian choreography but unknown to the town's undulating citizenry. Of the four, Monique had the most pleasurable but uneventful round with a man of good manners who'd been unsuccessfully courting the pretty woman since she returned to Haiti.

Reseated and enjoying survival, Alex and Elliot watched with wonder the inexhaustible celebrants' appetite for carnival. Leaning close to Elliot, although it was unlikely anybody could eavesdrop in this din, Alex told him DuBois had openly spoken with townspeople about his displeasure over the false hope for affluence the Americans were planting in the citizens, and the cruel letdown they'd suffer was risking the Haitians' well being. It seemed a prelude to a classic move by DuBois to tighten control of the town.

When those with the greatest endurance finally drifted from the plaza, stilling the out-of-tune band's last note, the weary, honored guests felt it would not be discourteous to leave for their beds. Having said goodnight to DuBois, his lieutenants and the priest, already asleep on his wooden chair, Monique and J.C. lingered with Alex and Elliot, discussing rumors DuBois was plotting to get control of the garbage revenues and consolidate power exceeding his jurisdiction. J.C. had heard DuBois, when re-elected, would expect bribes before allowing the garbage barge to be unloaded and then dictate the twenty-five thousand dollars be spent at his discretion.

"With election three days away, there's no time to lose," Elliot said. "J.C., get the word out that the Steele Company, whom I represent, will only release the funds to a non-political, urban improvement agency chosen by the people which will disburse monies for projects approved by the people's vote. This will require proposals and surveillance for each project. You've got a lot of work ahead of you getting your name on the ballot as chairman of some revenue watchdog agency."

"But there is no such agency," J.C. said.

"You can create one and call it something simple that explains its purpose—like Port de Paix Independent Improvement Aid."

"Isn't this what you came back for?" Monique asked, sensing J.C.'s hesitation to take on the responsibility.

"You know you can rally the people for some real project that benefits the town. Remember how many turned out today to welcome us?" Elliot emphasized. "And you need to stress the Steele Company won't release funds until they're sure drug dealers and crooks can't get control of the money."

"When should I start?" J.C. asked.

"Right now," Elliot answered, "and don't stop running until you're elected."

"Goodnight, Monique. This has certainly been an exciting evening. Good night, J.C.," Alex said.

"Goodnight," Elliot called as he and Alex walked toward the tug. "And, by the way, you may want Sister Felice on your side. You may need some voodoo."

"When should I tell her?" J.C. asked.

"Right now wouldn't be too soon."

"You know, Elliot, you're pretty good at winging it," Alex said, putting her arm around his waist as they strolled along the dock.

By dawn the day following fiesta, J.C. was campaigning for the chair of the proposed Port de Paix Independent Improvement Agency. He first called on Sister Felice, whose only remark, according to J.C., 'I expected you last night' energized him to work straight through the day without stopping for lunch. Utilizing an adaptation of the chain letter technique, he multiplied his coverage of voters, and along the way he discovered more enthusiasm and coverage was possible by encouraging a friendly competition among his supporters to see who could acquire the greatest number of commitments in his behalf. His creativity, surprising not only his mother but himself, was contagious and started a voter turnout unlike any before in Port de Paix.

During the remaining two days of campaigning, the tug and barge lay a mile out of port in perfect view to remind voters only a victory for J.C. and the Port de Paix Independent Improvement Agency could make the twenty-five thousand dollars a reality. The anchorage also served as a precaution against any unexpected visitors coming aboard without permission. Twice Monique rowed out with fresh fruit and vegetables for Elliot and Alex and updated them on the campaign while they ate breakfast together. At each meeting, she displayed determination to help bring reform to the town's administration, and her good common sense and ability to make quick adjustments to outflank DuBois's underhanded moves were reassuring.

In the dark of the night before election day as Elliot and Alex were preparing for bed, they heard the sound of a one-lunger motorboat drawing closer. Curious to see who was in the harbor at that hour, they went on deck as the boat drew alongside.

Its sole occupant yelled, "Captain Elliot, may I come aboard?" The unmistakable accent of DuBois warned them this was no social visit and probably concerned the election.

"Of course, Monsieur," Elliot replied, watching the newcomer pull his bulk aboard with difficulty. "Come into the cabin and let me get you a drink."

DuBois extended his hand to Alex who shook it but remained silent.

"Sit here, Monsieur, it's the only comfortable seat we have to offer you," Elliot said in his most obsequious tone as he drew up the chair behind DuBois and warned Alex with his eyes to stay alert.

"Now tell me, Monsieur DuBois, what brings you all the way out here on such a night?"

"It is a matter of deep concern and such sensitivity I can only discuss it with you and you alone," DuBois said, indicating he did not want Alex to hear.

"Have no concern," Elliot said, pouring DuBois another glass of wine, "This matter you wish to discuss will be between you and me. No other ears will hear it."

"What about the woman?" DuBois asked, jerking his head towards Alex.

"Oh, Monsieur, she's handicapped—can't hear a thing we're saying," Elliot rose, handing Alex a copy of *Moby Dick* and arranging a chair where she'd be sitting with her back to DuBois. "Spends much of her time with books."

"Ah, Captain!" DuBois challenged, "but I saw her talking with you at fiesta."

"Indeed you did, Monsieur. That's because she signs and reads lips. Listen, I'll show you she can't hear. Alex, you are the worst dancer I ever saw. You embarrassed me at fiesta. The only good thing is you don't talk back to me," Elliot said. "Have some more wine, Monsieur, that row must have made you thirsty. How far do you calculate that is from the dock? Would you say a mile, maybe more and not in a very sea-worthy boat?"

DuBois poured another glass of wine from the bottle set on the table before him. "But I did not come to discuss rowing."

"Oh, that's too bad because I'm quite a rower, single boats, you know. I rowed three years on the varsity crew of Oxford, Oxford University, England."

"Yes, yes," DuBois interrupted and took another glass of wine before he began a lengthy discussion on Haiti's form of government, executive, legislative and judicial, and how honored he was to serve Port de Paix as their chief executive. He emphasized the importance of cooperation among the three branches of the town's government and the necessity of obeying authority. Slowly he moved to Port de Paix's excruciating poverty and how deeply it saddened him. Becoming more eloquent with every glass, he described the relief he envisioned the twenty-five thousand dollars would bring to the people, but now some radicals were trying to upset the order of things. He bemoaned the unspeakable hardship many would suffer at the hands of a few subversives. DuBois was giving more focus to the reason for his visit as the consumption of his wine increased. He became more reckless and almost identified by name those he claimed as enemies of the people but pulled back until Elliot indicated sympathy for his civil concern.

"It is hard for me to believe, Monsieur, someone would stand in the way of your administration. Who could this be?"

"Captain, perhaps you've guessed the well-intentioned J.C. and his mother have put themselves in grave danger by pursuing their foolish course."

"Monsieur, you can't mean they would bring hardship to their own people?"

"Oh yes, Captain, and there are some who will do violence to stop them."

"Do you know of such violent men?"

"I know of some who when aroused may stop at nothing to preserve order."

"I'm glad you warned me," Elliot said.

DuBois reached to pour more wine and, finding the bottle almost empty, asked if he might use the bathroom.

"Of course, Monsieur, right down here," Elliot replied.

As soon as DuBois left the cabin, Elliot told Alex to go immediately to the pilothouse and take the tug out to sea if he improvised signing presumably directing her to the deck locker for more wine. Then he removed his flare gun from a cabinet and readied it for firing.

"Incidentally, I resented that crack about being handicapped," she said.

When DuBois returned to the cabin, Alex was reading and Elliot tried unsuccessfully to get more wine from the bottle.

"Well, Monsieur, I suppose an influential man like you would know how to contact these people intent on saving the town from extremists like J.C."

"I hear things."

"Could you contact these people right now from the boat if I persuaded J.C. and his assistants to quit?"

"I'm sure that can be arranged."

"Right from this boat using the ship-to-shore telephone."

"Oh, yes, Captain."

"That calls for another drink," Elliot said. "I'll sign for the woman to get us more wine." In a moment, she put down her book and left the cabin. "I'm glad we had this talk, Monsieur. You can't imagine how much you've eased my mind."

"My God, we're moving," DuBois said as the throaty sound of the engines confirmed the tug was underway. "Where are we going?"

"We're going out to sea."

"Stop the boat. Take me back, I'll have you jailed for this," DuBois yelled.

"I think not, Monsieur. You see the captain of a vessel is the law on the ocean and can take whatever steps are necessary when lives are threatened."

"But I never threatened your life."

"Quite so, but nobody else knows that. Now I suggest you sit down and listen carefully while I tell you what your options are. First, you can write down the names of the people who do your dirty work and then call them on the ship-to-shore phone and in English make it clear they are to harm no one. If they ask where you are, tell them you're on vacation for a few days—but only if they ask and that's all you tell them."

"And the other options?" DuBois asked, feeling he was losing control.

"The other option is we'll take you out to sea and dump you overboard and capsize your motorboat. If anything is found of you, it will look like a tragic accident."

"You don't leave me any choice, Captain."

"I thought you might rather feel that way. Now write down the names and then we'll call your friends. And don't try any funny business," Elliot said, pulling out his flare gun. "I've heard these things will fry a man at close range."

Chapter 22

J.C., Monique, Alex and Elliot stood at the waterfront watching the townspeople unload the last bales of garbage from the barge. It surprised Elliot how much vegetable matter the gulls had removed, revealing even more metal, wooden and plastic solids than he or J.C. had estimated. The amateur stevedores were undeterred in their labors by the smell and surprisingly cleared out material manually that had required machines to stow.

"Tell them not to hose out the barge, J.C. I'd like to leave scraps for the gulls. It will be nice to have some company on the way home," Elliot said, receiving a jab in the ribs from Alex.

"You have been so good to J.C. and me, to all our people," Monique said. "They would like to hold another fiesta for you."

"Please thank them for Elliot and me, but we haven't recovered from the first one."

"Now remember, J.C., the twenty-five thousand dollars has been transferred to the Port de Paix bank for deposit in the account of the Port de Paix Independent Improvement Aid. As soon as your signature is verified and sent to the Steele Company in New York, the funds are freed up. Mail or fax your signature right away and you have Jim Steele's phone and address if you need him."

"I know, Elliot. I've gone over it in my head a hundred times."

"And you also have our ship-to-shore number."

"Yes, thank you again, but before you go, tell us what you did with DuBois for a whole day till the election was decided."

"Oh, that was easy. Alex thought he had such an interest in garbage he should get a close look at it, so we arranged for him to spend some time on the barge."

"Good byes are not easy," Monique said, "but you will never be away from our prayers." She hugged Alex and kissed her forehead. "God bless you, Monsieur Elliot. Take care of each other."

In turn, J.C. embraced Alex and Elliot. "See," he said, "I've made you some going away presents." He opened his hand to offer two rings braided from very fine copper wires found in the trash.

"Goodbye, goodbye," Alex and Elliot said in unison and, wiping their eyes, boarded the tug.

They were several miles at sea with the empty, towed craft bobbing behind them before either spoke. A single gull made a long glide over the tug to circle and land on the barge.

"There's your company," Alex said, needing to break their silence. "Elliot, you wouldn't have really thrown DuBois into the ocean, would you?"

"Why not? I catch things in the sea. Why wouldn't I throw things back in?"

"Thanks a lot," she said, snuggling up to him.

"Are you happy to be going home?"

"In a way," she replied. "How about you?"

"There were times when I couldn't wait for this trip to end, but now it's different. I was concentrating on the garbage so much at times, I forgot it wasn't the main event. Little by little, you've changed all that for me, and now the end of the trip in some way is going to affect us, and not knowing how is uncomfortable. I don't really like the prospect of having some Immigration officer handcuff me and pack me off to England without you."

"But I'd follow right away. I wouldn't wait for anything."

"Even to get out of those grubby sweats?"

"Not even for that."

"Alex, I love you. Will you marry me?" He'd felt it before, and now he'd said it out loud. What would he do if she said no?

"Oh yes, Elliot, oh yes, as soon as we find a preacher."

"Maybe we don't need to look for one," he replied, purposely looking smug.

"What do you mean?"

"The other night I told DuBois and I meant it that at sea the Captain is the law. By that right, I'm empowered to marry us."

"Let's do it right now," she replied.

"Wait a minute. I need the proper rhetoric to give this marriage the respect it deserves, and you can bet the only books aboard are *Moby Dick* and the log."

"I have an idea," she said, excited with the prospect, "we'll call Rich and have him find the marriage rites to read us. Why don't you get a hold of him while I change into my skinny pants and slinky blouse."

It was an hour before Rich returned their call—sixty long minutes to examine and revisit their lives and reflect on the selflessness of a new life in marriage. A simple lunch, partially eaten, didn't speed the clock or divert niggling uncertainties, and when the ship-to-shore transmitter was activated, they were startled by its noise but relieved the wait was over.

"Hello Elliot, 'lo Alex. Where the hell are you guys?"

"Mission accomplished, we're towing an empty barge on the way home."

"Sorry I didn't get back to you right away, but I was out rowing, getting in shape for our face off."

"That's fine," Elliot said, "we'll talk about that later, when we get back."

"Well, it's good to know everything worked out; we missed you here. Immigration has called a couple of times, but we can work on that when you make port. Is there anything else we need to go over?"

"Yes, Rich, I want you to get a copy of the marriage vows right away and call us back."

"Elliot, I don't know where to find that stuff."

"How about a church to start with," Elliot suggested.

"I haven't been in a church since I was baptized."

"Then it's time you got back to one. Or try the Justice of the Peace's office."

"May I ask why the hell you want a copy of the marriage vows? Is this some kind of a scavenger hunt?"

"We're getting married. I'm going to marry us, and you need to read what I should say. And hurry up, my bride's already dressed for the ceremony."

"Why don't you get married when you land here?" Rich asked.

"Because we want to get married right now. Hurry up, will you, Rich, and call us back."

They broke off their communication and Elliot, not to be outdone by the bride, put on the handsome shirt she'd bought him. Now afternoon, they decided to look for a place to moor for the night, choosing a cove on the northern point of La Tortue Island. It was a lovely retreat to quiet and calm. For a while, they sat satisfying themselves with idleness, and then Rich's call brought a heightened excitement that something extraordinary was about to take place.

"Hello, Elliot, this is Rich. Can you hear me?"

"Just fine."

"I have a copy of pretty fancy marriage vows. Shall we begin?"

"Let's get to the meat and potatoes part," Elliot said.

"No, darling, I'd rather hear the whole service. I'm only getting married once," Alex replied.

"Okay, okay, you two can quarrel later. Here goes."

"Shouldn't he hold my hand?" Alex asked.

"Not yet, okay here we go. Now remember, Elliot, you're the marrier so you say—'We have come together in the presence of God to witness the joining together of this man and this woman in Holy Matrimony.' Go on, say it, Elliot."

"Wait a minute, we know what we're doing here. Let's get on with it."

Rich started again, "We have come together, etc., etc. The union of husband and wife in heart, body and mind is intended by God for their mutual joy, for help and comfort in prosperity and adversity, and—"

"Hold on, Rich, I can't remember all that."

"I can," Alex said.

"But you're not the Captain," Elliot replied. "Just get to the important part."

"No," Alex said, "I want to hear the rest of it."

"All right," Elliot said, "but make it snappy."

Rich read on, "and when it's God's will for the procreation of children."

"And when God wills children," Elliot paraphrased.

"Therefore marriage is not to be entered into lightly," Rich read.

"That's okay with me. I can't remember the words so pretend I said it," Elliot replied.

"Now Elliot," Rich said, "you must state 'If anyone knows why these two people should not be married, speak now or forever hold your peace.'"

"Any objections to our getting married?" Elliot asked.

"Now it's my turn to speak as a witness," Rich said. "I want to know if it's going to interfere with our rowing. Then I'll know if I want to object."

"You can have him to yourself every Friday of the month that falls on the thirteenth," Alex offered, joining the nonsense. "Aren't you having a good time, Elliot?"

"All right, you guys, stop fooling around, this marriage business is serious stuff," Rich said, trying to gain control of things. "Let's get back to the ceremony. Now, Elliot, you're the marrier so say to yourself, 'Elliot, will you take this woman Alex to be your wife? Will you love her, honor her and keep her in sickness and health so long as you both shall live?'"

"I'm familiar with that part of a wedding," Elliot said and proceeded to recite the passage flawlessly. "Wait a minute," he said and left the pilothouse for the cabin.

"Where did he go?" Rich asked. "He certainly is a nervous groom."

"He's back, Rich, and says he'll do all those things."

"Elliot, you ask Alex if she will take this man to be her husband? Will you love him, honor him and keep him in sickness and in health so long as you both shall live?'"

"I will," Alex said, "as long as he shaves off his beard."

"I know the rest, Rich," Elliot said, putting one of J.C.'s copper ring presents in Alex's hand and keeping the other.

"With this ring, I thee wed," he said to Alex.

"With this ring, I thee wed."

"By the power vested in me as captain of this tug, I pronounce myself and you man and wife."

"And by the power vested in me as your wife, I pronounce you a United States citizen."